Andrew Martin grew up in Yorkshire. After qualifying as a barrister, he became a freelance journalist, writing about the North, class, seaside towns and eccentric individuals rather than the doings of the famous, although he did once loop-the-loop in a biplane with Gary Numan. He has also learned the rudiments of driving steam trains, although it will be a long time before any passengers are foolish enough to ride with him.

In praise of *The Necropolis Railway*, his first Jim Stringer adventure, the *Evening Standard* said 'the age of steam has rarely been better evoked', while the *Mirror* described the book as 'a brilliant murder mystery'. This was followed by *The Blackpool Highflyer* and *The Lost Luggage Porter*. The next books in the series, *Murder at Deviation Junction* and *Death on a Branch Line,* were shortlisted for the Ellis Peters Historical Crime Award and, in 2008, Andrew Martin was shortlisted for the CWA Dagger in the Library Award.

He has also written a book about housework for men: *How to Get Things* ⬚⬚⬚⬚⬚⬚⬚⬚⬚ *g, Dusting and Other Househ* ⬚⬚⬚⬚⬚⬚⬚ *stliness, Ghoul Britannia*, wh ⬚⬚⬚⬚⬚⬚⬚ *vn.*

Andrew M⬚

www.jimst⬚

It is to be stressed that the adventures of Jim Stringer can be read in any order, but they do chart a biographical progress.

He was born in 1884 in Robin Hood's Bay (Baytown) in Yorkshire. His mother died giving birth to him, and he was raised by his father, a well-meaning but snobbish butcher. Jim grew up into a dreamy, observant, possibly moustachioed youth, enamoured of trains. Aged seventeen, he 'got his start' as a lad porter at Grosmont on the North Eastern Railway. Following an encounter with an enigmatic stranger outside the gentleman's lavatory at that station, Jim was invited to apply for work as a cleaner – first step to firing engines – on the London and South Western Railway.

This gave Jim the chance to train for the footplate, but he found himself in a part of the LSWR's operations that he hadn't reckoned on (see *The Necropolis Railway*). After untangling (sort of) a very dark conspiracy, Jim married his landlady, Lydia, a proponent of women's suffrage, and probably Jim's intellectual superior (she certainly thinks so). The two then moved to Halifax where, in the summer of 1903, Jim fired engines on the Halifax–Blackpool line for the Lancashire and Yorkshire Railway, or 'the Lanky'. However, further obstacles were put in the way of his career – literally so, since he came up against a determined train wrecker.

Jim was then sacked from the Lanky for running a locomotive into a wall. (But it wasn't his fault! The brake wasn't properly warmed!) His path to engine-driving now barred, he was persuaded by Lydia – materially ambitious in spite of her Labour activism – to enrol as a railway policeman (plain clothes division), working for the North Eastern Railway force from their office on Platform Four of York station.

In *The Lost Luggage Porter*, Jim grappled with safe-crackers and worse under relentlessly falling rain in York and Paris. In *Murder at Deviation Junction*, he pondered the disappearance of an entire carriage-load of rich men in the snowbound wastes between Whitby and Middlesbrough. In 1911, Jim, now a Detective Sergeant, unravelled aristocratic murder in the pretty/creepy village of Adenwold with Lydia aiding, or at least criticising, his investigative methods (see *Death on a Branch Line*). In *The Last Train to Scarborough*, Jim took up residence in a Scarborough guest house during the storm-swept off-season, his aim to discover which of the shabby-genteel residents did for a railwayman-guest.

Forthcoming is *The Somme Stations*, in which Jim goes to the Western Front with the 'pals' battalion raised by the North Eastern Railway. Let's just say for now that events lead him to develop a heavy cigarette habit – preferably Woodbines.

In his investigations, Jim comes up against real people, whose crimes arise from moral dilemmas . . . Well, all right, some of them *are* violent nutcases. He proceeds circuitously, by observation, inevitably making mistakes. He is a rather melancholic man, slightly bullied by his wife and his 'Chief', the sinewy old soldier, Weatherhill. He remains keen on trains, to the bemusement of Lydia ('What are you, Jim? Ten years old?'), but he usually comes up to the mark in the cases assigned to him, while doubting himself along the way . . .

by the same author

Bilton
The Bobby Dazzlers

In the 'Jim Stringer, Steam Detective' series:

The Necropolis Railway
The Blackpool Highflyer
The Lost Luggage Porter
Murder at Deviation Junction
Death on a Branch Line

Acknowledgements

I would like to thank, in no particular order: Roy Lambeth of the Durham Mining Museum; the World Ship Society and especially Mr Roy Fenton; Drene Brennan of the Postcard Club of Great Britain; Dr E. M. Bridges of the Museum of Gas and Local History at Fakenham, Norfolk; Tony Harden of the Railway Postcard Collectors' Circle; Andrew Choong, Curator of Historic Photographs and Ships Plans at the National Maritime Museum; Mr N. E. C. Molyneux of the National Rifle Association; Adrian Scales of the Scarborough Railway Society; Sue Pravezer, QC; Clive Groome of Footplate Days and Ways; Rod Lytton, Chief Mechanical Engineer at the National Railway Museum and Karen Baker, librarian at the Museum.

All departures from historical fact are my responsibility.

THE LAST TRAIN
TO SCARBOROUGH

Andrew Martin

faber and faber

First published in 2009
by Faber and Faber Limited
Bloomsbury House, 74–77 Great Russell Street, London WC1B 3DA
This paperback edition first published in 2010

Typeset by Faber and Faber Limited
Printed in England by CPI Bookmarque, Croydon

A CIP record for this book
is available from the British Library

ISBN 978–0–571–22970–3

4 6 8 10 9 7 5 3

For all the people in the Quiet Carriage

PART ONE

Chapter One

As I awoke the thought came to me: '*Where has Scarborough got to?*' and it caused me a good deal of pain. I knew I was near coal – too near. I was *on* it. Or was it a great black beach, for I heard waves too? There was darkness above as well as below, but not quite complete darkness above, for I could make out thin strips of light. Each thought caused me a blinding pain behind the eyes and I did not want any more to come.

I inched a little way to the left, and the coal smell was stronger. It disagreed with me powerfully, and I saw in my mind things to do with coal and burning as the nausea came on: a locomotive moving coal wagons in an empty station that ought to have been packed with holiday-makers; a man making coal-gas tar at the works on the Marine Parade at Scarborough, and evidently doing it for his own amusement, for he was the only man in the town. A storm approached across the black sea behind him.

I saw the booklet that gave directions for use of an incandescent oil lamp – it gave sunshine at night through a red shade, one hundred and twenty candles – and I saw smoke over Scarborough, and further general scenes of that sea-side town in the hour before the lamps are lit: the funicular railway closed and not working; the locked gate at the entrance to the underground aquarium and holiday palace. I figured an orchestra locked inside there along with a troupe of tumblers, and a magician who was the wonder of the age but nevertheless troubled by a leaking kettle.

I saw the harbour of the town with the boats at all angles, as though they'd been *dropped* in only moments before, and were still struggling to right themselves.

I saw a public house with a ship's figurehead on the front, a marine stores, the sign reading 'All Kinds of Nets Sold' lashed by waves . . . and nobody about. I pictured the great hotel – I could not recall its name and knew it would cost me pain to try and do so. I saw the high, windowless wall to the side, streaked with rain – the place was a prison viewed from that angle. I heard a great roaring of water on the other side of that wall. Flags flew from what might have been flagpoles at the top or might have been masts, and in my mind's eye the monstrous building slid away from the Promenade, and began bucking about on the dark sea.

These scenes were mainly without colour, but then some colour came, and it was wrong, too bright, done by hand: a red baby in a sky-blue cot set in a yellow room. That baby was on a post card – that was *its* trouble, and at the thought my stomach lurched fruitlessly while the head-racking pain redoubled. I moved on the coal and the same convulsion came again, only worse. My stomach was trying to do something it could not do. I thought of a short cigar taken from a cedar-wood box. It was a little dry. But what was dry? Box or cigar? At any rate the room containing the cigar was too hot, yet how could it be, for it was part of heaven? No, not quite heaven. A voice echoed in my head: 'It's turned you a bit bloody mysterious, this Paradise place.' Paradise. Somehow, a secret file was involved, a paste-board folder containing papers that everybody looked at, and yet it was secret. I saw a jumble of razor blades, a fast-turning dial on what might have been a compass, but surely ought not to have been. My mind could hold ideas and pictures but could not make the connections between them.

I looked up again at the light strips. I raised my arm towards them, and they were a good way above the height of my hand. My arm wavered and fell; it was not long enough, and that was all about it. I was perhaps underneath the floorboards, in some species of giant coal cellar, and this notion came with a new sensation: a fearful sense of eternal falling. Some of my memories were coming back to me, and coming too fast. I closed my eyes on the great coal plain and raced down, down, down.

Chapter Two

And there in place of Scarborough was the city of York, or the outskirts thereof: our new house, 'the very last one in Thorpe-on-Ouse', as our little girl, Sylvia, used to say, the house that put off the beginning of open country. It was evening – early evening, spring coming on; a kind of green glow in the sky, and I sat in my shirt sleeves and waistcoat. They had been ploughing in the fields around the village, but I'd not seen the work carried on, for I'd passed all day in the police office in York station.

I sat on the front gate with Sylvia, and our boy Harry. They both liked to sit up high – well, it was high to them, Sylvia especially, and I had my arm around her to stop her falling, which she didn't like. Not the falling I mean, but the arm. She wanted to sit on the gate unsupported like Harry, who now pointed along the lane, saying, 'Here he comes', and old Phil Shannon, who lit the lamps in Thorpe-on-Ouse and at Acaster Malbis, was approaching on his push bike, with the long lamp-lighter's pole held at his side. I fancied that it was a lance, and Shannon a sort of arthritic knight on horseback. He leant alternatively left and right as he pedalled, like a moving mechanism, some species of clockwork.

'You could set your watch by him,' I said, as he came to about three hundred yards' distance from us.

'You could not,' said Harry. 'It's twenty past six. Last night he was here at five past.'

'Take your arm away, father,' said Sylvia.

I removed my arm, and we watched Shannon come on.

'He looks all-in,' said Harry.

'Well, we're the last house he does,' I said.

'I know that,' said Harry. (He was a bright boy and it seemed that he knew most things of late.)

'I think it's ever so nice of him to come all this way,' said Sylvia, who then tumbled forward onto the cinder track that ran under the gate. She was quite unhurt, and climbed straight back up, saying, 'Don't worry, my pinny's still clean.' It was clean on, and she knew she'd catch it from her mother if it got muddy.

'It's not *nice*,' said Harry. 'He's paid to do it.'

'Keep your voice down,' I said.

'Why?' said Harry. 'It's fact.'

As Mr Shannon came up, we all said, 'Good evening, Mr Shannon,' and he growled out a 'Good evening' in return, which tickled me. He wasn't over-friendly, except when he'd a drink taken, but even he couldn't ignore a greeting from three people at once. He was an idle bugger into the bargain, and remained on his bike as he lifted the pole up to the lonely gas lamp on the standard over-opposite.

'Does he bring the flame on the end of the stick?' asked Sylvia.

'You know very well he doesn't,' said Harry.

'There's a hook on the end of the pole,' I said. 'He uses it to push a switch. That sets the gas flowing. Then he pulls a little chain with the hook, and that ignites the gas.'

'Let's *watch*,' said Sylvia, as though what I'd just said wasn't really true, and needed to be proved.

We watched, and when he'd done, Shannon circled on his bike in the pool of white light that he'd made, and set off back for Thorpe and, if I knew him, the Fortune of War public house.

'I love Mr Shannon,' said Sylvia as he wobbled off between the wide, darkening fields.

'He's quite useful about the village,' I said.

'That's exactly what I mean,' said Sylvia.

'He hasn't changed the water in the horse trough for a while,' said Harry. 'It's all green.'

'How does he take the *old* water out?' asked Sylvia.

'Harry?' I said, turning to the boy. 'How does he do it?'

Harry watched the gas lamp for a while, keeping silence.

'Not sure,' he said, after a while.

'Perhaps he drinks it,' said Sylvia, and she gave a quick little smile.

'That might not be far off the mark,' I said, thinking of Shannon sinking his nightly five pints of Smith's.

We turned and walked back to the house, across our land, which we called 'the meadow'. It smelt of cut grass just then because I'd gone at some of the taller stuff with a scythe in my work suit only an hour before. The house was a long cottage, half tumbled-down, but it was big, getting on for three times the size of our old place on the main street of Thorpe. You could look at it as a terrace of three with a barn or, with a bit of knocking-through, it would be one good-sized cottage with built-on barn.

We lived in four rooms at one end of it, but the whole thing was ours, and on the day we'd moved in the wife had turned to me in our new parlour and said, 'Well, Jim, we've got *on*.'

She was before the house now, beating a Turkey carpet that

hung from the washing line. I had never seen that carpet before, but the house had come furnished, and the wife was turning new things up every day.

'I still can't believe it's our house,' said Sylvia as we came up.

'Well, you can thank Mr Robert Henderson for that,' I said.

'He must really like us,' said Sylvia.

'He really likes mother,' said Harry, and I eyed him as we stopped to watch the beating of the rug.

It was true enough.

I watched the wife beating away. With each stroke, a wisp of her brown hair flew forwards, and she pushed it back behind her left ear. But her left ear was too small to keep it in place. You'd think she'd have worked that out after thirty years. As she went at it, the colour rose in her face – not to redness, but a dark brown. I had often wondered whether there might have been a touch of the tar brush in the wife's family, to account for the blackness of her eyes, and the brownness that went all the way down. I thought of Harry's paper, *The Captain*, which he had on subscription every week, and how one of the stories was 'Tales of the Far West'. There were Sioux Indians in these tales and at odd times a Sioux squaw would appear, supposedly a different one every time. But all of them looked like Lydia.

'Feel free to just stand there gawping,' she said. 'Harry, you'll take the water up for your sister's wash.'

Harry went off to the copper in the scullery. He was good about helping around the house. His main job was to look out for his sister. Their bedrooms were both at the end of a long corridor, over the top of the in-built barn, and this made Sylvia nervous, even though it was these two rooms that had decided us – or decided the wife – to rent the house from Henderson at the knockdown rate of seven shillings a week. It was the view over the fields that had done it. There was a gas mantle in the corridor between the two rooms, and Sylvia believed that it was kept on all night. But this was because she had never yet been awake beyond eight o'clock. In fact, Harry was under orders to come out of his room and switch it off at nine, after his hour of reading, which was often more than an hour.

The children went off through the opened front door, and I said to the wife, 'I'm not sure you should be beating that carpet with washing still on the line.'

I said that just to see the look she would give me, but she didn't take the bait. Instead, still beating, she said, 'Mr Buckingham has been riding the railway again.'

'Oh Christ,' I said.

'On his departure from the station –'

'Which station?'

'Any station . . . He found that the carriage door had been left unfastened by the company's servants . . .'

'Which company?'

'You won't put me off . . . Mr Buckingham endeavoured to fasten the door himself, and . . .'

Mr Buckingham didn't exist but I could picture him quite easily. He had pop eyes, a red face, and a thin moustache; he looked permanently put-out and was always ready to fly into rage. He was smartly dressed, in clothes often dirtied by the negligence of whatever railway company had the ill-luck to carry him, according to terms and conditions that might or might not have been correctly set out or somehow indicated on the backs of their tickets. He carried a portmanteau (containing valuable items) which was regularly mislaid or damaged by the company's servants. Everything he did was reasonable, or reasonably foreseeable, or so he said, and everything the company did was unreasonable, or so he also said.

'In endeavouring to fasten the door,' said the wife, who had now left off beating the carpet and was enveloping herself in linen as she took down the laundry, 'Mr Buckingham injured himself –'

'Seriously, I hope.'

'And he is contemplating suing. What are his prospects of success?'

The wife said that last part with two clothes pegs in her mouth, and she now walked to the laundry basket, which was over by the chicken run.

'This is something to do with Adams versus the Lancashire and Yorkshire Railway Company, isn't it?' I said.

'It might be,' the wife said, as she dropped the white sheets into the basket. Some of them went in, and some went onto the bit of cinder track that skirted the chicken run.

'Oh heck,' said the wife.

She was no great hand at housework, but she knew more about *An Introduction to Railway Law* by Harold Andrews – in which the adventures of Mr Buckingham featured – than I did myself, which was a bad look-out, since I was the one about to be tested. She picked up a tea towel that had missed its mark, and tried to brush off the muck.

'I'd say *that* was reasonably foreseeable,' I said.

'I forgot to mention', said the wife, standing upright again, and turning to me, 'that Mr Buckingham attempted to close the door while the train was in motion, and that there was a sign fixed to the door expressly forbidding opening or closing it while the train is moving.'

'Right,' I said.

' . . . which Mr Buckingham didn't see.'

'Had he been drinking, by any chance?'

The wife glanced anxiously down again at the basket, looked up at me, and brushed her hair behind her ear.

'Come on, Jim,' she said. 'You're supposed to know this.'

And her hair fell forward.

Chapter Three

Now York retreated at a great rate, and I was back in the coal cellar, which was now rising bodily at speed. I was not rising in it, for the floorboards remained the same distance from my face. I would be sick at the peak of the rise, I knew; but when the peak was reached and the next fall began, I changed my idea: I will be sick at the lowest point of the fall, I decided, but instead I turned my head, finding once again a kind of coolness on the coals, and an easing of the pain in my head as York came back.

There came first scenes of the kind I'd once seen at the Electric Theatre with the wife: the great cathedral, the gates of the city wall, only the pictures were not moving, just as they had not moved at the Electric Theatre, except for scenes of the river Ouse – or *some* such moderately wide and dirty river – meant to suggest the passing of time. That had not been enough for the wife, who had leant across to me, and said, 'Two shillings for this, it's a swiz.' But the scenes showed that York was an important place. Important and beautiful, and I ought not to have left it for Scarborough.

I saw in my mind's eye the mighty station waiting as the trains waited within it, the notable churches of the city, and some of the very old buildings of the centre. I saw a display of the new electric trams, and then I was with the newest of them all, following the newest *route* of all. The side of it said 'Singer's

Sewing Machines' and the board fixed to the front said where it was going: the terminus of Line Nine, the Beeswing Hotel.

That had been the start of it all, but before that there'd been an earlier start. Of course, this too had to be in York, for that was where *I* started. But the outskirts . . . and again I was back in Thorpe-on-Ouse.

When? Some time before or after my journey to the Beeswing. No, it must have been before. We were in the front parlour of our new house, which had several parlours, depending on how you looked at it, but only one so far cosy. Again, it was spring time: primroses in prospect – in the very air – but not yet appeared.

And the fire blazing in our new front parlour, rows of tins of paint lined up ready near the door.

Thursday 12 March, 1914: in the National Gallery, London, the Rokeby Venus had been attacked. The event was reported in the *Yorkshire Evening Press* and the account lay on the table between us. Mary Richardson, feminist and suffragette, had gone at the painting so named with an axe. Earlier in the day, Robert Henderson, who was the son of Colonel Robert Henderson, whose smooth looks and smooth *name* I did not like, had stopped the wife in the high street of Thorpe – stopped the wife, I stress. I, walking alongside her, he had quite ignored.

'I do not know the female equivalent of the word "confederate", Mrs Stringer,' he had said.

'Nor do I,' Lydia had said.

'But your confederate, Miss Mary Richardson, has destroyed one of our greatest paintings.'

'Has she?' the wife had said, not yet having seen the *Press*.

'The report was in *The Times* this morning,' said Henderson.

14

'Which painting was it?' enquired the wife. 'Just out of inter-est.'

'You seem pretty sanguine about the whole business,' he'd replied. 'But then you are part of the women's Co-operative Movement and you agitate on behalf of the suffragettes.'

'Agitate!' said the wife. 'I wouldn't know how to agitate if you paid me.'

'Oh, I think you would,' he said, at which I had to cut in.

'We're just off actually, Mr Henderson,' I said.

He tipped his derby hat at me, but continued to address the wife: 'I do believe you are a symptom of the malaise afflicting the country, Mrs Stringer.'

And then of course he'd given a grin.

'You are a symptom of the malaise afflicting the country,' I said to Lydia as we walked on down the dusty road, in the light rain, making for the boot maker and mender's with the lamps overdue for lighting but old man Shannon nowhere in sight. 'What do you make of that?'

'I'm rather flattered,' she said, as we turned in at the gate of the boot maker's long front yard.

'Yes,' I said, 'I could see. You coloured up.'

'I certainly did not,' she said.

But she had done, and the colour was up in her face still as she lay on the sofa in our new front parlour, in the new (and also very old) house a little way outside the village, the house that had been practically given us by that same Robert Henderson: seven shillings a week for a place three times the size of our earlier one, and with a contract giving us the option to buy at some equally favourable rate.

It was nine o'clock, as I knew by my watch rather than by the clock of St Andrew's church, which did not now reach us, we being so far out.

'I mentioned the business about the Venus to Peter in the Fortune earlier on,' I said.

'Oh yes?' said the wife, who was not in the least interested in the sayings and doings of Peter Backhouse, who was the verger of St Andrew's, even though she counted his wife, Lillian, amongst her best friends.

'He said, "Somebody did *what*, you say? To the Rokeby *what*?"'

The wife sighed.

'And to think it was done for publicity,' she said.

She sat back down. The law books were on the tab rug between us.

'I don't know about all this business,' I said, indicating them. 'All I wanted was to be an engine man, and when that came to nothing, I settled for being a railway copper.'

'Don't fib, Jim,' said the wife, and we listened to the ticking of the clock, the ticking of the fire, and then the mooing of a cow, of which we heard a good deal in our new house, along with wood pigeons.

We were more thrown together, living so far out, and that was good *and* bad. The wife's aim was to set us up with our own little empire, and her work for the women's cause was starting to take second place to that, although she would never have admitted it. She'd gone all out for the country life, stealing a march on me, for I was the Yorkshireman. I was the one who'd taken her north, having struck that bad business while apprenticed for the footplate with the London and South Western Railway. For me, life in the North Eastern Railway police was next best thing to life on the footplate. I'd been promoted detective sergeant in double quick time, and I now made fair wages. But the wife wanted to make me a sort of gentleman farmer-cum-solicitor, and her pushing had earned its reward. I was on the point of giving in my notice, with a view to starting as articled clerk in the offices of Parker and Wilkinson, an arrangement subject to my performing satisfactorily during what was billed as a 'conversation' with Mr Parker himself about railway law. His outfit was one of several firms that did work for the North Eastern, and their particular speciality was cases of personal injury: the paying off – or, better yet, fending off – of passengers' claims for damages.

I knew very well that this conversation was to be a test, albeit of a gentlemanly sort, and it was now less than twelve hours off. Going into the office of Parker and Wilkinson would entail at first a cut in my earnings, but the wife had told me to see this as taking a step back in order to make a great leap, and she was prepared to dip into the inheritance she'd had from her father in order to help fund my training for the law.

'Shall we have another look at Buckingham?' she enquired.

'Go on then,' I said, and she picked up the book.

'The train he's waiting for is running late,' said the wife, after an interval of reading lying down with her head propped in her hand. 'He takes a carriage instead, and then sends the bill to the railway company. Will they settle?'

'They'd be better off just paying him not to use the railway,' I said. 'They should pay him to leave the bloody *country*.'

The wife eyed me.

'It depends on the lateness of the train,' I said. 'If it's only running half an hour late, that would be a reasonable delay. A day late would be unreasonable. Anything in-between, you argue about.'

The wife yawned as she said, 'That's about right, Jim. I'm

sure you'll do brilliantly tomorrow.'

'Are you?'

'It's really nothing to worry about. Mr Parker said it would be a formality.'

'That's just what bothers me.'

She came across and sat on my sofa, lifting her skirts as she stepped up, like a tomboy climbing a hill.

'You'll have a lovely day of it tomorrow,' she said. 'Your meeting with Mr Parker will be over in no time, and when it's done, you'll be on the road to being a solicitor . . . I know you've the whole day off, but you might call into the police office to let them know how you get on.'

'To put on swank, you mean?'

' . . . You'll perhaps take a turn in the Museum Gardens, then perhaps go to Brown's to see how your new suit's coming on.'

Owing to the slowness of Brown the tailor my new suit would not be ready in time for the interview, and I would be making do with my *best* suit.

'I think I'll sit by the river and watch the trains going over the Scarborough railway bridge. They've the new Z Class on the Scarborough branch. They're just running her in, you know.'

'What are you, Jim? Ten years old?'

'I'm pushing thirty, which is too late to be starting a new job.'

'It's not a job, it's a profession. You might come back here for a nap, then you've your office "do" at the Beeswing.'

'The Chief says he has an important bit of business he wants to mention to me at the Beeswing,' I said, and the wife frowned.

'But you've practically left.'

Silence for a space. I had deliberately stirred the wife up, and felt rather bad about it.

'It's not a dangerous bit of business, is it?' she enquired.

Would she be so concerned if she knew that *Robert Henderson* might be put in the way of violence? I liked to think not.

Chapter Four

A needle hung before me. It was the common run of needle –
it had an eye in it – only much bigger, and it did not go away
until I started to count the seconds of its persistence, where-
upon it vanished immediately. I saw next a line of paint tins
against a wall in a room. They were not opened, and I knew
that I did not want to see them opened, for I did not like the
smell of paint. Close by, I strongly suspected, was a rattling
window and beyond that the sea, which was black with something . . . something starting with the letter B, and ending in S.
The sea was black with *butlers*: dark-coated men bathing. No,
couldn't be. That wasn't the word.

Now bells rang about me on the dark coal plain, and the
floorboards over my head were being lifted one by one. It
appeared that they were not nailed down, for they came away
very easily. Two men worked at the job. Both wore rough
guernseys and some species of gumboots, and as they
worked they rose and fell with the coal plain, and with me.
Above them, a night sky was gradually being revealed: a
mighty and expanding acreage of stars and racing wisps of
cloud. I fixed on one very bright star, and that was a mistake,
for the act of watching it brought back the sickness, and the
French word came to me: *mal de mer*. I had heard that somewhere of late.

As I watched in wonder, I counted the bells. Had there been

eight strokes in all? One of the two men wore a hat that might have been a captain's peaked cap, but there was no braid and no badge, as though he wanted to keep back his identity. His face was brownish and square. The other's face, beard and hair were all grey, and he was now down on the coal with me, fastening up a tunic with two rows of brass buttons. The man who remained above, standing on the edge of the ragged skylight that he'd had a hand in making, shouted a question to the one standing over me, and I could not make it out, but I knew from the tone that he must be the governor, and I heard the reply: 'They're all aft, skipper.' He was foreign in some way, this second man. He put a bit of a 'd' sound at the beginning of 'they're', in a way that made the word seem babyish. But he looked a hard case, as did the other.

Another bell was rung – a bell that existed in an altogether different world – and it brought me to wakefulness sitting alone in my best suit on the top deck of the Number Nine tram. Friday evening and the tram running along, and my memory doing so once again as well. We ran along under the York lamps and only a scattering of stars, making for the place where easternmost York came to a stop: the Beeswing Hotel. The conductor was hanging off the platform, and joshing with various street loungers that we passed, like a performer on a moving stage. His high, cracked voice floated up the staircase but hadn't kept me from sleep. I had not slept in the afternoon as the wife had suggested, and I was dead tired, for I'd been awake all night fretting about my meeting with Parker.

In fact, our 'conversation' had been just that, and we had not touched on the doings of Mr Buckingham, reasonable or otherwise. 'I have satisfied myself that you are not a fool, Mr Stringer,' Parker had said, but he'd taken two and a half hours about it, in the course of which he'd introduced me to every man in the office. He'd asked me a good deal about Lydia, and I wondered at first whether he was one of her not-so-secret admirers like Robert Henderson, but I decided he was more nervous of her than anything. 'She is a rather forward party,' he had said, which I thought rather forward of *him*. Then again, in the summer of 1913 she had intercepted him on his bicycle in the middle of York, and put it to him that I might have a start in his office.

'How did she know it was me?' Parker had asked, towards the end of our interview. My answer was pretty well-greased. I told him he was a famous York character, often mentioned in the *Yorkshire Evening Press* as chairing the police court or speaking at society events, or addressing the Historical Society on the Merchant Adventurers of York, on which he was an expert.

'Yes, but there's never a photograph, is there?'

That was true enough. The *Press* only ran to photographs for convicted murderers.

' . . . So how did she know?'

The truth was that Mr Parker had made the mistake – if that's what it was – of bicycling out to Thorpe-on-Ouse one summer's evening. As he went on his stately way along the high street, Harry had called out, 'That's an A1 bike!' It was one of the best made: a Beeston Humber. As Harry went on about the bike – he was excited over the expanding sprocket on the rear, which gave half a dozen different gearings – I explained to the wife about the rider: about how he was the star of the police court, the top man in the office to which I often took our witness statements should a prosecution be under consideration. The wife had taken note of the man, or perhaps most particularly the bike, and flagged it down in central York not a week later, just as people stop the knife grinder on *his* bike when they want something sharpened.

As we clattered on over the new-laid tram rails, I saw from the windows that a light rain was falling, and the wind getting up. After the stop at the Spotted Cow, I caught the whiff of the gas works at Layerthorpe, and heard drunken chatter coming up the stairs. I turned about and saw Constables Flower and Whittaker from the York police office, the conductor shouting some jest up after them. I'd known that Whittaker lived some-where hereabouts. They were on their way to the 'do' but half canned already. They nodded along the gangway when they saw me, but took care to sit well short of where I was.

Everyone likes having the top deck to themselves, and the arrival of Flower and Whittaker annoyed me. I knew they thought me a queer fish, and they could never quite hide the fact. I tried to imagine myself as they saw me: a railway copper genuinely keen on railways – that marked me down as a nut, for a start. Neither Flower nor Whittaker would have cared a rap for the Class Z.

I was in addition a plain suit man – the only one in the office just then – and they were uniformed. I was their superior, and Chief Inspector Weatherill's favourite into the bargain. But being the Chief's favourite . . . well, it came with complica-tions. He had a great liking for danger and excitement but, since he was nearly seventy, his days of experiencing bother directly were about done. So he put all the trouble my way, perhaps suspecting I enjoyed it as much as he had. Or was it just that he thought I had the makings? That I might be trained up to enjoyment of tangling with the really bad lads if only I was given enough experience in that line? I didn't know, and it certainly wouldn't do to ask. The Chief was a force of nature: you took what came from him.

I'd had the solving, after a fashion, of three murders, while the constables' quarry was of the order of fare evaders, card sharpers and makers of graffito on carriage windows. I had a wife who went out to work, and who thought herself superior. She was one of those suffragettes, very likely a bomb thrower in the making, and on top of all that I was practically a solicitor already, and the lawyers were the enemy. They decided on who we could or could not go after, and in the serious cases they took the prosecution – and the victory, if it came – all for themselves.

I thought again of Parker and his office. It commanded a view of the old station, which was now used as an overflow siding for coal wagons, but it was a world away from those wagons, with the oil paintings on the wall, the thick carpets, the law books as heavy and handsomely bound as bibles. There were rows of silent ledger clerks, who recorded the decisions of the office brains, and everything flowed smoothly and silently on a river of black ink.

Behind me, Whittaker and Flower, who'd fallen silent on first seeing me, had regained their pep and were bickering after their usual fashion.

'How many drinks have I stood you over the years?' Flower was saying (or maybe Whittaker, but it hardly mattered).

'I've no idea,' came the reply, '. . . Not many.'

'No, no, think about it. Tot it up.'

'I should say it comes to about exactly half the amount *I've* bought you.'

'I should say it does *not*.'

There hadn't been a single cross-grained individual in that

law office; every face had smiled at me at every turn. But when I got out of there I was relieved . . . in which case how would I stand a lifetime of it? The money I'd be earning after five years would smooth the way, of course: I would eat luncheon at dinner time, and ride in cabs. Or I saw myself atop my own Beeston Humber, with a gearing to meet every condition of road.

And I would be James, not Jim.

I looked up at the window, and thought: *Lightning!* but it was the conductor flashing the electric lights and bellowing up, 'Terminus!' I looked back: Flower and Whittaker had bolted. They would already be inside the hotel, the name of which filled the top deck windows on the left side: BEESWING. Just the one word. The letters were green, and seemed to glow in the blustery night even though they were not illuminated. For some reason, I knew they meant trouble.

As I stepped off the tram, I gave the conductor a cheery enough 'Good night!', but I was thinking that we ought not to have been dragged out all this way for the 'do'. It ought to have been held at the Railway Institute, which was hard by the station and our office, but the Chief had had a falling out with Dave Chapman, who ran the bar and booked out the social rooms there. Chapman had found the baize scraped and a little torn after a billiards session involving some of the men from the Rifle League. He had sent the bill for repair directly to the Chief, who was one of the high-ups of the League. Well, there'd been a hell of a row. The Chief wouldn't pay the bill. He made out that Chapman was down on all shootists because his flat was right next to the shooting range, and he was kept up at all hours by the firing. The Chief had turned on Chapman even though the two had been great mates, which was how the Chief had come to know the whereabouts of Chapman's flat and so on. He had a habit of turning on people, especially lately, and I marvelled at the way I managed to keep in his good books, and wondered how long it would last.

The Chief had set about trying to get Chapman stood down, and meanwhile started looking out for another venue for the 'do'. Favourite was the Grapes in Toft Green next to the railway offices, which was really called Ye Grapes, but not by the railway police blokes, who preferred it to all the nearby Railway Taverns and Railway Inns, and pubs named after locomotives, perhaps because the new landlord of it had been in the railway police himself before my time. But he hadn't had a licence for functions, or was short-handed or something. So that was out, and the Beeswing was in.

The place was brand new but meant to look old; handsome enough, but more of a pub than a hotel . . . and where the wings of bees came in, I couldn't guess. Fastening up my Macintosh, I decided to take a turn down the road rather than going straight in. This was the edge of York, and my way led me first past a muddy building site. A sign read: 'Construction by Walden and Sons', and I wondered why anyone would want to lay claim to what presently looked like a battleground. Further, I came to a children's park. One loutish-looking kid went back and forth in the gloom on a brand-new swing that creaked even so. He had an unpleasant look of not being content with the swing but waiting for something else to happen. I walked on beyond the limit of the York lights, and walked past cows standing stock still in fields, as though for them too time had stopped.

I turned and went back towards the hotel. The tram that had brought me up was rocking away into the distance, and another Number Nine was drawing up, about as thinly patronised as the previous one. I watched as one man climbed down: the Chief. I tipped my bowler at him (saluting had somehow long since gone by the board between the two of us), and he lifted his squash hat clean off his head, at which the wind made his few strands of orange hair rise up as well, in a kind of double salute.

'Evening, sir,' I said.

'Don't stand out here nattering, lad,' he said. 'The beer's gratis until nine o'clock.'

As we entered the hotel by a side door, I unbuttoned my top-coat, and the Chief saw my smart rig-out. He looked taken aback for a second. He hadn't been in the police office himself that day – he was in it less and less often – but he knew I'd been away from it too, and he knew why. He didn't mention my interview with Parker, however. He'd never either encouraged me or discouraged me in the plan to turn solicitor. But I knew he didn't like it, and this because he couldn't stop it. The Chief liked to control people – he was like the wife in that way – and now he was losing control of me. The Chief said, 'I've a spot of business to mention to you, lad.'

'I know,' I said.

I followed him over to the bar, where, instead of talking to me, he fell in with Langbourne, the charge sergeant, so I was left dangling.

We railway coppers had been kept apart from the Beeswing regulars (if such a class existed) by being put in what might have been the function room. It smelt of new wood varnish, and I half expected to see pots of the stuff lying around. There was a stage, and a new piano, but there would be no turns. There would just be free beer, followed by cut-price beer, and that would be quite sufficient. There were about a dozen from the police office, and a few station officials and hangers-on besides. The fellow at the bar gave me a glass of ale without needing to be asked, and old man Wright, the Chief Clerk, came up. He looked rather canned already.

'You're off, then?' he said, wavering slightly.

'Very likely,' I said, 'but not yet a while.'

He took a belt on his drink, and cocked his eye at me.

'*When?*' he enquired, quite sharply.

Old Man Wright was inquisitive to a fault, which was indecent somehow in a man of his age.

'It's not settled yet,' I said.

'How's your missus?' he said.

'All right,' I said. 'Yours?'

Our wives both worked part-time for the Co-operative Women's Union, and were both strong in their feminism.

'They're opening a new store, Acomb way,' he said.

'I know,' I said.

Silence for a space.

'And that little lass of yours,' said Wright, 'what's she called again?'

'She's called Sylvia,' I said, taking a belt on my beer and grinning at Wright. 'I don't suppose I need explain why.'

Wright frowned down at his pint.

'Why?' he said, looking up.

'Sylvia *Pankhurst*,' I said. 'It was the wife's doing. But it's a pretty name.'

Another silence, in which I drained my glass. Wright drifted off, and I asked the barman the time of the last tram.

'Ten thirty,' he said.

'Because I don't want to be stranded here.'

'You do *not*,' he said, 'take it from me.'

'Are there any sandwiches laid on?' I asked him.

28

'Laid on *what*?' he said, and I knew he was not a York lad.

I decided that I would be on that last tram, and that I might as well put away a fair few pints beforehand. I sank a couple more in the company of Shillito, the uniformed sergeant, and Fred Thomas, who was not a copper at all but the deputy night station manager. The talk wasn't up to much. Trams came periodically crashing up beyond the windows. They made more noise and vibration than was needful, and each time I thought some disaster was in the offing.

The Chief was now talking to a fellow called Greenfield, who'd come up specially from the Newcastle railway police office. I watched the Chief's face as he spoke. It had been scorched by the sun in the Sudan, pounded by heavyweights in his army boxing days, and set about by whisky and baccy smugglers in the docks of Hull, where he'd had his start on the force. Consequently the Chief's face was irregular: no two photographs of it looked the same, and it would have been hard to draw.

Presently, Wright came wobbling back over, and he was not only drinking but munching at something. I saw the carton in his hand: liver capsules.

'You ought not to be drinking if you've liver trouble,' I said.

No reply from Wright, who just eyed me for a while.

'Here,' I said, 'any idea what the Chief's got in hand for me?'

He looked sidelong, and I knew he knew; but to old man Wright, information was valuable, which is why he was forever asking questions and why he hardly ever answered them.

'Why do you want to know?' he said presently. 'Do you have the wind up?'

Behind him, the Chief was approaching with papers in his hand.

Chapter Five

The Chief handed me one of his small, bitter cigars, which meant 'down to business'. He never gave a cigar to any other man in the office. He lit his, and lit mine. As he did so, I eyed the documents he'd put on the bar top. The top-most ones were cuttings from newspapers.

'Why are you mentioning this to me now, sir?' I said.

'Nothing else for it,' he said, and gave a quick grin – a *very* quick one. 'I want you on to it day after tomorrow.'

That meant Sunday. The wife would just love that, what with all the work we had to do about the house. But this was the Chief all over. He liked to keep his men on their mettle. He had many times taken me for a drink-up in the middle of the working day, so I ought not to have been surprised that he should talk shop in the middle of a 'do'. But there was a look on his face I didn't much care for: a kind of excitement. How much beer was he shipping? He passed over the first cutting. It came from the 'Public Notices' page of a Leeds paper.

MISSING, Mr Raymond Blackburn of Roundhay, Leeds. Aged 30, 5ft 10in high, medium-large build, brown eyes, dark hair. Last seen at the Paradise Guest House, Scarborough, on 19 October last, and has not since been heard of. Any information to be addressed to the Inspector of Police, Roundhay, and the informant will be suitably rewarded.

'Know the name?' said the Chief.

'No. Why do you ask?'

Old man Wright was lying down on the stage. It looked pretty final.

'The same notice has been posted in the *Police Gazette* the last few months . . . Have you not seen it?' The Chief was rocking a little back and forth, eyeing me quite nastily. 'Blackburn was a fireman,' he said.

'On the North Eastern?' I asked, because other companies ran into Leeds besides ours.

The Chief nodded.

'On 19 October last year, he fired a passenger train into York from Leeds New Station. It was meant to be taken on to Scarborough by another crew, but the fireman booked to take over from Blackburn was off sick, so Blackburn stayed with the engine and took it all the way through with the second driver. It was a Sunday, and Blackburn's train was about the last one into Scarborough station. The engine was needed next day in York, so the driver ran it back that night with another York bloke who was waiting in Scarborough after an earlier turn.'

'Why didn't Blackburn go back with them?'

'Because he knew he wouldn't get into York in time for the last Leeds connection.'

'Well then . . . he could overnight in York.'

'But he chose to do it in Scarborough.'

The Chief was eyeing me; I glanced down at the newspaper clipping.

'Paradise,' I said at length. 'It's a good name for a rooming house.'

'It might be,' said the Chief, blowing smoke and grinning at the same time, 'and it might not be. It just depends what it's like.'

'And you want me to find out?'

The Chief looked away, saw Wright on the stage, looked back.

'Of course it's odds-on he made away with himself,' he said. 'All his belongings were left in his room except the suit he wore. He was a gloomy sort, by all accounts. He probably just went off in the night and jumped in the sea.'

'But then the body would have been washed up?'

'Not everything that falls in the sea off Scarborough is washed up,' said the Chief, '. . . thank Christ. Now our lot in Leeds have been looking into the matter with the Scarborough Constabulary.'

'And what have they found out?'

'Fuck all,' said the Chief, who then removed a bit of tobacco from his front teeth and said again, 'Now . . .'

But this was followed by silence, as the Chief again eyed old man Wright, who was sitting *up* on the stage now, looking somehow like a little boy. The Chief was looking daggers at Wright; he then fixed me with the same evil stare, as though Wright's behaviour was somehow my responsibility.

'It struck the *Leeds* blokes', the Chief continued, 'that they ought to send a man to stay over at this house, and see how things stand, and to do it on Sunday so as to get the Sunday lot of guests.'

'Why have they not done it then?'

'Well, they've been a bit short-handed.'

The Chief had softened his tone now. He was so variable in his speech that you did wonder whether fifty years of hard drinking and blows to the head might not be catching up with him.

'I see,' I said. 'And that's why they've taken five months to get round to the idea?'

'What brought it on was that the house has started advertising for railway men again.'

'Where?'

'In the engine shed at Scarborough. Other places beside.'

'If they're posting adverts in the engine shed they must be on the List.'

There was a list of private boarding houses close to stations that had been approved by the Company for taking in railway men on late turns. Sometimes the Company paid the boarding houses directly; sometimes the railway blokes paid out of their own pockets and claimed the money back later.

'They were on it all right,' said the Chief, 'and they've never been taken off it.'

'How many engine men had gone there before Blackburn?'

'None. He was the first.'

'So you might say that, so far, no railway man has gone to the Paradise guest house and survived to tell the tale?'

'Well,' said the Chief as once again the smoke spilled from the sides of his grinning mouth, 'I'm hoping you'll be the first. You see, the Leeds blokes thought it'd be quite a clever stroke to send a copper who could make on he was a North Eastern fireman – just to see if there was anyone in the house who might have a grudge against the Company, or against railway blokes as a breed. Only they don't have any men who can fire an engine.'

Silence between the Chief and me; he dropped his cigar and stood on it.

'You're a passed fireman, aren't you?' he said at length. 'You fired engines until you ran that loco into the shed wall.'

I was not having *that*.

'It was my mate who ran it into the wall. He'd jiggered the brake. I just happened to be standing up there when the consequences of his error became manifest.'

'I like your way of putting that,' said the Chief. 'You'll turn up at the house with just the right amount of coal dust and muck on you, just the right engine smell.'

'It's customary for engine men to have a wash when they've finished a turn, sir.'

'Yes, well don't be too thorough about it. I've a driver all fixed up for you,' said the Chief. 'He's just the man for the job.'

'Why? Is he the man who drove the engine that Blackburn fired?'

'No, that bloke's out of the picture – taken super-annuation, retired last month. I have in mind a bloke called Tommy Nugent.'

But he would say no more about this Nugent apart from the fact that he knew him through the North Eastern Railway Rifleman's League, which the Chief practically ran. Blackburn had also been in the League, and both the Chief and Nugent, it seemed, had said the odd word to him at inter-regional shooting matches.

'Will Nugent be staying at the house too?'

'Could do,' said the Chief. 'You might be glad of a mate . . . Some pretty queer types in this house, apparently.'

'They've all been questioned, I assume. Statements have been taken.'

'They have, lad.'

'Answers not satisfactory?'

'They *en't*,' said the Chief.

The Chief was grinning at me. I was growing anxious, and he liked that.

'Do you have the case papers to hand, sir?'

But I somehow knew he wouldn't have. Clerking was no part of real police work, at least not to the Chief's mind.

'Well now, there's been a mix-up over that,' he said. 'They were meant to've been sent but they've not come. The earliest I can get them now is Monday morning, but it'll do you good to go in there blind. You'll bring a fresh pair of eyes to it all.'

'I think that's what's called a mixed metaphor,' I said, and I left off the 'sir', which I would generally add, as an insurance policy, when talking to the Chief. '. . . Or maybe not,' I said, seeing the way he was eyeing me.

'When do you start in that fucking solicitor's office?' he said.

'It's not decided yet, if you recall . . . sir.'

'It's already rubbing off on you.'

The Chief took a pull on his beer. More was coming, I knew.

'Bloody *infected*, you are.'

Was this Scarborough job his way of penalising me for leaving the force? Of course it was. The Chief was down on all lawyers. In court, they had a habit of asking him, 'And what accounts for the injuries sustained by the accused in your custody, Chief Inspector Weatherill?'

I asked, 'Was Blackburn married?'

'He was not,' said the Chief, 'but he was engaged – had been for ages.'

'Might be an idea to talk to her.'

'I think the Leeds blokes have had a word. She's a bit flighty, moved about a lot, very different from Blackburn.'

'What was *he* like?'

'Grave bloke,' said the Chief. 'Quiet. Bit of a lone wolf . . .

Big Catholic, as a matter of fact.'

I tried to figure him in my mind: a big, quiet, dark bloke. But the picture that came was of a big, quiet, dark Catholic *church* I'd seen hard by a railway line in Leeds. St Anne's, I believed it was called.

'Tell you something else about him,' said the Chief. 'He was a bloody good shot.'

I bought another pint, and the Chief climbed onto the stage and made a speech. Well, it was more a reading of notices. The office was doing creditably well. More crimes solved than last year. A collection would shortly be taken for the North Eastern Railway super-annuation fund. The Riflemen's League was always looking out for new members, ditto the York Territorials. A fellow ought to be able to fire a rifle – he never knew when it might not come in. Vote of thanks to the landlord of the Beeswing, and that was that. The drinking was carried on for another hour, and then we all piled on the last tram back to York.

I sat next to Shillito, the other sergeant, and behind Flower and Whittaker.

'My cousin's six foot seven,' Whittaker was saying.

'You en't half a spinner,' said Flower.

'You *reckon*?'

'Don't ask rhetorical questions.'

'Are you bloody well accusing me of asking rhetorical questions?' Whittaker asked Flower.

'There, you've just asked another,' said Flower. 'You don't even know what one bloody is.'

Wright was kipping on the front seat.

'Is Wrighty okay?' I asked Shillito.

'He has his troubles just now,' he said, which was a very

36

Wright-like reply.

My head reeled a little, and I felt it best to avoid looking through the windows, for the street lamps would rush up rather fast. As the tram jolted and jerked its way, I felt the motion to be unnatural. It was a heartless machine – no fire burning in its innards. I closed my eyes, and then we were at the railway station and piling off. The Chief was first down, and straight into the cab shelter. I watched him amid all the rattling of horses' hooves and cab wheels, and the loud, echoing goodbyes of all the blokes. The Chief was walking fast towards a bloke coming out of the station. He looked behind and saw me as he advanced on this bloke. The Chief collared him by calling out, 'A word . . .!' and then a name I didn't catch. The two closed, and began talking, the Chief twice more looking around in my direction, which was not characteristic of him, since he didn't usually bother about other people. Was the Chief going down the hill? He was too often juiced; too often out of the office; too careless of his paperwork; too old. I eyed the bloke the Chief was talking to. The bloke glanced my way once, and then looked down, rather shamefully I thought, as though I was the subject under discussion. Who was he? I knew him from somewhere.

I walked away towards the bike rack, which was under the cab shelter. I was taking the front lamp from the saddle bag, prior to fixing it on, when old man Wright walked up.

He said, 'I've a bottle of whisky in the office, if you fancy a nightcap,' and he was trying to steady himself, as though he was on board a ship.

It was such a strange turn-up that I immediately agreed, and re-stowed the lamp in the saddle bag.

'What's brought this on, Wrighty?' I asked, as we stepped

through into the station.

He made no reply, but just concentrated on walking straight.

In the station, I saw few people. Instead, the trains were in charge – they had the run of the place. There were not many, it being late, but the night-time trains seem to make more noise and let off more steam than trains of the day. The last Leeds train was making hard work of pulling away from the bay platform, Number Six. We were on the main 'up' platform, where the police office stood, and Wrighty was veering wide, approaching the white line of the platform edge. Then, half running, he climbed the steps of the footbridge and crossed to the main 'down'.

'Wrighty!' I called out. 'What's going off?'

But I was drowned out by the thundering of a great coal train coming up on the 'down' line. The loco was black, the *smoke* was black, and every wagon thoroughly blackened. It was as if the English night itself had been put on rails and carted north. I crossed the footbridge as the train ran underneath, and I saw Wright on the very edge of the main 'down'.

'What's up, Wrighty?' I shouted at him.

'Nowt,' he said.

'Well then!' I shouted, and Wright kept silence but the train did not. It seemed to come on eternally, like the turning of a wheel, and Wright stood at the platform edge facing the wagons as though expecting them to stop so that he might climb aboard. He stood too close to them for my liking. I pulled at his sleeve to draw him back away, at which he turned about, and I saw that his face was quite different. He didn't look as if he was blubbing, but I knew that was what the alteration signified. He said something, and I couldn't make it out for the thundering of the wagons.

'Come away from here, Wrighty!' I shouted.

But he made no move, and once more addressed the flying coal wagons.

'Jane's left me.'

'Eh?'

'She's left me!'

I could hardly credit it. Wrighty had been married to Jane for forty years. I couldn't think what to say, but after a dozen more wagons or so, I shouted, 'Don't take on, Wrighty!'

'I was always home to her directly!' Wright shouted at the train. 'I was never a stop-out!'

'Your missus is a decent sort!' I shouted back, 'You must be able to . . .'

But I couldn't think what.

Suddenly a flying, flimsy brake wagon signified the end of the train, and Wright and I stood in silence, the empty tracks before us.

'Let's go into the office and put a brew on,' I said, but Wright shook his head. I tried to pull him back from the platform edge in case he had it in mind to wait for another train, and pitch himself in front of it. I thought: This is more like the kind of drama that happens when you've *missed* the last tram, and I pictured Jane Wright: a sensible woman with a lot of grey hair. She smoked cigarettes and had a smile that was fetching on account of teeth that went *in*. I'd never been able to make out what she saw in Wright, who didn't have a nice smile, or any at all come to that. After forty years of marriage, that might become rather wearing.

Wright turned away from the platform, saying, 'Weatherill's told you what's going off in Scarborough, has he?' and he was about back to normal, in that he was asking questions instead of answering them.

'He has that,' I said.

I saw that the offer of whisky had just been a ruse on Wright's part to achieve . . . well, something or other to do with his own difficulties.

'Walk you home, shall I?' I said, and he gave a half nod.

'When are you off, then?' he said, as I collected my bike.

'To Scarborough,' I said. 'Sunday.'

'You going on your tod?'

'No, the Chief's fixed me up with a mate. A driver. We're going there as a footplate crew. Don't tell anyone, mind you,' I added, grinning at him.

'Weatherill's putting a train driver to police work?' said Wright. 'That's rum.'

So he hadn't heard *that* part.

'The Chief has it all planned out,' I said.

We'd come out of the station, and turned down Leeman Road. I was pushing my bike, and Wright was occasionally colliding with it as he walked. We came to the beginning of Railway Walk, which was a kind of dark alleyway running along by the main line. Only you couldn't see the railway for the hoardings that were all down that side. From the railway they were bright, cheerful things advertising Heinz Beans, Oxo and whatnot, but on Railway Walk you just saw the shadowy backs of them, and the tall sooty timbers holding them up. Wright lived along one of the terraced streets that ran off the Walk on the other side.

Why had he been glooming at the coal train? Perhaps he was a regular on the main 'down' at eleven o'clock? That train came through every evening at about that time. It wouldn't stop in under half a mile and so presented a nightly opportunity for anyone wanting to make away with themselves.

'This is you, I think,' I said to Wrighty as we contemplated Railway Walk. But he made no move.

'Has the Chief let on?' he said '. . . He's dead certain that Leeds bloke was done-in.'

'Well . . .' I said.

'And that it was somebody in the lodging house that did him.'

'I'll get in there,' I said, 'and I'll run the bugger to earth!'

I eyed Wright, giving him the chance to say, 'Good luck with it,' but he moved off without a word, zig-zagging somewhat.

I climbed onto my bike, and set off for Thorpe. As I rode, it came to me that I ought to have asked Wright whether I might mention his trouble to Lydia, who was quite pally with Jane. I was assuming she'd stick up for marriage in general. But maybe she in turn would leave me for Robert Henderson. She wouldn't have to coach *him* up to being a big earner. He was that already.

Chapter Six

'They're all aft, skipper.'

The words revolved in my mind, a problem waiting to be solved. I first thought: That grey man talks just as though he's a sailor; wears a sailor's coat too. I did not *want* him to be a sailor, for sailors were in the habit of travelling further afield than it was normally convenient for me to go. But I took heart from the way that he was lighting a small cigar. Any sort of man anywhere might light a cigar.

'I feel ill,' I said, or anyhow I *thought* the words, and there was some sort of a connection between my thoughts and my lips, for some sound came out and it must have served well enough because the man replied:

'Just wait until we get some sea,' although it was really more like 'Just wade undil we get shum sea.'

'You'd best look out either way,' I said. 'I'm going to be sick no end.'

I tried to rise from my coal bed, and the two men, one above, one below, watched me do it. I found my feet after a couple of goes but it took an effort to stay up; I wanted to go back to sleep on the coal. I slowly looked down at my boots, feeling myself to be thinner than I was before . . . and there was stuff all down my suit-coat. I contemplated it while trying to steady myself on coal. I raised my hand to the stuff, and I did not know my own hands. They were red, and I could not shake the notion that they had been stained by beetroot juice. When had I been near beetroot? I looked hard at them in the night sea light, which was partly moonlight, and partly something ghostly made by the waves. It was not beetroot. The redness was under the skin. Poison. I wiped my hand again over my suit-coat. The stuff was vomit . . . and my North Eastern company badge was missing.

'Where's my top-coat got to?' I said, and then: 'I've a hell of a thirst.' The top man, the skipper, seemed ready for this because he held a bottle of water. He dropped it down to the man below, who passed it to me. I held it with my stained left hand as I drank, and stood with head spinning as the water took effect. It made me feel better in some ways, worse in others. The grey man held out a tin of cigars.

'Do shmoke?' he seemed to say.

I could not read the words on the tin; there seemed to be a picture of a blue church but it was covered in coal dust. I took a cigar.

'What's happened?' I slowly enquired. 'Have I been pressed into the fucking navy?'

No reply.

'Why are my hands red?' I demanded, but there came no answer, only the flare of the match rising up to my face. The cigar was lit, and the grey man threw the match onto the coal. There was just enough light for me to see it go out.

I looked up. The man above, the skipper, had been away – must have been away, for he now returned. He held a ladder, and he too now wore a tunic with brass buttons. He lowered the ladder, and placed the top of it by a wooden beam that helped support the roof of the great coal hole I was in. The grey man indicated the ladder with a turn of his head. Was I supposed to be smoking the cigar, or climbing the ladder? I contemplated the burning cigar, and dropped it. I was not up to smoking just then, and it struck me that I had been far too long on my feet. I wanted to sit down on the coal again, but at the same time it was necessary to rise from it, and escape the black air of this underworld. I climbed the ladder using not so much my feet as the memory of climbing ladders, and when the rungs ran out I was for a moment in a cool breeze at the top of the highest tree in my home village. The name came to me slowly: Thorpe-on-Ouse. But I stepped from it onto iron, where I stood face to face with the one set in authority over the grey man.

He held a small revolver, and behind him was a whole ship with more than a breeze blowing over it. I saw the expanse of the fore-hold running up to the great bulk of the mid-ships, with high-mounted lifeboats either side, tall masts, where derricks with steam winches were fitted, great white-washed ventilators for sucking air into the iron worlds beneath, and the whole thing set upon the roaring, crashing sea under the thousands of stars. I wanted to congratulate the fellow on the effect, to shake his hand, ask him, 'Now how did you manage all this? And how do you ride the thing with only the two of you on board?' For there wasn't another soul to be seen.

Chapter Seven

Before, in our old house, when I reached our front gate I knew I was home, but now the gate was the start of a fairly long walk – across the dark meadow. One light burned in the house, and Lydia was sitting up in bed. I knew my interview with Parker would be uppermost in her mind, and as it turned out, she mentioned it the instant I stepped into the bedroom.

'You've done brilliantly, our Jim,' she said, and she stepped out of bed in her night-gown, and handed me a little envelope. It was a telegram from Parker himself. 'Much enjoyed our meeting of today. Very happy for you to start in April. Particulars follow by post.'

'I'm very proud of you,' she said.

We kissed, and I said, 'You should be very proud of yourself. I mean, it was all your doing.'

She watched to see whether I smiled at this. I did, and the smile was meant. Parker was obviously a decent sort, and I found that I didn't mind too much the idea of being a solicitor, providing I didn't think too much about it.

'Wait until we tell your father, Jim,' she said. 'He'll just die of pleasure.'

My dad was a lovely old fellow, but an out and out snob.

'Actually,' the wife ran on, frowning, 'I think that really is a danger in his case. You're to break the news gently. At first, just tell him you're going into a law office and work up from there.'

She sat back on the bed, and picked up another letter.

'This came as well,' she said. 'It's postmarked London.'

She looked a little worried as I opened it, as if she thought it might contain something that would stop me becoming a solicitor. It was from *Railway Titbits* magazine, from the editor himself. He was delighted to inform me that I had won the competition in the January number: I had successfully named all ten termini pictured and placed them correctly in order according to date of construction. A one pound postal order would shortly be despatched to me. I showed it to Lydia, who said:

'It really is a red letter day.'

'There must have been hundreds got the answer right,' I said. 'I expect I was just the first name picked out of the hat . . . I probably shouldn't have entered, being a railway employee.'

The wife rolled her eyes.

'Send the pound back, why don't you?'

'It's the first competition I've ever won,' I said.

'How many have you entered?' the wife asked.

'One.'

'Well then,' she said.

'What did you get up to today?' I asked, as I undressed, for it had not been one of her days in the Co-operative Women's office. I knew that as long as Robert Henderson's name didn't come up, then I'd be happy.

It didn't. She'd worked about the house, dug some of the plot that was intended as the kitchen garden, pulled up two more sycamore saplings that had taken root in the wrong places, and gone for an evening walk into Thorpe with the children. I turned down the lamp, and we tried to sleep.

'I can't get off,' the wife said after a while. 'I'm so excited.'

'Let's read, then,' I said, and I turned up the lamp, and picked up my *Railway Magazine*, while the wife reached across to the night table, where she found a book that I knew to be called *The Practical Poultry Keeper* by T. Thornton.

'Now let's see what's what,' she said, and opened the book at the beginning. It was the umpteenth time she'd started it, and after five minutes she tossed it across the counterpane.

'That flipping *book*,' she said. 'But they're getting on with it now, you know ...'

'Who are?'

'The hens. Three eggs today.'

Was that a good rate of production for fifteen hens? The answer to the mystery lay in *The Practical Poultry Keeper*, but it was a stiffer read even than *An Introduction to Railway Law*.

Half an hour later, we were still not asleep.

'What are you thinking about?' the wife asked.

It'd been a while since we'd done any lovemaking, what with all our changes of life, and I thought this might be the moment. But then I thought of old man Wright.

I said, 'Did you know that the Wrights have separated?'

'Oh yes, that's very sad. Well, it's sad for him. *She's* overjoyed about it. She's gone off with Terry Dawson.'

'Who's he when he's at home?'

'Honestly, don't you pay any attention to Co-operative business?'

'No.'

'He's assistant manager of the Co-operative butchers on South Bank. You go there every week, Jim, just in case you've forgotten. But as from next month he'll be managing the new store in Acomb.'

'So he's the coming man of the York Co-op? Wright's very

cut up about it. Do you think you might have a word with her?'

'I could do, but I wouldn't hold out much hope. He's such a misery. A woman's entitled to a bit of fun in her life, you know.'

'I can think of a way of giving you a bit of fun,' I said, and I put down the *Railway Magazine*. 'It only *would* be a bit, mind you.'

'Ten termini,' said the wife, as I inched over to her side. 'That's going some.'

'*Railway Titbits . . .*' I said. It isn't for the true rail enthusiast, you know. Come to think of it, I don't suppose most of its readers could name *one* railway termini.'

'You can't have one termini,' said the wife, as we fell to.

Later on, we *still* weren't asleep.

'What are you thinking about *now*?' Lydia asked.

'Just thinking on,' I said. '. . . I've been promised a lot of things lately: ownership one day of this house, perhaps; a start at Parker's office; a pound from *Railway Titbits*. Only thing is . . .'

'What?' said the wife.

'I've got to go to Scarborough first.'

The wife eyed me.

'When?'

'Sunday.'

'What? For the whole day?'

'For the night.'

'The night?'

And that, somehow, was what bothered me: the idea of staying the night in Scarborough during the off-season, and the suspicion that the Chief hadn't so much given me a job as set me a trap.

Chapter Eight

The sky was not quite black. Proper blackness rolled upwards from the funnel, and the sky was different to that: a dark, drifting grey. The ship plunged and rose with no land in view as I walked before the Captain's pistol. The ship was about the length of an ordinary train and it moved straight, both over and under the waves like a needle going through cloth. The thread it dragged was a long line of white in the blackness of the water. Parts of the decks were picked out with the white light of oil lamps hung from railings, and here the decks shone with rolling water. The sea flew at the three of us as we walked. We were getting some weather now all right, and it was waking me up by degrees. To my right, a sail was rigged. It was higher than a house and a constant shiver rolled across it diagonally. It was both white and black, covered in coal dust. I knew that a steam ship would sometimes rig a sail if the wind served. We were advancing on the mid-ships, the bridge housing. I couldn't have named all the ship's points, but some of the right words came to me from Baytown, the sea-side place where I'd been born. In going to Scarborough I had returned to the sea and that had been a mistake, but I could not just then have said why or how. I had gone too near the edge of land and somehow fallen *off* the edge, and the sea had taken me.

I turned about and saw the Captain, with gun held out.

'Where are we going?'

'Aft,' he said.

Another sea came, breaking white over the decks and soaking me through, but that was quite unimportant. The pressing matter was the pain in my temples. Coming fully awake seemed to have brought it on. I did not want to look left or right – that was one result of it; and I wanted to sit down. I wanted badly to sit down and be sick. After that, I wanted breathing time to remember who I was. I had been imagining myself in all the places I knew a certain Detective Stringer to have been and I knew that I had at one time kept a warrant card in my suit-coat pocket that would very likely carry that name, but I did not want to look at it just in case I had confused myself with someone else. We stopped at another ladder, and another wave flew at us. We were like the clowns in the circus who attract buckets of water wherever they go. I was meant to climb this ladder; the Captain held my arm as I did it.

'We must get to the bottom of this business,' I said, and he made no reply. I made two further remarks to him as I climbed the ladder: 'Are you two the whole ship's company?' and then, 'This is a bad affair.' All three remarks went unanswered, and no wonder.

The ladder took us to a low iron door that was on the jar. I pushed at it, and we were into a saloon: here was a lessening of the coal smell. White-painted planks had been fitted to the iron to make wooden walls. I noted an oil lamp on a bracket, two couches, a wooden chair; books on a folding table. Another ladder, or something between a ladder and a staircase, came down into the middle of this room.

'Do go up,' the grey man seemed to say. It sounded as though he was asking politely, but that wasn't it. 'Go,' he repeated, as I eyed him. There was spittle always behind his

50

teeth when he spoke, as though the sea rose and fell inside him as well as all around.

At the top of the stairs was a bare wooden chart room, if that be the right description. It was the room set behind the bridge, anyhow. The for'ard side of it was all window save one slatted wooden door that was *half* window, and this banged constantly so that the sight of the ship's bows, and the wild seas breaking over them, came and went. The Captain walked directly through this door onto the bridge, and I was left alone with the ghostlike foreigner, who kept silence. The water rolled thickly and slowly over the window like quicksilver; the door clattered, and I glimpsed for an instant the edge of the ship's wheel, the binnacle alongside, and a hand upon the wheel. It was not the Captain's hand – so there was at least a third crewman in the know. I heard a rapid pass of words between the Captain and this new man, but I could make out no word in particular over the crashing waters, the rising wind and the banging door, save perhaps the single faint bell of the telegraph as an order was passed from bridge to engine room. The Captain came back in, removed his cap, and drew his sleeve once over his forehead, which was all that was needed for him to recover from exposure to the storm, just as though he'd been walking fast on a summer's day and worked up a light sweat. The door continued to clatter behind him, and I wished he would shut it permanently, for I was half frozen, and the iron stove in the corner of the room burned too low.

The Captain's hair was practically shaved right off, which made him look foreign. They went in for shaved heads in France, and I fancied there was something about his square face not quite English. The word came to me at length: his face was too *symmetrical*; but he *was* English – north of England too, going by the few words he'd spoken. He stood directly opposite to me, with the chart table in-between us. The uppermost chart was quite as big as the table top, and showed a sea full of tiny numbers, but I could not make out *what* sea. A parallel ruler rested upon it, together with an oil lamp and a black book. To the side of the table stood the grey man – the grey Dutchman, as I had now decided – who indicated a chair at the table, and seemed to say, 'Sit down, I dink you want shum corfee.'

I will set down his words normally from now on. He was always only a little 'off' in his English, and of the two he seemed the better disposed towards me. But I did not think he was fit for life beyond this ship. Where the Captain was per-haps in the middle forties, the other was in the middle fifties; his beard and face tried to outdo each other for greyness, and it was the dead greyness of driftwood.

The Dutchman quit the room, perhaps to fetch coffee, and I sat down. This ought to have brought some comfort, but instead the movement brought a worsening of my headache. It was a pain that came as a kind of mysterious brightness, a kind of electricity. But the room we were in was dark, and the Captain's face was dark. He laid the small revolver on top of the chart, took his own seat, and lit an oil lamp that stood on top of the chart. He then took a pen from his pocket, and briefly scrawled something in the book that lay on the chart. I sup-posed this to be the ship's logbook, but nothing about the book gave away the name of the vessel, and it was impossible to read the Captain's handwriting – which seemed to me illegible in any case – in the brief instant of time before he shut the book.

'Why do you have the gun?' I enquired.

'Because we're minded to shoot you,' he said, blowing out the match.

He sat back in his chair, and picked up a pencil. He looked at it.

'You are the Captain,' I said, after a space.

He nodded once, in a mannerly sort of way, still inspecting the pencil. A further interval of silence passed.

'Being the Captain, you might at least take a glance at that fucking chart occasionally.'

No answer.

'And the other one, the one who's gone for the coffee . . . he's the First Mate.'

The Captain nodded again, put down the pencil.

'I want a change of clothes, hot water and soap,' I said.

I considered letting this fellow know that I had a family, but it would have been wrong to bring them into it. I had considered them too little of late. In fact I had done them some wrong that I could not quite bring to mind, and this was the penalty: I would be removed from their lives altogether.

'*Sea captain*,' I said, looking up. 'In the town where I was born every other bloody *man* was a sea captain.'

'Who *are* you?' asked the Captain.

I raised my hand to the inside breast pocket of my suit-coat. The pocket had survived whatever had happened to me; the warrant card had not.

'You *know*,' I said.

'But, you see . . . we want to hear it from you,' said the Mate, returning with coffee.

I nodded slowly at him, and the thing was: I didn't know the half of it.

PART TWO

Chapter Nine

The North End shed, a quarter mile beyond the station mouth, was where the Scarborough engines were stabled. I felt a proper fool, approaching the Shed Superintendent's office with my kit bag, just as I had in the days when I'd been working with a company rule book in my inside pocket, and not as some species of actor.

It had turned into a nothing sort of a day – I would have had it hotter or colder, darker or sunnier. The church bells of the city would not leave off, and their racket drifted over the complicated railway lands that lay at the very heart of York. I was tired out. I'd hardly slept on Friday or Saturday night. There were many new noises in our new house: Sylvia reckoned that the branch of the big sycamore tree tapped on her window – 'but only at nights'.

'It taps when there's a wind,' Harry had corrected her.

The thought of taking articles and becoming a railway solicitor made me hot and cold. It was like a fever. One minute, I could imagine the whole enterprise going smoothly on and myself going to the Dean Court Hotel alongside the Minster – which was the refuge of the top clerks in the North Eastern offices – wearing a grey, well-brushed fedora hat. But it would keep coming back to me that the profession I was entering was unmanly. It came down to this: the lawyers only talked about the railway, instead of doing anything to make the trains go.

I wore my great-coat on top of my second best suit. I had on a white shirt and white necker, and I carried in my kit bag a change of shirt and a tie in case the boarding house should turn out to be a more than averagely respectable one. I carried no rule book, but on my suit-coat lapel I'd pinned the company badge, this being the North Eastern Railway crest about one inch across. All company employees were given one on joining, and the keener sorts would wear it every day. You'd be more likely to see a driver or a fireman wearing his badge than a booking office clerk because the footplate lads took more pride in their work.

I had taken off my wedding ring, partly because it didn't do to fire while wearing a ring – there were plenty of things to snag it on – and partly because Ray Blackburn had been a single man, and I wanted to place myself as far as possible in his shoes. (He'd been engaged, evidently, but surely no engine man would ever wear an *engagement* ring.) My railway police warrant card I carried in my pocket book, which was in the inside pocket of my suit-coat. I'd need it if it came to an arrest, but I did not envisage having to produce it, and it must be kept out of sight for as long as I was passing myself off as an engine man.

The Super guarded the shed from his little office, which was stuck onto the front of it like a bunion, spoiling what would otherwise have been a perfectly circular brick wall, for the North Shed was a roundhouse. He was expecting me, and seemed to have been thoroughly briefed by the Chief. He had me sign the ledger which was kept underneath a clock in a little booth of its own, the whole arrangement putting me in mind of a side altar in a church. The ledger was really a big diary. The left hand page for Sunday, 15 March 1914 was the booking-on side, and that was clean. But the booking-off side was dirty because those blokes had spent the past ten hours at close quarters with coal, oil ash and soot. It came to me that this was just how it had been at Sowerby Bridge shed when I'd been firing for the Lancashire and Yorkshire railway eight years since.

As the Super looked on, smoking a little cigar, I signed my name.

'What shall I put under "Duty"?' I asked

'Well,' said the Super, inspecting the end of his cigar, 'you're working the last York train of the day to Scarborough, then running back light engine . . . Only you're not, are you?'

And he practically winked at me.

'I've no notion what I'm doing,' I said. 'All I know is I'm stopping in Scarborough.'

'Your engine'll break down there, lad,' said another voice, and it was the Chief, who had now entered the booth, and was lighting his own cigar from the Shed Super's. 'That way you'll have a good excuse for staying.'

'What's going to be *up* with the engine?' I said.

'Injector steam valve's shot,' said the Chief.

'Leaking pretty badly,' said another voice, and there was a fourth man in the tiny booking-on place. 'Just come and have a look!' he said.

In the confusion of us all getting out of there, and walking into the shed proper, the new man was introduced to me by the Chief, and he was Tom, or Tommy, Nugent. He didn't look like an engine man – too small and curly-haired, and too talkative by half – but he would drive the locomotive to Scarborough. He'd then come on with me to the boarding house called Paradise and obligingly make himself available as a second mark for any murderers that might be living there. He would also be a kind of guard for me, and it did bother me that the Chief thought this should be necessary, especially since he hadn't seemed over-protective of me in the past.

We entered the great shed, and the galvanising coal smell hit me. I thought: How can blokes keep away from a place like this? But there were not many in there and not many engines. Half of the berths, which were arranged like the spokes of a wheel, stood empty. Tommy Nugent led the way, talking thirteen to the dozen. I couldn't quite catch his words, which were directed to the Shed Super and the Chief, but I saw that he walked lame, and I liked the combination of his excited patter and his crocked right leg. He was half crippled but didn't appear to gloom over it.

The air in the shed was grey, and every noise echoed. A shunting engine was being cleaned by a lad I'd often seen about the station, and as he went at the boiler with Brasso, an older bloke, who sat on the boiler top near the chimney, was saying, 'It's a half day and double time, so what are you moaning about?'

They both nodded at Nugent, who seemed a general favourite in the shed. We then passed one of the Class Zs; a bloke lounging by the boiler frame nodded as we went by.

'Aye aye,' he said, and gave a grin, as if to say, 'Look what I've got to lean on.' ('An engine of exceptional grace and power', the *Railway Magazine* had called the Z Class.)

But now our party had come to a stop before a little tuppenny ha'penny J Class. It was in steam, and too much of the stuff was trailing away from the injector overflow pipe beneath the footplate on the right hand side.

'*And* the fire door's jiggered into the bargain,' Nugent was saying. 'It jams on the runners and it's a right bugger to shift it.'

'Seems a bit hard on the passengers,' I said. 'I mean, we are going to *take* passengers, aren't we?'

'You're the 5.52 express,' said the Chief. 'I'll say you're taking bloody passengers!'

'She's been in this state for ages,' said Tommy Nugent. 'She'd get us back home tonight with no bother, but we don't *want* to come back, do we?'

'We want to come back eventually,' I said.

'Paradise,' he said, climbing onto the footplate with some difficulty. 'They've got a nerve calling it that, when they're killing off the fucking guests. Here, what shall I call you when we get there? Not Detective Sergeant Stringer, I suppose?'

The Chief looked at me, and gave a grin. He seemed more easy-going today, perhaps pleased that his plans on my behalf were running smoothly.

'No flies on Tommy,' he said.

'Just call me Jim,' I called up to Tommy.

'But that's your real name.'

'I don't see any harm in using it,' I said.

I didn't see the need of all this palaver either. The aim was to kid any spies the Paradise guest house might have in Scarborough station or engine shed, but it seemed highly unlikely there'd be any.

'Either there's something going on in that house,' I said, 'in which case the offenders will be brought to book, or there isn't, in which case we have a pleasant Sunday night in Scarborough.'

'Or they kill you,' said the Chief, blowing smoke.

The Chief knew I was inclined to nerves, and so would rib me in this way, and I preferred this open style of joshing to the strange smiles he'd given in the Beeswing Hotel.

'Just let 'em try,' said Tommy Nugent. 'I hope they bloody *do*!'

Having collected an oil can from the footplate, he was now touring the lubrication points of the engine. He carried on talking as he did it, but sometimes he'd go out of sight and in one of those moments I said to the Chief:

'Seems a pleasant enough bloke, but he talks a lot . . . might be a bit of a handful in the house.'

'He's plucky though.'

'How'd he come by the leg?'

'Shot wound. Tom was in the York Territorials . . . wandered onto the target range at Strensall barracks.'

No wonder he was in with the Chief then. The Chief was not in the Territorials himself, but as an old soldier he had many connections with them. And he liked any man who shot. He was forever trying to get me at it – and he'd described the missing man, Blackburn, as a good shot.

Nugent's voice had gone muffled as he oiled underneath the engine, but it came clear again as he climbed up out of the inspection pit:

'The good thing is, Jim, that I really am a driver, and you really were a fireman or so I've heard.'

'I was a passed cleaner, but I did plenty of firing. Then I turned copper . . . and now I'm very likely off to be a solicitor.'

'Blimey,' said Tommy Nugent. 'Restless sort, en't you?'

'He has a restless *wife*,' said the Chief, 'which comes to the same thing', and so saying he shook both our hands and went off. I watched him hunch up as he retreated between two engines. He was lighting a new cigar. What did it say on the firework tins? Light the blue touch paper and retire. The question biting me was this: did he know more about the situation in Paradise than he was letting on?

The Shed Super had gone off too, and I was left alone with Tommy Nugent and the busted engine. Tommy took his watch from his waistcoat pocket.

'All set?' he said.

'Aye,' I said,

'Be a lark, this, won't it?' he said.

'Aye,' I said. 'Hope so.'

Chapter Ten

'I want this rolling to stop,' I said.

It helped not to look at things – to keep my eyes closed. But there was no help *for* it; I had to look. On the table beside the chart was the coffee pot, a tin of Abernethy biscuits, a box of wax matches (the label showed a cat with glowing eyes and the words 'See in the Dark') and the Captain's pocket revolver. It had a beautiful walnut stock, worn from use by the looks of it. The chart itself I had given up on. It showed only sea: there was a fold where there might have been the beginnings of land. A north point was drawn at the top of it: a sort of glorious exploding star with a capital N riding above, and I felt we must be moving in that direction for the chart room was growing colder by the second. If I had thought on, I might have come to a different conclusion about our direction of travel, but all I knew was that the sun was rising somewhere and making the sky violet, which was more or less the colour, I also knew, of one of the last rooms on land that I had been in.

As the light rose, the rain had eased a little and the figure on the bridge stood a little more clearly revealed as a man in a great-coat and a woollen hat. He hardly touched the wheel, but just stood by it with arms folded, looking always forward (I had not seen his face) where the prow of the ship plunged and rose with great determination. I could see it all through the windows of the chart room: the fore-deck rising one second, half under swirling waves the next.

Until I'd fallen to staring at the objects on the table I had been talking, but I could not now quite remember what I had been saying or for how long. I could not lay hands on my pocket watch, and I could not see any clock in the chart room. I'd started by demanding – in-between the head racking electric pains – to know how I had come to be aboard, and where we were going. I'd told them that I was a copper, and the Captain had said, 'I am the authority on this ship.'

I'd wanted to know whether my face was as red as my hands, whether or how the Captain and the Mate were connected to the Paradise guest house, and how long I had spent on the coal heap. But I'd given up with the questions after a while: the two would not answer, and the Captain barely spoke at all. I'd always known it would be like this on a ship: the man in charge would be the man who said least. It was a little that way on the railways.

Instead, and in return for a borrowed shirt, guernsey and oilskin, and coffee in a metal cup (they had offered me bread but I was not up to food), I had begun to tell them what had happened. I resolved to lay it all out, in hopes that the more I spoke the more I would know. There was much more to it than I said, but I began to give the Captain and the Dutchman the main points of the tale. I did not know what to leave out, so I left out nothing that seemed material and I was encouraged in my speech by the way the pair of them listened closely, and by the way they were not put off even when my own tales began to include the stories of others, as a ship carries lifeboats.

But the Captain was now looking at his pocket watch. I had not got to the meat of the story; I had not got to Paradise, but the Captain was nodding to the Mate, who turned to me and said, 'We are going, my friend.'

He motioned me to stand.

'Where?' I asked.

'For'ard,' said the Captain.

I rose with difficulty to my feet, and contemplated, through the windows of the chart room, the waves washing over the bows.

'You're too deep laden,' I told the Captain.

He nearly smiled, but it was the Dutchman who replied. 'We have a sea running,' he said, as if it was something the two of them had arranged between them.

The Captain remained in the chart room, but gave his revolver to the Mate, who followed me down the steps we'd come up, and back alongside the fore-hold. It was now full morning, although not much of one: grey light and wild, grey waves, and the white moon still hanging in the sky, waiting to see if it was really day, but its turn of duty done. The grimy fore-sail shook, like something troubled – it wanted to take wing and fly.

'You don't let any man come for'ard,' I said to the Mate. 'You keep the whole ship's company aft.'

All save the man at the wheel. But I left him out of it.

'You save your breath, I think.'

'For what?' I said.

'Sleeping,' he replied, and I heard myself asking, 'Was there something in the coffee? The second pot? Something for sleep?'

Or was it the return of the thing that had done for me the first time?

At any rate, the foc'sle took an eternity to arrive. With the movement of the ship, our way was all up and down and not enough *along*, and the sight of the sea exhausted me. It stretched away on all sides, with no vestige of land to be seen. At the end of our walk the Mate held open an iron door which gave on to a short ladder, and this I was meant to climb down. 'I'm all-in,' I said, more or less to myself, and I would have slept at the bottom, in the metal corridor, the companion way as I believed it was called. But another door was held open for me, and I stepped into an iron room about the size of an ordinary scullery.

'What's this?' I asked.

'Let us say . . . sick bay,' said the Mate.

The Captain would not have tried a crack like that, I thought, but the Mate was a livelier sort, for all the greyness of his face. He closed the door with a clang and seemed to have trouble locking it, for the grating noise carried on for minutes on end, but it hardly mattered since there was no handle on the inside. On the floor, I could just make out a tarpaulin and a great, roughly piled chain with links about a foot long; one end of the thing rose up and disappeared through a hole in the roof, and that was about it as far as entertainment in the iron room went. So I put the tarpaulin about me, lay down in the space between the chain and the wall, and fell instantly to sleep.

Chapter Eleven

I was curious to discover whether I still had the knack of firing but did not get away to a good start: as we stood waiting to run onto the turntable, I couldn't open the firehole door, so Tommy showed me the trick of the lever.

'It wants a light touch,' he said. 'The harder you try, the harder it is.'

That went for the business in general, of course. It was all in the relaxed swing of the shovel. Tommy was now stowing two biggish-sized kit bags in the locker, ready for the off. (My own bag was already up.)

'What've you got in there?' I asked him.

'Toothbrush,' he said, 'and all that sort of doings.'

'Who usually fires on this run?' I asked.

'Oh, we have various,' he said, and he explained how that complication came about, which was something to do with the mysteries of Sunday rostering in the North Shed – and a bloody nuisance too, since he had to run out with some right blockheads. 'Here, do you think it'll be safe to drink the water in Paradise?' he ran on. 'What's the programme?'

'My immediate aim,' I said, 'is to find the blower.'

I was searching for it in all the mix-up of levers and little wheels, and without a murmur of complaint Tommy dragged his bad leg over to my side again.

'That's always the question when you're new to an engine,'

he said, putting his hand on a certain little wheel.

I put a bit of blower on to wake up the fire, then put coal in the four corners, where it was too thin. Being out of practice, I had trouble reaching the back of the box, but Tommy wasn't watching.

'We're booked to leave at five fifty-two,' he said, 'and we'll be in by three minutes past seven, or a little later depending on whatever slow freights are moving through Malton, and who's in the signal box at Seamer. There's one bloke there who . . .'

'What about this injector?' I cut in.

'Have a go,' he said. 'See for yourself.'

I turned the wheel of the injector that was on the blink (all engines have two and both have to be working *tolerably* well since their job is to put water in the boiler, and boiler water is what stands between any engine crew and an explosion). The wheel was stiff, but the injector made the right sort of singing noise, and the water level in the gauges rose without any bother. There was now more steam coming out of the overflow, however.

'Looks worse than it is,' said Tommy, going back to his side. 'You'll have to put a little more rock on, what with the falling pressure. But it's nowt to worry about really.'

'Good thing there's no hills on the way,' I said.

'No hills, no tunnels, nowt. It's that bloody *boring*.'

'I could never find engine driving boring,' I said.

'I could,' he said.

'When I was on the footplate, it was absolute life to me.'

'Just try doing it for twenty years,' he said, '*then* see.'

A clang on the boiler plate from a shed attendant told Tommy he could roll forward onto the turntable. He drove while sitting on the sandbox, to spare his bad leg – and while talking.

'Why d'you pack it in if you were that keen on it?' he asked, before he remembered what the Chief had said. 'Oh aye – your missus. She's the pushing sort, is she? Well, that's all right. You want a lass with a bit of go.'

'You married?' I enquired, leaving off shovelling as we came to rest on the turntable.

'Engaged just last week, Jim,' he said, as we began to revolve. 'Costly business that was: nine carat ring with garnet.'

But he wore no ring himself, of course. Tommy was saying something about how he was pushing fifty now, but it was better late than never and she was a lovely lass. The eyes of every man in the shed were on us as we revolved. It made me feel quite embarrassed.

Then we stopped with a jerk, and were arse-about-face to the shed exit. That was the first surprise, since I'd been banking on us going out forwards. I put the gear to reverse, and Tommy gave a gentle pull on the regulator while talking about his intended, who was called Joan, who was twenty years younger than him and pretty well placed, being the daughter of the fellow who owned the shop called the Overcoat Depot on Coney Street. I kept up my end of the conversation by asking who made the giant grey coat, about fifteen foot long and covered in bird shit, that hung from the flagpole near the roof of the Depot, and Tommy not only knew the answer, but had a tale to tell about it as well.

However, I left off listening as we came out of the shed into the heart of the railway lands, where the church bells were still ringing, but in colder and darker air. Over the tracks all around us hung red and green lamps, like rows of low stars, and each one meant something. I'd got my living in the middle of this mysterious web for years, but forgotten how it worked, and even Tommy Nugent had to keep silence for a while as he began to pick his way in the J Class.

We first raced backwards towards a pegged signal and a red lamp that I was sure would check us. But we ran on past them, because it turned out they belonged to another track after all. We carried on going through the railway lands just as though aiming for the main 'up' and a run backwards all the way to London. But after clattering over a diagonal mass of tracks we came to a stop, and Tommy indicated for me to put us into forward gear. We were still some way off from the station, and I was interested to see how we'd get into it.

We again clattered over the diagonal mass, this time heading forwards, and Tommy stopped us under the eye of the waterworks signal box, which was five hundred yards in advance of the station on the 'down' side. We then reversed into the echoing, bluish gloom of the great station, and buffered up to the little rake of Scarborough coaches that waited for us on a short platform, Number Ten, with Tommy talking again about what might or might not be waiting for us in the Paradise guest house, just as though what he'd done with the engine was of no account at all.

I wound down the hand brake, leant out, and looked backwards. The coaches we'd backed onto had been brought up from Leeds, for we were about to make the second part of the Leeds–Scarborough run that Blackburn had done in its entirety, owing to the sickness of the York man. Our service, in fact, would be exactly the same as the one he'd worked into Scarborough.

They were a miserable looking lot, the half dozen or so

boarding at York for Scarborough – didn't seem to want to drag themselves away from the gaslights of Platform Ten. In summer, Scarborough was a better place to be than York but in winter the scales tipped, and York was better. As the passengers boarded, our train guard climbed down from his van, and came walking up. Had he been briefed by the Chief? Had he buggery. He was a big bloke, with a blank white face behind blank glasses. I half turned away from him, and began shovelling coal as he handed a docket to Tommy. I could tell he was eyeing me, but if Tommy never had the same fireman twice it ought not to signify.

In fact, Tommy didn't even bring up the subject.

'Injector exhaust's playing up worse than usual,' he said to the guard, who might have worked that out for himself, since he was standing in the hot cloud the leak was making. He said nothing as Tommy talked but stood motionless on the platform until his glasses had completely steamed over from the leak. He then turned and walked back to his guard's van.

I left off shovelling when he'd gone, and said to Tommy, 'He's not a York bloke, is he?'

'Les? He lives in Scarborough.'

'Not at the Paradise guest house, I hope?'

'No – he has a flat near the goods station.'

'Quiet sort, en't he?'

'He's half blind is Les White,' said Tommy, as though that was somehow an answer.

He left it to me to look for the 'right away' from the platform guard. Tommy was nattering away as I looked out, and was still nattering when the whistle blew. He did hear it though, because he gave a tug on the regulator, and we started rolling.

' . . . Half blind,' Tommy repeated in a thoughtful sort of way.

'That's why the traffic office took him off the footplate.'

'He'd been a driver, had he?' I said, and we were making a new noise, owing to being on the iron bridge over the river Ouse, which rolled black under the riverside lamps.

'Passed fireman, Les was, but failed his eye test for driving. So now he's a guard. Just counts the carriages, makes up his dockets . . . then sits in his van playing chess.'

'Who against?'

'Himself. Seems rum to me – I mean to say, how can you ever win? There again, though, how can you ever *lose*? Funny thing about those cheaters of his . . .'

I was counting off the dark landmarks of retreating York: railway laundry, cocoa works, gas works.

'Cheaters?' I said.

'His blinkers.'

'You what?'

'Les's glims. Those bloody bins of his . . .'

'You mean his spectacles?'

Tommy frowned.

'Aye,' he said after a moment, as though the word would just about do at a pinch. 'He got 'em about a year since, and they somehow made him silent. I don't know how but they sort of choked him off. Trainload of crocks we are – him with his eyes, me with me leg.'

That's right, I thought, and the engine's jiggered into the bargain.

The junction for Hull was to the right, and we clattered over the complication of tracks. Next thing we were flashing through the little halt for Strensall barracks, and I said, 'This is where you did your leg, the Chief told me. At the barracks.'

Tommy nodded and half smiled.

'Didn't hurt too much, I hope?'

'I didn't know a deal about it,' said Tommy. 'I went unconscious, you see. Funny thing is, when I came around, I was chattering away like billy-o.'

'*Really*?' I said. 'About what?'

'About all sorts.'

And while Tommy Nugent talked about what he'd been talking about when he was accidentally shot, I tried my best to balance fire and water, periodically breaking off to look out of the side of the J Class.

It felt fine to be swinging the shovel again, and just after the village of Flaxton, Tommy, who'd been going on about what a white bloke my governor was, interrupted himself (so to speak) to come over to my side, clap me on the back, and say, 'I wish I had you firing every Sunday'.

I was quite choked by this, almost felt the tears springing to my eyes, and I said, 'You think I'm up to the mark then?' which of course I shouldn't have done but I wanted to hear it again.

'She's steaming like a fucking witch,' Tommy said, making his way with difficulty back to his sand box, and that was even better. No praise that might come my way as an articled clerk could ever mean so much, of that I was sure.

The ruins of Kirkham Abbey came up on the right – a standing shadow in the gloom – and I said, 'Tell me about Blackburn.'

'Hasn't your governor put you in the picture?' said Tommy. '*Well* then . . .'

Between Kirkham Abbey and Malton – which was our only booked stop – Tommy told me all he knew about the fellow.

Leeds and York were both in District One of the company's Rifleman's League, which was where Tommy did his shooting

74

after having been invalided out of the Territorial Army. He and
Ray Blackburn had first met two years ago at a shooting match
in the York range at Queen Street, behind the station, and since
there were only three other clubs in District One, they'd shot
against each other a few times since. Nugent said that
Blackburn was 'quiet – a slow and steady sort of bloke'. *Being*
slow and steady, he was 'better at the deliberate targets . . . not
a great hand at the quick-firing'. But a good shot all the same.
'He had a good eye,' as Tommy said.

After that *first* meeting, the Leeds and York teams had gone
for a drink in the York Railway Institute.

'They'd bested us,' said Tommy, 'and the losers generally buy
the winners the first drinks. But Ray came straight up to me,
put out his hand, and said, "Good shooting. Now what will you
have?"'

That had impressed Tommy no end, especially since his firing had been 'all over the shop' that evening. What had
impressed him still more though was that Ray Blackburn had
turned out to be a tee-totaller, so Tommy hadn't had to buy
him a drink back. 'Refused outright – wouldn't even have a
lemonade.'

'He never drank?'

'Never,' said Tommy. 'He would smoke the odd small cigar,
and that was it.'

When the two had met for a second time, after a shooting
match in Hartlepool, it had been the same story over again.
Blackburn had shot well, Tommy not so well, but still
Blackburn had bought the round, expecting nothing in return.
This combination of superb shooting and not requiring a
drink had quite floored Tommy – 'I mean, talk about gentlemanly' – and I had a suspicion that it was on this account,

rather than because of any deep acquaintance, that he'd come to Scarborough.

'If Ray Blackburn's been done in,' said Tommy, 'then I want to know who's done him, and I want to be up and at 'em.'

'Did the Chief ask you to come on this job, or did *you* ask the Chief?'

'I wanted to know if I could help at all,' said Tommy, drawing back the regulator.

'It does you credit to risk your neck for a stranger,' I said, and Tommy coloured up at that.

'I en't risking me neck,' he said, but whether because he doubted his own words or because he was embarrassed at being praised we went on in near silence for the next little while, with Tommy just occasionally adjusting his position on the sandbox, as though his bad leg was giving him jip.

'Of course, he was religious,' I put in, as we flew through the little station of Huttons Ambo. (It was too dark to see, but I knew the long platform signs there from memory: 'Huttons Ambo: serves also High and Low Hutton'.)

'That's right is that,' said Tommy. 'Catholic. I can't remember how I know that but he was the sort of bloke . . . you just couldn't *help* but know. Not that he was pi. It just came off him.'

'Radiated,' I said.

Tommy nodded.

' . . . Sort of thing. 'Course, with that particular lot, there's no bar on drinking, quite the opposite in fact. So there *again* he was just that bit different. Mind you, that lass of his . . .'

'His fiancée?'

'I only saw her once – easy on the eye but a bit of a tart, if you ask me. Led him a right bloody dance.'

76

'What did he look like?'

'Nice looking fellow. Dark, biggish – very dark eyes.'

As we closed on the market town of Malton, Tommy gave up on Ray Blackburn for a while, yawned and limped over a couple of paces to glance at my fire. 'Dead spot back centre,' he said. 'Big coal makes a dead spot,' he added, going back to his perch. 'You want it about the size of your fist.'

It wasn't a criticism, I told myself, so much as just a passing remark. He hadn't meant to take back his earlier praise. As I put on coal, I was half aware of Tommy opening the locker door. A little later, as I continued shovelling, he was pulling a night-shirt and under-drawers from one of his kit bags, and when I looked over at him again, he was pointing a fucking rifle at me.

Chapter Twelve

It was a short rifle – barely three feet long – and Tommy stood there grinning with it in his hand, and rocking slightly on the footplate.

'I'll be taking this in, if it's all right with you,' he said.

He reached again into his kit bag, and took out a smaller bag made of cloth. From this he took a cartridge, which he put between his front teeth.

'Hold on a minute,' I said.

'I've another in the kit bag, and *you* can have that one,' said Tommy, still with the cartridge between his teeth. He pulled a lever behind the trigger; the gun broke, and he put in the cartridge. He snapped the gun shut once again.

'See how it's done?' he said.

He then pulled the lever again and the cartridge flew spinning upwards before landing on the footplate. Tommy caught it up, and frowned. 'Dented, that is,' he said, and he pitched it through the fire-hole door into the rolling white flames.

'Shut the door, man,' I said. 'There's liable to be a bloody explosion.'

But as I spoke there came only a soft, single pop from within the fire. I stared at Tommy, as we rattled into Malton.

'You're a bit of a dark horse, en't you?' I said.

'It's only little,' he said, running his hand along the stock. 'Carbine, point two-two calibre. Handy if you're on horseback or if you're a lad – or both. Yours'll be just the same, but you can have a feel of both, and take whichever one suits.'

'Stow it, Tommy,' I said. 'Police don't go armed in this country . . . Does the Chief know you've brought all this ironmongery?'

'Why else would he send me?'

That *might* be right.

And as we rattled on through the night, I saw that in Tommy's eyes this gun – or these *guns* – made up for his crocked leg; gave him a value in this world that he didn't seem to get from driving an engine. The guns were the reason he'd come, and it was just like the Chief to have packed me off with someone like Tommy; part of his game of keeping me always on the jump. I was his favourite all right, but I paid the bloody price for it.

'Look, this is a fishing trip, Tommy,' I said. 'Do you know what that means? We go in and keep our eyes skinned. I come back and write a report saying whether further questioning is required. There ought to be no bother. We ought to be perfectly all right.'

'Ought to be?' he said. 'With these beauties, it's a surety. You know the firing positions, I suppose? There's standing . . .'

And he shouldered the weapon, with the dark streets of Malton rolling behind.

'Kneeling . . .'

At that, he did kneel down and aimed the gun in all the black dust of the footplate. I ought to stop him. Apart from anything else, the Chief had shown me the firing positions more than once, in hopes of getting me to take up shooting as a benefit to myself, the railway company I worked for, and the country I lived in.

'. . . And prone.'

Tommy baulked at that one, but I could tell he'd been contemplating lying flat to show me the third firing position. He was now stowing the rifle in the kit bag again. It appeared that he kept them wrapped in his clothes, towel, night-shirt; fairly buried they were by the time he'd finished. He then shut the locker door smartly, for Malton was coming up.

Three minutes later we were at a stand in the empty station. It was 6.35 p.m., but you'd have thought it was midnight. Of train guard Leslie White there was no sign. A couple of people had boarded, one had alighted, and we were waiting for our starter signal and the whistle of the platform guard, who stood a little way off with hands clasped and head bowed as though someone had lately died.

The signal gave a jerk, the platform guard looked up, and we were off. Tommy didn't wait for the whistle. For all that he seemed the most amiable of blokes, the business with the gun had set me thinking he was a bit crackers.

With one hand on the regulator, he was talking now about how he hadn't told Joan, his intended, what he would be about in Scarborough; how he'd tell her after the event, on Wednesday, when they were going to the Electric Theatre on Fossgate; how they reserved seats for every Wednesday; how you could get ninepenny seats for sixpence if you reserved but no seats there were very comfortable, which was why for *preference* they'd go to the City Picture Palace on Fishergate, only it wasn't possible to reserve there so you had to take pot luck, which was no use because Joan always wanted an aisle seat, not on her own account but so that he, Tommy, could stretch out his leg – this even though he always said he didn't care where he sat. 'The leg does not stretch out, and that's all about it,' he told me, before embarking on a further speech about how he was looking for a house over Holgate way to move into with Joan . . . and presently we were approaching Scarborough.

Only half the lamps were lit, and the wide, dark terminus stood nearly empty. A long coal train was parked at the excursion overload platform, as though to send out a message: *Forget about coming here for pleasure this time of year.* Other coal wagons were scattered about on the approach roads, and a little pilot engine waited with a bloke leaning out of the cab. He'd no doubt be put to rounding up the wagons; meantime, he was smoking and watching us come in.

Scarborough, being a terminus, had a strange arrangement that made the working complicated. We drew right up to the buffer beams on Platform One. We would then – as I supposed – uncouple our coaches, and the pilot would pull them back, releasing our engine. In the normal course of things we'd then work backwards to the engine shed, which was about a mile off, take on water, turn on the turntable, and head back to York. But our engine was not fit for the run back, or so we would make out.

Tommy Nugent was already on the platform, and making his lop-sided way towards a door under a big lantern: the office of the night station master. He knocked, the door was opened, and in he went to start lying.

I looked back, and the last of our half dozen passengers were stepping down from the carriages. They walked through the leaking steam and away towards the exit. Leslie White, the guard, was coming up through the steam as well. He stopped, and turned his specs in my direction.

'Where's Tom?' he said, and I saw there was a wooden box and a folded board under his arm. I read the label on the box:

'In there, mate,' I said, indicating the SM's closed door.

White's spectacles tilted that way, then back to me.

'You're running light back?'

'Reckon not,' I said.

And I indicated the steam whirling all around us.

He gave the shortest of nods, turned on his heel, and went off. There was a crew room somewhere about. He'd book off there. When he'd gone, I was left quite alone on Platform One. I saw the pilot engine simmering away on the approach road, but the driver of it made no move. The door of the night station master's office opened, and Tommy stepped out.

'He's telephoning through to the shed,' he said, and his voice echoed in the empty station. 'They'll look at the engine overnight.'

The bloke in the pilot engine had now stirred himself, and was buffering up to the back of our coaches. Tommy was heading for the platform edge, prior to climbing down and uncoupling. But to spare his leg, I said I'd do it. I jumped down onto the filthy ballast, and began unscrewing the brake pipe. As I worked, I saw Tommy's boots, and he was talking at a great rate once again, as though to keep my spirits up.

It'd only be the work of a moment, he said, to run up to the shed, make out the card describing our engine's defects, and book off. We'd have a bit of a spruce-up, but not too much because we did want to look like engine men after all, then it'd be off to Paradise to sort out that bad lot, perhaps with a stop for a pint on the way. He generally took a pint at the end of a turn did Tommy, if not several, and he didn't see why he should do any different this time. But I didn't know about that. Now that the journey was done I wanted to be off to the house of mystery as soon as possible, get in and out, have the whole business done with.

It would be another half hour, though, before we untangled ourselves from the railway lands of Scarborough . . .

The pilot pulled back our coaches and took them off to the darkness, making for the tunnel that led to the main Scarborough sidings at Gallows Close, where excursion carriages by the hundred were stored in winter much as a lad's train set is stowed in a cupboard when school term begins. We then worked the J Class back to the engine shed, where Tommy fell into a long, echoing conversation with a very tall fitter, whose long brown dust-coat looked as though it might be hiding the fact that he was really two men, one standing on the shoulders of the other. The shed was dark, and smelt of the dying fires that had been dropped into the pits below the engines. Tommy Nugent's voice came drifting through the floating wisps of smoke.

' . . . And that's how I know it's not the clack valve, you see. Now the stuff's not coming out full bore, so it's not completely shot, but of course the higher the pressure the faster the leak, and what it could really do with is . . .'

Why did he have to go on so? The valve needed replacing, and that was all about it. They'd be very unlikely to have the right one in the Scarborough shed so we'd have all the excuse we needed to hang about in the town for ages if we wanted. I wandered into the booking-on vestibule, where there was a little less floating smoke, and a little more light, thanks to two gas lamps sticking out over a wide, green North Eastern Railway notice board. I walked up for a look. I was informed that two new dummy signals were in place on the Scarborough approach, and a certain water tank had been discontinued.

Company employees were to refrain from removing the news-papers from the engine men's mess, otherwise newspapers would no longer be provided. A small quantity of gunpowder had been found under a seat on a train running between Scarborough and Filey and a general warning was accordingly issued to all employees of the railway. A fellow from the shed had won a barometer at cycle racing.

In one corner of the board was a space for notices of a more general nature. A seven-roomed house was for sale in Scarborough: 'In splendid condition – large garden.' My eye ran on to the notice directly beneath: 'PREPARE FOR A RAINY DAY!' I didn't read that, but moved directly to the one below.

Paradise Guest House. All rooms excellent and nicely furnished. Baths, hot and cold water. Sea views. Five minute walk from station. Railway men always welcome, cheap rates for short or long stay. Apply Miss Rickerby at Paradise Guest House, 3 Bright's Cliff, Scarborough.

Miss Rickerby – she sounded a respectable enough party. A picture composed in my mind of a thin, jittery woman who almost outdid her white dress for paleness, but I realised I'd called to mind a Mrs *Riccall*, who worked in the pharmacy on Nunnery Lane, York, and was known to the wife. Just then Tommy Nugent came limping into the vestibule.

'Well, I'm finally shot of it,' he said, meaning the J Class. 'I've told 'em we'll come back in the morning about ten to see what's what.'

'We'll try to,' I said. 'It all depends on events.'

Tommy stood still under the gas with his cap in his hand, and he made his eyes go wide, and blew upwards, which caused his curly hair to move.

'Quick wash and brush-up, then Paradise it is!' he said.

I didn't show him the notice posted by or on behalf of Miss Rickerby because I'd finally worked out what was making him talk at such a rate: Tommy Nugent was spoiling for a scrap, and I didn't doubt he'd prove a brave man if it came to it. But that didn't mean he didn't have the wind up.

Chapter Thirteen

I might have been sleeping in my metal quarters as I heard the sound of a bell amid the sea roar and the creaking iron. It might have been the bell that woke me. There came another, and I counted five strokes in all. Were we within earshot of a coastal church?

No, the bells were floating along with us; we had made away with them, carried them off. They rang them for the watches, and five strokes did not mean five o'clock. I thought again of the run to Scarborough, and how I ought to have known not to head for the sea. I figured a boat approaching the Scarborough harbour, lurching on the waves like a drunkard; I called to mind the clock tower above Scarborough railway station, white against the Scarborough night, a foreign look to it somehow. I thought of the porter who was keen to lock the station gate, as though he had secret and illegal business to conduct there; I saw a heap of razors, safetys and cut-throats, and a hot bluish room. I saw again the gigantic needle hanging in the air. I began to count, and the needle faded.

The station clock tower came up once more, and I knew I had a brain injury of some sort – a concussion perhaps – because I could not see why a station would have a clock, leave alone a clock *tower*? It was asking for trouble, because the clock would only prove the trains wrong. I adjusted my position against the chain. No. It was *churches* that had clocks in the main, but why did churches have clocks? They did not operate trains. They were not in the business of time, quite the opposite really. But they did have them, and that was fact. It seemed to me that my brain was befuddled as before, but I was no longer subject to the flashes of electricity, and the sea was perhaps a little calmer. The violent rocking had been replaced with a calmer up and down, like a great breathing.

More visions came. I saw in my mind's eye an oil lamp burning red, a gas bracket giving a shaking white light.

I saw a knife polisher on a kitchen table, a packet containing rat poison and again the lamp burning red, as though by thinking of light, I might *create* light.

The chain room was darker than when I had been put into it. A tiny amount of moonlight came down through the hole that the chain went through, and this only illuminated the remainder of the chain. There was no mystery about where the thing went. It was not the Indian rope trick. This was the anchor chain – it ran up to the windlass on the fore-deck – and I had a suspicion that the anchoring of the boat, the end of the voyage, would be the end of me as well, because there would be *policemen* where we ended, and law and order generally – and the Captain meant to avoid that. Yes, it would be very dangerous even to sight land, because it would remind the Captain and the Mate that they would have to account to someone for holding me prisoner and I did not think they were over-keen to do that.

I was too bloody cold.

I sat against the chain and pulled the tarpaulin around me. I was supposed to be becoming a solicitor, a notion that seemed more than ever mysterious. I tried to recall having done some lawyering but could not. I had stood up many times in the police court but only as a policeman-witness. I had meant to be going into a quiet office over-looking the sleeping wagons of the old station, but there had evidently been a change of plan, and I would be going to the North Pole instead.

Running my hand over the tarpaulin, it came to me that it was not smooth as a tarpaulin ought to be, and it did not have the tar smell that generally came off a tarp. The smell in the chain locker was paint and oil, and I wondered whether it might serve as a *sail* locker as well. I swept my hand again over the canvas – for that's what it was – and found the thing I was after before I knew I was looking for it: a stretch of rope. I could not find the end of it and for all I knew it was longer than the anchor chain, but a length of it between my hands made a weapon. I sat back holding the rope and feeling there would be no half measures from now on. When the grey Dutchman came back, I would be on him; I would be on him quicker than thinking.

But after a while I set down the rope. It was too cold to hold. A short interval of time later, I pulled the oilskin more tightly around me, and made also to wrap myself in the great sheet, which might have been a sail or might have been something else again, but as I counted the faint ringing of a further six bells, it didn't seem to matter one way or another, and the only thing to do was to give in to the darkness, the rise and fall and the deep cold, and to sleep.

Chapter Fourteen

We had a scrub-down in the engine shed wash room. Then we walked back to the station along a cinder track, and climbed up onto Platform One. We exited the station through the main gates that a porter stood ready to padlock. It was only just gone seven, but he was shutting up shop. It was depressing, some-how, that a fair-sized station like this should close so early.

I said to the porter, 'Leslie White, our guard . . . has he come by?'

'Ten minutes since,' he replied.

With the station behind us, we stood at the top of Valley Bridge Road. A few wagons rolled through the streets but there were no trams to be seen, and precious few people.

Turning towards Tommy, I said, 'Paradise is on Bright's Cliff – it's on the south side, off Newborough.'

'Not far, is it?' he enquired, as we began to walk.

He came to Scarborough a lot but evidently did not leave the station very much. I mended my pace to his as we made our way along the dark canyon of the Valley Road. Tall houses stood a little way off on either side, beyond the Valley Gardens. They were beautifully tended, those gardens – and famous for it – but now they were enclosed in darkness. Halfway along, the sea came into view below us, with the white of the wave tops standing out clearly on the black water.

'It's getting up,' said Tommy, when he drew level with me.

He'd expected the sea to be quiet, like the town.

The tide was coming in, and the waves were like an invasion sweeping right up to the empty Promenade. The Grand Hotel was in view high on our left, the four turrets making it look like a great castle – a fortress against the sea. Lights shone at barely a quarter of the windows. The flags on the roof were all stretched out to the utmost by the sea wind.

'Bright's Cliff is on the other side of it,' I said. 'We've come a bit out of our way.'

'Oh, wait a bit,' said Tommy. 'I'm missing a bloody bag.'

It was true enough: he only carried one of his two.

'Reckon I left it at the gate,' he said. 'I put it down when you asked the bloke about Les White. Will you just hold on here?'

'Is it the one with the guns in it?'

'One of 'em,' he said, which I didn't quite understand.

'I'll go,' I said, because I was twice as quick as him and I wanted to get on, but Tommy wouldn't have it. He would fetch the bag himself.

'Look,' I said, pointing to a lonely-looking bench under a lamp on the Promenade. 'I'll wait for you there.'

'Right you are, mate,' he said, and he turned to go.

'Leave your other bag here at any rate!' I called after him, but he didn't seem to hear that, and I stared after him until he was claimed by the darkness of the Valley Gardens.

I sat down on the bench, and watched the waves for a while. Then I looked to my right, where the Prom curved around towards the Spa, which was like a little mansion with a ball-room, restaurant and orchestra. But this Sunday evening the Prom curved away into darkness, and the Spa might as well have been spirited clean away.

Because I was looking the wrong way, I didn't see the

woman who approached out of the darkness from the left and sat on the bench alongside me. She wore a blue dress, which came out from underneath a grey-blue double-breasted coat, which she hugged tight about her. Her hair was a mass of dark curls under a fetching hat with a peaked brim and a feather in it. I thought: She looks like a hunter. Who was the Greek female who was the hunter? I couldn't recall.

She looked out to sea, and I watched her face from the side. It was squareish, darkish, a little plump with wide green eyes. She was wrapping the coat tight around herself, and I thought: If she's so cold, why is she sitting here and not walking briskly? But then she left off with the coat, and gave a sort of startled gasp, as though she'd just remembered something. I thought: She'll go off now. But she crossed her legs right over left instead, and began waggling her raised right boot. The wife would do that when she was restless, but this woman was not restless; she was bored, more like – and idle with it. I liked the look of her though, and I thought I'd better stop eyeing her in case it became obvious.

I craned my neck backwards to see whether I could catch sight of Tommy Nugent coming out of the gloom of the Valley Gardens. But there was no sign of him, so I looked forward again, and counted three wide waves as they came in, turning themselves inside out and going from black to white in the process. I knew the woman was eyeing me, so I tried to watch the sea as though I had some special understanding of its moods and movements.

Another night walker came up out of the darkness to the left: a man in a great-coat and a high-crowned bowler. He walked a little white dog with the lead wrapped around his wrist, and he was eating a fried fish from a bit of paper. He

91

stopped just in front of the bench, and leant against the railing, half looking out at the wild sea, half at the woman on the bench. He might have nodded at her and nudged his hat when he'd come up, or he might just have been setting it right after a gust of wind.

The fish didn't half smell good, and the dog thought so too, because it would sit down, begging to be given a scrap, then shuffle about and sit down again, just in case its master hadn't noticed the first time. The man ate the fish with a superior look, as if conveying to the dog: 'Well yes, I suppose you would like a piece, but then who wouldn't? It happens to be excellent grub, otherwise *I* wouldn't be eating it.' After a few moments, the woman spoke up, and I was glad – encouraged, somehow – to hear that her accent was mild.

'Will you give your dog some of that fish, for heaven's *sake*?' she said.

'He doesn't like fish,' said the man, and I couldn't tell whether the two knew each other or not.

'You could have fooled me,' said the woman.

'It's cats that like fish,' said the man.

'Try him,' said the woman.

'Oh all right,' said the man, and he dropped a bit of fish that the dog caught and ate in an instant.

'I saw Jepson in town today,' said the woman.

'The magician?' the man asked, rather unexpectedly, as he finished off the fish and crumpled up the paper. '*He's* in town early.'

'Or late,' said the woman. 'He was in Boyes's.'

'Oh aye?'

'Household Goods department . . . Returning a kettle. He was after a full refund.'

'Why?'

'It was faulty.'

'How?'

'In the only way that a kettle can be faulty, Mr Wilson,' replied the woman (and she gave me a look as she did so). 'It had a hole in it.'

'Well,' said the man (evidently Wilson), 'what about it?'

'He was very angry.'

'He's entitled, isn't he?' said Wilson, who was surprisingly off-hand with the woman, considering how pretty she was. 'If I bought a kettle with a hole in it, I'd do my nut.'

'Yes, but *you're* not The Magical Marvel of the Age,' said the woman. '. . . With all due respect.'

The man pulled a face, which might have meant anything.

'It doesn't do for a man who's supposed to have mysterious powers to get all worked up about a faulty kettle,' said the woman.

'Well, that's his look-out,' said the man, and, giving a half nod to the woman, he went off into the windy darkness as the woman said, partly to herself: 'He put on such a lovely show at the Winter Gardens, as well.'

The woman now stood up and sighed at the sea. She took off her hat, and drove her hand into the mass of curls. Then she turned and headed off into the Valley Gardens. I watched her for the space of three lamps, and at the instant she disappeared there was Tommy Nugent coming the other way, grinning and limping, kit bags in hand.

'You all set?' I said, standing up.

He gave a nod; there was no mention of taking a pint. He seemed minded to get on with it now. We walked towards the funicular railway that led up towards the Grand, and I read the

famous sign: 'Two hundred and twenty steps avoided for 1d.'
But it wasn't working. The two carriages were suspended
halfway up, like two signal boxes dangling from a cliff. It was a
strain for Tommy to climb the steps, but he never moaned. As
we toiled up, we had the high north wall of the Grand Hotel
towering alongside us. There were no windows in it, and a dark
slime ran all the way to the top.

Tommy was saying about he'd had enough of the J Class;
he'd try to lay his hands on one of the Class Qs. They had a
good height to the cab roof; you weren't all cramped up in
there as with the Js. They'd been express engines, but were now
coming off the main line, and were ideal for the medium distance, semi-fast trips like the Scarborough runs. He was talking to cover up nerves, I felt sure of it.

At the top of the steps, we were in the square that stood
between the Grand and the Royal hotels. No-one was about. A
horse whirled a hansom away from the front of the Grand, and
I had the idea that every last person was fleeing the town. We
turned right, making for Newborough, which was the main
shopping street of Scarborough, but dead and abandoned now
apart from the shouts of a few unseen loafers.

We went past a furniture store that showed in the window
its own idea of the perfect living room, lit by a low night light.
Next to it was a marine stores: 'All Kinds of Nets Sold'. After
half a dozen shuttered and dark shops I saw the sign: 'Bright's
Cliff'. It was a short stub of a street at a slight angle off the
Newborough – put me in mind of a drain leading to the cliff
edge, a sort of cobbled groove over-looked by houses older
than the common run of Scarborough buildings. At the end of
it stood a single lamp that marked the very edge of
Scarborough, and a steep drop down to the Prom. Near by

stood an upended hand cart with a couple of old sacks tangled up in the wheel spokes. It might have been connected with some stables that looked half derelict.

The end property was turned somewhat towards the cliff edge, as though disgusted with the rest of the street, and a derrick stuck out from its front, from the forehead of the house's face, so to say. This must be for drawing things up the cliff. I walked directly to the end of Bright's Cliff and looked down. I saw an almost sheer bank, covered in old bramble bushes and nettles; then came a gravel ledge, then the rooftops of some buildings on the Prom: a public house, a public lavatory, and the Sea Bathing Infirmary. A little light leaked out of the pub, and, as I looked down, with Tommy Nugent breathing hard behind me, a man walked out of it – well, he was just a moving hat from where we looked, and the hat revolved on the Prom, and doubled back into the public lavatory, which must still have been open. I doubted that the sea bathing place was open. There'd be very few takers for its waters in March.

Tommy tapped me on the shoulder, and I wheeled about.

'Paradise is that one,' he said, and . . . Well, I didn't know about paradise but, as far as Bright's Cliff went, the house indicated was the best of a bad lot.

Chapter Fifteen

It was a house of white-painted bricks, and the paint was falling away a little, like the white powder on the face of a pierrot. It was perhaps a hundred years old, and sagged somewhat. The windows were rather ill-assorted as if they'd been bought in a job lot at knockdown price, no two being the same size. The door was blue; over it was a fanlight of coloured glass with the name of the house set into it, the letters being distributed between the different panes like so: PA-RAD-ISE.

'You knock,' said Tommy, and he held one kit bag in each hand, as though he was ready to march straight in.

I knocked, and there came the sound of a woman's laughter from beyond the door as I did it. The door opened slowly, and there stood a trim, well-dressed man, perhaps in the middle fifties. The laughter had stopped but the man was smiling pleasantly. He was the very last sort of person I'd bargained for, and I was silenced for a moment by the sight of him. He tipped his head, preparatory to asking our business. But Tommy was already speaking.

'We're two railway men,' he said. 'He's the fireman, and I'm the driver.' (I thought: Don't say that, it's not convincing.) 'We've just come from the station, and we're having to overnight in Scarborough.' He took a deep breath before continuing: 'Now we've heard . . .'

But the man cut in, turning a little to one side, and saying,

'Miss R! Two gentlemen in need of a bed – they're railway men,' he added, in a way I didn't much care for.

The trim man was now replaced in the doorway by a woman – and it was the one who'd been sitting on the bench. She'd evidently just come in, for she had her grey-blue coat and hunter's hat still on. She looked a bit distracted, flushed and very pretty. I took off my hat, and she whipped hers off at exactly the same time, as though we were playing the looking glass game; and then she shook her curls.

The hall was rather cramped. The landlady stood on a brownish carpet, a little worn, under a swinging gas chandelier, with three of the four lights burning. The wallpaper was green stripes, also a little faded; there was a faint smell of paint. On the wall was a thin case with a glass front. Above it a sign said, 'Today's Menu,' but there was nothing in the case. The stairs were narrow, and rose up into darkness. The thin banister was rather battered . . . and the hall was too hot. In spite of this, the woman seemed highly amused at something or other – and she *was* beautiful.

I was on the point of speech, but Tommy was under way again.

'Our engine's broke down,' he said. 'It's an injector steam valve that's giving bother.'

'I'm awfully sorry,' said the woman, 'but you see . . .'

'Steam's pouring out of the overflow, and when that happens . . .'

The woman was eyeing me, half smiling. Did she remember me from the bench?

'We saw your notice in the engine men's mess,' I interrupted, for fear that if I didn't speak up soon she'd think me dumb.

'Ordinarily,' Tommy was saying, 'we'd have taken the engine

back to York tonight but it's not up to the trip, so we've left it at the Scarborough shed, and in all likelihood they'll have it sorted out by morning.'

'*Good*,' said the woman, by which she no doubt meant: 'Shut up.' Then she said, 'We hate to turn railway men away, but we only have the one room available tonight.'

'Single bed, is it?' I asked.

'If *that*,' she said, with half a smile.

I turned about and looked at Tommy; then back to the woman, who looked as if she was trying not to laugh. It was fascinating to watch the movement of her lips over her teeth.

'Do you mind if we step away for a moment to talk it over?' I asked her.

'Not a bit,' she replied, and she retreated into the house, leaving the door on the jar.

I walked with Tommy towards the gas lamp at the end of Bright's Cliff.

'I'm going to take the room, Tommy,' I said. 'I'm the investigating officer and . . . well, do you see?'

He put down his two bags on the cobbles, and, opening one of them, said, 'Fair do's, Jim. But you'll take a rifle, won't you?'

I'd forgotten about the bloody rifles.

'No,' I said, and Tommy looked put-out. 'I mean . . . they're a bit small,' I said.

'Dangerous to a mile these are, Jim,' he said, 'and I should think the average room in that house is about ten foot across.'

'But they're meant for target shooting. I mean, they're *miniature* rifles, aren't they?'

'How big a hole do you want to make in their bloody heads, Jim?'

He was unwinding one of the great bandages he'd made of

all his under-clothes.

'Well,' I said, 'I don't want to make a hole in their heads at all. I'm not trained up in rifle shooting.'

'No need to be a dead eye,' he said. 'Not inside a house. You're not going to need orthoptic bloody *spectacles*, Jim: just pull the bloody trigger. And I'll tell you something else: you're well away with this because it's about the only gun you could loose off indoors and not deafen yourself.'

He was obviously a good deal more concerned for the one firing than the one being fired *at*. I looked down at the kit bag, where one of the rifles was in clear view.

'I just don't fancy it, Tommy,' I said. 'I shan't bother.'

'Jim,' he said, glancing back over towards the door, 'those people are *strange*.'

The door of Paradise was still half open, spilling coloured gaslight onto the cobbles of Bright's Cliff.

I said, 'They didn't look strange to me.'

Tommy now held a third bloody shooter in his hand: a pistol this time. It was very small and thin – there was nothing to it. It looked like a pop gun of Harry's.

'Two-two pistol,' he said.

'How many more have you got in there?'

'What do you say, Jim? You can carry this beauty in your pocket.'

I shook my head, and he fastened up the kit bag, covering over this final offering.

'Remember this,' he said, 'if Ray Blackburn *was* killed, and you click to the reason, they'll come after you no matter what.'

'Tommy,' I said, 'I can't hang about or it'll look funny. I'll see you at the station tomorrow, all right?'

And it appeared that I really had offended him, because

without another word he marched along the short cobbled road until he came to the junction with Newborough, where he hesitated for a moment, before turning left and disappearing from sight.

I returned to Paradise and knocked on the opened door. The woman came again, and I liked being able to make her appear in this way – like Aladdin with his lamp. She now carried a cup and saucer with a bit of cake on the side. She'd disposed of her hat and coat, and wore a dress, more lavender than blue. I thought: What a pity that, being a married man, I can't fuck you, because you'd certainly make a very nice armful.

'My mate's gone off,' I said. 'I'll take the room if that's all right.'

She opened the door wider to let me in, turned and put her cup down on the bottom stair, and held out her hand. The house was boiling warm. The woman raised her arm over my shoulder and pushed the front door to.

'I'm Miss Rickerby,' she said, as the door closed behind me.

'Pleased to meet you,' I said. 'Stringer.'

And I found that we were exchanging smiles rather than shaking hands. I could tell immediately that she was at odds with the house. The place ought to have belonged to an older person. A clock ticked softly, and I thought of people's holidays ticking away. Would this hallway look any different in the summer months? It seemed all faded, and with a suspicion of dust. Also, it was kept hot as the houses of old people – those that can afford it – generally are. And the paint smell made it seem more, not less, old. Even the fanlight over the door was old, I thought, half craning round towards it, with old colours in it: a mustardy yellow, a green and a red of the sort seen in church stained glass.

'Shall I help you with your coat?' the landlady enquired. She seemed very keen to do it, and I thought: Is she sweet on me?

'No thanks,' I said, 'I'll manage.'

But I made heavy weather of the operation as she looked on.

'I like your badge,' she said, when the lapel of my suit-coat was revealed, and she leant forward and nearly touched it.

'Oh,' I said, with face bright red, 'that's the North Eastern company crest. Really it's three other railway company crests in a circle.'

'Why?' she said.

I tried to peer down at it. I must have looked daft in the attempt.

'It's the companies that were amalgamated to make up the North Eastern,' I said. 'The top one is the York and North Midland Railway. That has the city of York crest on it. The bottom left hand one is the Leeds Northern Railway and that has the Leeds crest and a sheep to show the woollen industry, together with ears of corn to show *that* side of the business, and a ship to show ... well, shipping ...'

As I rambled on it struck me that there was a good deal more to this badge than I'd ever thought, so I said, 'Do you really want to hear about the third crest?'

She was looking at me with an expression of wonderment.

'Would you like a cup of tea?' she said, seeming to come out of a trance. 'Or would you rather see the room first?'

At the back of the hallway, to the right of the stairs, I could see the man who'd answered the door. He now wore some species of dressing gown over his suit. It was perhaps a smoking jacket – not that he was smoking, as far as I could make out, but just generally taking it easy. He too held a cup of tea. He nodded as I looked at him.

My coat was over my arm. A coat tree stood in the hallway, beside a small bamboo table on which stood an ornamental tea pot, a dusty circle of sea shells, some framed views of Scarborough, and a black album of some sort, closed. I reached out towards it, thinking it might be a visitors' book, that Blackburn's name might be in it, but something in Miss Rickerby's look checked me. However, after eyeing me for a moment, she said, 'Open it.'

I did so. It held more views of Scarborough.

'The sea from Scarborough,' observed Miss Rickerby of the first one I turned up. 'Scarborough from the sea,' she said of the second.

'I thought it might be a visitors' book,' I said, closing it again. 'I thought I might have to sign it.'

'We do have a visitors' book, but it's in the kitchen. I'm going through it just now.'

I nodded, not really understanding.

'You see,' she explained, 'I write to the visitors asking if they'd like to come back – the ones I *want* back, that is.'

I should've thought they'd all want to come back, looking at her.

I glanced up, and the man had gone from the side of the stairs.

'It's hardly worth keeping it out this time of year,' the land-lady said.

'You've not been busy then?'

She smiled, eyeing me strangely.

'We had a Mr Ellis last week.'

'An engine man, was he?' I enquired, and it seemed my investigation had begun sooner than I'd bargained for.

She shook her head.

'He travelled in galoshes, if you see what I mean. Now . . . tea or room?'

'I'd rather see the room, I think,' I said.

'Quite right,' she said, 'because you might just hate it. What did I put down about it on the notice at the station?' she asked, turning towards the staircase.

'You said all the rooms were excellent,' I said, and she made a noise like 'Ha!'

I thought of the wife, who'd been a landlady when I first met her – *my* landlady in fact. She had a good sense of humour, but it would not have done to rib her about the rooms she let out. Being so keen to get on, she never saw the funny side of anything touching business or money.

Miss Rickerby carefully moved her teacup aside with the toe of her boot, and began climbing the stairs. Without looking back, she said, 'Follow me.'

I did so, with my coat over my arm, and of course it was a *pleasure* to do it, at least as far as the view of Miss Rickerby's swinging hips went. But the stair gas burnt low. The paint smell increased; the stair carpet seemed to deteriorate with every new step, and the green stripe wallpaper became faded, like a sucked humbug. We came to the first landing: black floorboards with a blue runner, none too clean. It led to closed doors.

'The sitting room is on this floor,' Miss Rickerby said, indicating the nearest closed door.

The staircase narrowed still further as we approached the second landing: a dark corridor where one bare gas jet showed tins of white-wash and rolls of wallpaper leaning against the wall.

'These are all the rooms you can't have,' said Miss Rickerby

– and this was evidently why Tommy Nugent had been turned away.

'Decorating,' I said.

'You're very quick on the uptake, Mr Stringer.'

I followed her up another, still narrower staircase, and we came to a short corridor, running away ten feet before ending in the slope of the house roof. A gas bracket – unlit – stuck out of the wall to my left. A little further along, also on the left, was a small white-painted door with a sloping top to accommodate the roof – evidently a cupboard or store room. Immediately to my right was a somewhat bigger white-painted door, with a low, reddish light coming out from underneath. The landing being so small, I was rather close to Miss Rickerby who smelt of talcum, perhaps, but also something out-of-the-way. She made just as good an impression close to, anyhow.

She said, 'You haven't asked the price.'

I said, 'No, that's because . . .'

' . . . You're stupendously rich.'

She took a small match box from her sleeve, turned the gas tap on the bracket, and lit the mantle, allowing me to see that the wallpaper was a faded green stripe alternating with an even more faded green stripe.

'It's because in your notice,' I said, breathing in Miss Rickerby, 'you put down "economical rates for railway men".'

'And because the North Eastern company will refund you,' said Miss Rickerby . . . which was what *I* should have said.

'Two shillings,' she said, and she reached for the handle of the bigger door, pushed it open and retreated.

The room was practically *all* bed. The head of it was just alongside the door, while the end fitted neatly under the windowsill. The window itself was about three feet with a wide ledge and red velvet curtains, which had perhaps once been very good, but now showed bald patches, and were parted, so that the whole window was like a tiny theatre stage. I went in, shuffled along by the edge of the bed, and looked out and down. There was a kind of staircase of dark house roofs to either side, but directly below was the Prom (which was deserted), then the lights of the harbour, with its cluster of cowardly boats, unable to face up to the wild black sea beyond.

'That's a grandstand view all right,' I said.

But Miss Rickerby had most unexpectedly – and disappointingly – gone, so I continued my inspection of the room alone.

Well, it was like a ship's cabin, or some sort of viewing booth: you'd sit on the bed with your feet up, and marvel at the scene beyond your boots. I took off my great-coat, set my kit bag down on the counterpane, and sat on the bed in the manner just described. The room was tolerably well-kept, although I fancied it wouldn't do to look too closely. On the hearth, I could see fire dust that a brush had passed too lightly over.

At my left elbow, as I sat on the bed, was the door, and there was a key in the keyhole. To the left of my left leg was a wardrobe with, as I imagined, just enough clearance between it and the bed to allow for the opening of the doors and barely any between its top and the ceiling. Beyond my boot soles was the window. To the right of my right boot was a small table covered with a tartan cloth. On the table was a box of long matches, a red-shaded oil lamp, with the wick burning low – as though in expectation of a tenant – and instructions for the lighting of the lamp. There was also a black book.

To the right of my right knee was a small fireplace, not laid for a fire but with kindling and paper ready in one scuttle, and coal in another. At my right elbow was a wash stand on a scrap of red and black tab rug, which ran partly under the bed as any rug in that room would have to do. For the rest, the floor was black-painted boards.

I sat and watched the black, brooding sea and listened to the wind rising off it, which periodically set the window clattering in its frame. I then leant forward and picked up the book that lay by the side of the lamp. It was *Ocean Steamships* by F. E. Chadwick and several others, and the owner had written his name on the inside page: 'H. D. R. Fielding'. Who's he when he's at home? I thought, and I settled down on the bed with it. Turning to the first page, I read: 'It is a wonderful fact in the swift expansion of mechanical knowledge and appliances of the last hundred years that while for unknown ages the wind was the only propelling force used for purposes of navigation . . .'

At that, I put the book back on the table and picked up the directions for the lamp. 'Sunshine at Night,' I read. 'The "Famos" 120 Candle-Power Incandescent Oil Lamp. The management of the lamp is simplicity itself . . .' Tucked into the pages of the little booklet was a handwritten note evidently meant for guests at Paradise and left over from the summer: 'Please note that teas can by arrangement be served on the beach. Please place requests with Mr Adam Rickerby.'

So there was more than one Rickerby. I didn't quite like the thought.

I replaced this and the lamp directions, and looked at the wallpaper, which was of a mustardy colour, bubbling here and there, and showing the same small ship – a black galleon – entangled dozens of times over in the same curly wave. I was just thinking that it would have made a good pattern for a lad's room when I heard a stirring to my left and there, looming in the doorway, was the over-grown boy who might have spent his childhood years gazing at it.

'Does it suit?' he enquired.

'Adam Rickerby?' I said, and he nodded.

'Will it do?' he said.

The words fell out of his mouth anyhow, in a sort of breathless rush, and with a quantity of flying spittle. He was a gormless lad of about eighteen and, depending on how he grew, he might be all right or a permanent idiot. For the time being, he was unfinished. He wore a shirt of rough white cloth, a thin white necker tied anyhow, and a dirty green apron, so that he looked like some monstrous sort of footman.

'It's cosy enough, en't it?' I said.

He made no answer.

'But it suits me fine,' I said.

'It's two shilling fer t'night,' he said, and he put his hand out.

'Who sent you?'

'Our lass,' he said, and so he was the brother of Miss Rickerby. I was glad he wasn't her husband.

While *her* face was made pretty and friendly-seeming by being rather wide, his was pumpkin-like; and while her mass of curls was fetching, his were . . . well, you didn't often see a man who had too much hair but his allowance was excessive, as though sprouting the stuff was about all he was good for. While his sister was well-spoken (for Scarborough, anyhow) he spoke broad Yorkshire, and his blue eyes were too light, indicating a kind of hollowness inside.

I paid over the coin, and he dropped it directly into the front pocket of his apron.

'Winder rattles,' he said.

'I know,' I said, and he skirted around the bed until he came to the window. There he crouched down and found a bit of paste-board, which he jammed into the frame, afterwards remaining motionless and gazing out to sea for a good few seconds. Rising to his feet again he indicated the paste-board, saying, 'You've to keep that *in*,' as though it was my fault it had fallen out. I could clearly read the words on the card: 'American Wintergreen Tooth Powder: Unequalled for . . .' and then came the fold. At any rate, it worked, and the best the wind could do now was to create a small trembling in the frame.

'Seen t'toilet?' enquired the youth, who was standing in the doorway once more.

I gave a quick shake of my head.

'It's on t'floor below . . . Yer've not seen it?' he repeated.

'Is there something special about it?' I said.

The lad kept silence for a moment, before blurting:

'There en't one in't back yard.'

'But you don't *have* a back yard, do you?' I asked, thinking of how the rear of the house gave on to what was practically a sheer drop.

He shook his head.

'So it'd be a bit hard to have a toilet in it, wouldn't it?'

I glanced down under the bed, and Adam Rickerby looked on alarmed as I did so. A fair quantity of dust was down there, but not the object I was looking for.

'There's no chamber pot,' I said.

He eyed me sidelong, looked away, eyed me again.

'This room doesn't *have* a chamber pot,' he said.

'I know,' I said. 'That's what I'm saying.'

'Want one, do yer?' he said, very fast.

'Yes,' I said, 'that's what I'm also saying.'

A note of music arose: the sea wind in the little iron fireplace – a very pure sound, like a flute.

'Cabinet fer yer clothes,' he said suddenly, indicating the wardrobe.

'Yes,' I said, and the silence that followed was so awkward that I said, 'Thanks for pointing it out.'

Had he taken the point about the chamber pot? It was impossible to tell.

'Coal an' wood in't scuttles,' he said – and just then there came a great bang and a scream from beyond the window.

The lad remained motionless, as I barged the bed aside to get a look. Red lights, like burning embers, drifted peacefully down through the black sky towards the harbour.

'I'd say a maroon's just been let off,' I said, and I looked at the lad, who was frowning down towards the bed.

''Appen,' he said.

'What does it mean?'

'Could mean owt,' he said.

'Well,' I said, 'that can't be right,' at which he looked up at me quite sharply. 'If a maroon could mean anything, they would-n't bother firing one. I'd say a ship's been wrecked.'

And the lad didn't seem to think much of that idea, because he just turned on his heel and quit the room. I went out after him, and caught him up on the floor being decorated.

'There's t'toilet,' he said, indicating a white-painted door. 'Paint's all dry.'

Evidently, then, he did not mean to supply me with a cham-ber pot. It struck me that he was a very inflexible youth.

'Where's everyone else in the house?' I said. 'I want to see

109

about this shipwreck.'

'Sitting room,' he said. 'Next floor down.'

I followed him down towards the first landing. On the way we passed three framed photographs I hadn't noticed on the way up. I turned towards them expecting to see sea-side scenes. Instead there was an old man giving me the evil eye. He hadn't mustered a smile for any of the three, I noticed, as we descended under his gaze.

'Who's that?' I enquired, although I knew the answer in advance on account of the pile of grey curls atop the old man's head.

The lad stopped on the stairs, but didn't turn about.

'Our dad,' he said.

'Is he in the house?'

'No.'

At the bottom of the staircase, the lad had paused to straighten a crooked stair rod.

'What do you mean?' I said. 'Is he not in the house just at present, or is he never in it?'

The lad straightened up, standing foursquare before me in the narrow space and folding his arms. He looked bullet proof, and big with it. Did he mean to put the frighteners on me? I stood my ground.

'Never,' he said.

'Well, let me see now,' I said. 'Would your old man be dead?'

'He would. How do you take yer tea?'

'What's that got to do with it?'

'I'll be attending yer in t'morning,' he said, taking a step closer towards me. 'I'll be bringin' yer 'ot water in a jug and tea . . . in a cup.'

'Well, that's just how I like tea,' I said. '. . . In a cup.'

No flicker of a smile from the lad.

'Two sugars,' I said. 'When did your old man die, if you don't mind my asking?'

'Two year since. Milk?'

I nodded. 'And plenty of it.'

'Seven o'clock suit?'

'Fine.'

The old man hadn't killed Blackburn at any rate . . . Unless the lad lied, but I somehow didn't think so. He was indicating the nearest closed door, and saying, 'Sitting room. Fire's lit in there.'

He then told me a cold tea was served on Sundays in the dining room, and carried on down the stairs. Remembering about the shipwreck, I approached the door of the sitting room. It faced the right way to give a view of the sea. I could hear muttered voices from within.

Chapter Sixteen

I looked up as the iron wall of the chain room cracked. The door was slowly opening, and it seemed that I was returning to this dark corner of the ship from hundreds of miles away. Blue cigar smoke came in first, like something curious, and I wanted it to go back because it brought the sickness rising up again. The grey Mate stood in the doorway, and he held up an oil lamp, which swung with the ship, and gave his face a bluish tinge.

'The old man wants a word,' he said, the white foam rising at the backs of his teeth.

'What are you talking about?' I said. '*You're* the old man.'

But I knew from Baytown days that the captain was always 'the old man' on any ship, regardless of age.

'Wants a word about what, exactly?' I then enquired, just as though there were many other things I ought to be attending to on the ship.

'You are to continue your story,' said the Mate. 'Your recollections.'

And he seemed to be trying out a new English word. The best thing would be to have it out with him straight away. His lamp had illuminated the length of rope, but I could hardly stoop to catch it up and I doubted that my hands would work properly anyway. He opened the first hatchway, and I stumbled into the companionway. He opened the second, and we were out onto the fore-deck under a dark blue sky and a moon that was full. The fore-sail was still rigged; it trembled in the wind, and so did I. The Captain waited a little way ahead, standing by the mid-ships ladder. One of the two of them must have held the revolver, but I could not see it just at that moment.

I looked up. The smoke from the funnel was pale blue and ghostly against the dark blue of the sky. It would come out at odd intervals, not connected to the beat of the engines. Smoke was unburnt carbon; the stuff could kill you if inhaled in a confined space, but that didn't mean that the fellows who made smoke were evil. Any man with an honest job made smoke in quantities, and I wondered about the men in the engine room of this no-name ship. Did they know about me? I doubted it, for the engines and the stoke hold were aft, and no man was allowed for'ard when I was out of my prison.

We walked on red-painted iron. Sea swirled over it, although not so much as before, and now the waves were almost pretty against the full moon. Some were set on following us, others drifted off crosswise, and they made the deck slippery in parts. What's wanted here, I thought, is a mop – and a big one. Mr Buckingham would scarcely have approved of the situation. Was he a real man? I could not decide. He was the fellow who bought a mill that was kept idle through the negligence of the railway company in not delivering a piece of machinery. Would the carrier be liable for profits lost by the mill being kept idle? No. Loss too remote. My ability to think was returning by degrees, but try as I might to recall those final hours in Scarborough, my recollections stopped somewhere about a giant needle, a quantity of razor blades, a wax doll, a paper fan and a paraffin heater in a blue room.

We walked on the starboard side of the ship, and as I looked over the sea, I thought I made out some deepening of night at a mile's distance, but it was more than that.

'Land!' I called ahead to the grey-faced Dutchman.

'Nobody knows you there, my friend,' he said, not turning around.

It looked homely enough all the same. I saw in silhouette two houses and what might have been a church clustered together on a low cliff. We were going at a fair lick, and they seemed to be riding fast the other way, but I kept them in sight as long as I could. Lights burned brightly at the retreating windows, and I was grateful to whoever had lit them.

The Mate had motioned me to stop. I looked beyond him towards the mid-ships, and another man had taken the place of the Captain at the ladder, this one much younger, hardly more than a boy. I saw him clear by the lamp that hung from the rail near where he stood. He wore the regulation galoshes but also a thin, ordinary sort of suit. I was certain that he was not the man who'd been at the wheel during my first visit to the chart room, which meant that there were four at least in on the secret. The kid had made some signal to the Mate, who was now leaning somewhat against the gunwale, and looking aft. Some delay had occurred in taking me into the bridge house, if that was in fact the programme. Perhaps there were some loiterers aft who might catch sight of me unless they were put off.

I looked again towards the land. It was not above a mile away, and the famous Captain Webb had swum twenty-five, or whatever was the width of the Channel. But he had trained for years; he was in peak condition and had covered himself in grease, whereas I was half dead from cold to begin with. A sudden burst of sea came, and the crash of the wave was replaced by the sound of a bell in the darkness, and this one was *not* aboard the ship. It approached – or we approached *it* – at a great rate, and it came into view after half a minute, clanging inside a revolving iron cage. Here was a warning buoy of some sort, a tattered black flag flying from the top of it. Perhaps we were too close to land; perhaps this was the best chance I would get to strike out for the shore. But there were no welcoming windows to be seen now, just a low line of cliffs that rose and fell, but always in darkness. I wondered whether such continuous blankness could occur in my own country, or whether some disaster had over-taken the place since I'd left.

I was still held in check by the Mate. I glanced at the face of the kid at the mid-ships. He looked pale in the white light of the moon and the white light of the lantern; his eyes were restless, but I did not care for the expression that came over his face when they landed on me.

'I would not be you, mate,' that look of his said, 'for *worlds*.'

Chapter Seventeen

The sitting room seemed to be filled with the night sky and the black sea. A man with his back to me stood at one of two tall windows, gazing out. Another, younger man lay on a couch. The room was surely the biggest in the house, and it might once have been two rooms – something about the way the floorboards rose to a gentle peak in the middle made me think so; and the way that the two tall windows did not quite match. They seemed to go in for knocking down walls in that house, as I would later discover.

The room was very old. The cornices were crumbling a little, the fireplace was small. Worn blue rugs were scattered over the black boards, but they were too widely spaced. Black and blue: they didn't set each other off right; they were the colours of a bruise. The articles of furniture seemed few and far between. Most notable of these was a very black upright piano, which had a wall to itself and was set somewhat at an angle by the slope of the floor. The man at the window stood some distance from an occasional table that held two books. I could make out the title of one: *A History of the British Navy*. The man at the window turned about. He was the fellow who'd answered the front door to me, only he looked older now. He stepped aside, as though politely allowing me a view of the sea.

On the harbour wall stood the harbour master's house and the lighthouse, both white. Against the black sky, the two together looked like a glowing white church with a round tower. The man who'd stepped aside was watching me as I noticed the scene on the dark beach, just to the right of the harbour. Two lines of men holding ropes hauled a boat towards the waves, beckoned on by a man at the front, who wore a long oilskin. From this distance the men looked tiny, the whole scene ridiculous.

The guardian of the window put out his hand.

'I'm Fielding,' he said.

'Stringer,' I said. '. . . I saw a maroon fired.'

He tipped his head to one side, as though questioning what I'd just said, although he was smiling as he did it.

'I saw it from my room,' I said. '. . . the room on the top floor.'

'Yes,' he said. 'It is the only one presently available.'

The man Fielding was trim, probably in the late fifties or early sixties, with carefully brushed grey hair, a high waistcoat, spotted tie very neatly arranged with a silver pin through it, and a decent, if rather worn, black suit under the smoking jacket. He seemed very proper and mannerly, although he had not yet introduced me to the man lying on the couch, who had not yet troubled to rise. I gave a bolder glance in his direction. He had a droopy moustache, and, as I thought, a lazy eye.

'Are you coming aboard tonight?' Fielding enquired.

'Coming aboard?' I said, shaking his hand. 'Well, I don't see why not!'

It was an idiotic answer, but the man smiled kindly.

'This is the ship room, after all,' he said, and he tilted his head again, as though I should really have known that already.

'That's because you over-look ships, I suppose,' I said with a nod towards the harbour.

'And are over-looked by one,' said Fielding, and with a neat little gesture, he indicated the wall behind me where hung a painting of a ship – two ships in fact, not sailing ships but steam vessels moving with great purpose through moonlit black and blue waters, the one behind looking as though it was trying to catch the one in front. What did you say about a painting if you wanted to come over as intelligent and educated? That it was charming? That it was in the school of . . . something or other?

'But we are diverted tonight by the one below,' said Fielding, and he faced the window again, spinning on his heel. He wore little boots, with elasticated sides – good leather by the looks of it, but perhaps with the cracks covered over by a good deal of polish, like boots in a museum. They made him look nimble, anyhow.

'But is there a wreck?' I said, for I was determined to crack the mystery of the maroon.

'I should hope not,' said the man on the couch.

He lay completely flat, like a man waiting to be operated on. He looked to my mind . . . naïve. It was a word of the wife's. I was naïve too apparently, but surely not as naïve as this bloke. His drooping moustache and long hair looked like a sort of experiment. He'd have a different moustache in a month's time, I somehow knew. He wore a greenish suit and a yellow and brown waistcoat, and that was naïve too. It was meant to make him look like a swell, but he just looked as though he'd been at the fancy dress basket.

'Rehearsal,' he said, nodding down towards the beach.

'It is a lifeboat *practice*,' Fielding corrected him, in a tone not completely unfriendly, but which suggested he'd held off from introducing the horizontal fellow because he hadn't really thought it worth doing.

'I don't like the look of that sea,' said the man on the couch, who had rolled to face the windows. 'It's sort of coming in sideways.'

He was perhaps five years older than me – middle thirties. Thin, with a high, light voice and long nails, not over-clean, I noticed, as at last he stood up, crossed the room, and put out his hand. He did not exactly have a lazy eye, but a droopy moustache, which pulled his whole face down, as though trying to make a serious person of him. We shook hands, and I saw that there was a black mark where his head had been on the couch.

'Stringer,' I said.

'Vaughan,' he replied.

He then gave a friendly smile that clashed with the downturn of his moustache, nodded towards the man at the window, and said, 'I believe it ought to be first name terms in this house, even if Howard here won't have it.'

'Then it's James,' I said.

'Now is it Jim or is it James?' he said, and he pitched himself back onto the couch in a somehow unconvincing way. I had him down for a clerk and the other, Fielding, for a *head* clerk, in which case I would outrank them both if and when I became a solicitor. But they both talked to me in the way people do when they want to make themselves pleasant to the lower classes.

'I'm Jim to my friends,' I said, feeling like a prize dope.

'I'm Theodore, which is a bit of bad luck,' said Vaughan. 'You can call me Theo if you like, Jim.'

'*Theo*, meaning God,' said Fielding from his post near the window, 'and *doron*, meaning gift. You are a gift from God, Vaughan. What do you say, Miss Rickerby?'

And he tilted his head at the beautiful landlady who was watching us from the somewhat crooked doorway, leaning against the door frame with folded arms, which I did not believe I'd ever seen a respectable woman do before. She said nothing to Fielding but just eyed him, weighing him up.

'A gift from God?' Mr Fielding said again. 'What do you say to that, Miss R?'

'His *rent* is,' she said, and smiled, but only at me, causing me to blurt out 'But. . .' without the slightest notion of what I was objecting to. I turned to the window, and found a way out of my difficulty in the scene on the beach.

'But . . . who's the one at the head?' I said, looking down at the men dragging the boat on the beach.

'That's the captain of it,' said Vaughan.

'The *coxswain*,' said Fielding.

'Cold tea tonight is it, Miss R?' enquired Vaughan, who was still lying down, but now propping his head on his right arm.

'In honour of the new arrival,' she replied, smiling at me, 'we are to have a *hot* tea.'

'Oh,' I said, 'what time?'

'About nine,' she said, smiling and backing away from the door.

'Of course Mr Stringer is not likely to be keen on that word,' said Fielding, who was still looking through the window, now with a rather dreamy expression.

'Supper?' I said. 'I should say I *am* keen on it.'

'"About",' said Fielding, still gazing down at the sea. 'You're a railwayman. No train leaves at *about* nine o'clock.'

'Well,' I said, 'you'd be surprised.'

'Perhaps,' he said, smiling and turning towards me, 'but I do have some experience of railways.'

120

Nice, I thought. I've an expert to contend with.

'Me too,' said the man on the couch.

But somehow I didn't believe Vaughan.

'It's not tolerated on the railway,' Fielding said, 'but in this house it is the lynchpin: "about" . . . "roughly" . . . "there or thereabouts". It's the Lady's way.'

I couldn't tell whether he was cross about it, or just making fun.

'What did you say was wrong with your engine, old man?' enquired Vaughan, who'd evidently had the tale from Miss Rickerby.

'Leaking injector steam valve,' I said.

'Doesn't sound too bad. Couldn't you sort of wind a rag around the blinking thing?'

'There were other things up with it as well,' I said.

'Like what, Jim?' said Vaughan, as Fielding looked on smiling.

I thought: *Are these two in league?*

'Oh,' I said, 'stiff fire hole door . . . some clanking in the motions.'

'You know, I think *I've* had *that* . . .' said Vaughan.

Fielding shook his head at me, as if to say: 'Whatever are we to do with him?'

'You worked on the railways, you say?' I asked Vaughan.

'After a fashion. Tell you about it over a pint, if you like?'

This was a bit sudden.

'Where?' I said, feeling rather knocked.

'I know a decent place in the Old Town.'

I was thinking: *What is he? Alcoholic?* Because we'd barely met.

'I generally take a pint before supper,' he said.

Howard Fielding had turned towards the window and gone dreamy again. There seemed no question of him coming along.

'Hold on then,' I said to Vaughan. 'I'll just get my coat.'

'Meet you in the hallway in two minutes,' he said, and it seemed he meant to remain in the room with Fielding until then.

Besides fetching my coat I would change my shirt and put on my tie in place of my necker. This way, I'd be able to hold my own at supper, which was to *be* supper after all, and not 'tea'.

As soon as I stepped from the sitting room, the door closed behind me.

Who had closed it?

Odds-on it had been Fielding, except that he had been over by the windows, and furthest off.

I climbed the narrow stairs between the faded green stripes. The stair gas made more noise than light – a constant, rasping exhaling. Bronchitic. It troubled me somehow, and here came the old man, glaring from under his curls. He ought to have been happy with hair like that. I reached the attic storey, pushed open the door of my room, and I was checked by a sharp bang.

By the low, red light of the oil lamp I saw what had happened: the card had once again fallen from the window frame, and a surge of sea wind had hurled itself at the glass. I sat down on the bed, inched along towards the end of it, and jammed in the card once more. Coming away from the window, I swung my legs in such a way that my boots clattered against the first of the two scuttles on the hearth – the one that held the kindling and paper – and knocked it over, spilling the papers.

There were many folded sheets from the *Scarborough Post*. 'Yesterday the sea was black with bathers,' I read, under the heading 'Shortage of Lifeguards Complained Of'. The paper was dated Tuesday, 25 August. There were also handwritten papers headed 'Menu'. The first offered a choice of celery soup or shrimp paste and biscuits; then beef and macaroni stew could be had, or cottage pie. No date was given, but just the word 'Wednesday'.

I looked down again, and saw another piece of paper – this one printed – and it looked familiar. It was a fragment torn from a booklet I'd often seen but never owned: the rule book for North Eastern company engine men. I reached down slowly, and with shaking hand caught it up: 'On Arriving at the Shed', I read. And then, beneath this heading, 'On arriving at the shed, your engine requires to be thoroughly examined.'

Was it Blackburn's? Had this been his room? I thought of his black eyes reading it. Or had they had another engine man in since? If it was Blackburn's property, how did it come to be in the scuttle?

I began to put the papers back, including the torn page from the rule book, but I was checked by a further discovery: a thin item, small, brown and reduced almost to the condition of scrap paper, but still recognisably a cigar stub. According to Tommy Nugent, the limit of Blackburn's vices was the smoking of the odd cigar.

I sat still and heard only the eternal sighing of the gas from the landing beyond; I looked at the wallpaper: the ship in danger over and over again. I thought of Blackburn. Surely he was at the bottom of the sea.

I sat breathing deeply on the bed, telling myself that I could breathe whereas Blackburn could not. That was the main difference between the two of us. I thought of the Chief, who had sent me to this old, faded house and its queer inhabitants. Who, I wondered again, was the man the Chief had been talking to in the station when I'd come down from the tram?

I quickly changed my shirt and fixed the smarter of my two neckers in place without aid of a mirror. I stepped out of my room and was confronted by the cupboard door over-opposite. The man Vaughan would be waiting in the hallway but . . .

I pulled at the little door. At first, it wouldn't come. I tried again, and it flew open. The gas was saying 'Shuuuuush' as I looked down to see a crumpled paper sack: 'Soda 6d' read the label. There was a bottle of ammonia, a beetle trap. Propped against the wall a shrimp net with a long, uncommonly stout handle, two faded sunshades, two folded wooden chairs. I closed the door feeling daft for having opened it. What had I expected to find? The bleached bones of fireman Blackburn?

In the hallway, Miss Rickerby waited instead of Vaughan. She looked very grave, standing sideways before the front door, under the old glass of the fanlight, with arms folded. She turned and saw me, and slowly and surely she began to smile. She seemed to find great amusement and delight in the way we kept coinciding about the place, like two holiday makers repeatedly clashing in a maze. Vaughan now appeared from the side of the stairs, with coat over his arm, and hat in hand.

'Old Jim and I are just off for a quick pint, Miss R,' he said.

'We keep a barrel of beer in the scullery so that the gentlemen don't have to bother,' Miss Rickerby said, addressing me directly as before.

'But it's the Two X,' said Vaughan, putting on a brown bowler, 'and I generally go for the Four. Besides, I like a smoke with my glass of beer.'

'I don't mind smoking in the least,' said Miss Rickerby, again addressing me even though it was Vaughan who'd spoken. 'I like to watch it.'

It wasn't a coat that Vaughan was putting on, but an Inverness cape, and he'd acquired from somewhere a paper package.

'Shall I hold that for you?' said Miss Rickerby, indicating the package. 'That way you'll be able to use your arms.'

Vaughan clean ignored her, but just carried on wrestling with the cape.

'What about the lifeboat?' Miss Rickerby asked him.

'They've got it into the water,' he said, the cape now positioned about his shoulders.

'Well,' said Miss Rickerby, 'I suppose that's a start.'

She was responding to Vaughan, but she addressed the remark, and the accompanying smile, at me. With the cape on, Vaughan looked like a cross between Dr Watson and Sherlock Holmes. Theatrical, anyhow. He was trying his best to stuff the package into the pocket of the cape, but it wouldn't go. Meanwhile Miss Rickerby had taken a step towards me. I thought: There's nothing for it but to reach out and touch her. Begin with the hair. It was a little way in her eyes. Move it aside. That would be only polite . . .

'Goodbye, you two,' she said, reaching out and opening the door for us. 'Don't be late back.'

And in spite of that word 'two', she'd again looked only at me.

Chapter Eighteen

We turned right at the top of Bright's Cliff, and were soon walking along the narrow cobbled lanes of the Scarborough Old Town. The gas lamps showed lobster pots, upturned boats and other bits of fishing paraphernalia at every turn, as though the sea had lately washed over and left these items behind. The sea wind came and went according to which way we turned in the narrow streets. Vaughan walked leaning forwards with his hands in his pockets and the mysterious paper parcel under his arm. Directly on leaving Paradise, he'd blown his nose on a big blue handkerchief, and this had left a trail of snot hanging from his moustache.

'Are there any other guests in the house apart from you, me and Fielding?' I enquired.

'Just at present? No, Jim. There was a chap in a week ago. Ellis.'

'What was he like?'

'He sold galoshes, Jim, and I don't think there was a great deal more to him than that.'

'How old was he?'

'*Old*.'

'Did you take him out for a pint?'

Vaughan stopped and looked at me as though I was crackers.

'Well, you're taking *me* out.'

'Different matter entirely, Jim,' he said, walking on.

'Did he stay in my room, the top one?'

'No, Jim. He was on my floor.'

'But that's all being decorated?'

He explained, under questioning, that there were four guest rooms in total on that floor, including his own, which was not being decorated, and there were no plans in hand to do so. As of last week, Adam Rickerby had only got round to white-washing two of the other three, so there'd been one spare for Ellis.

'Wouldn't you like your own room done?' I said.

'I like it just as it is, Jim.'

'It's a pretty good house, isn't it?' I said, cautious-like, because it only *was* pretty good at best. Then again, it might have been a palace to Vaughan.

'It's the best house in Scarborough at the price, Jim,' said Vaughan. 'They don't leave off fires until May; glorious views; and then you have Miss Rickerby into the bargain. What I wouldn't give for a rattle on the beach with her,' he added.

So that was *that* out of the way.

'How long have you been there?' I enquired, looking side-long at him and rubbing my own 'tache, in the hope that he'd do the same, and discover the dangling snot.

'Oh, since last summer,' he said, not taking the hint but just striding on.

That would comfortably put him in the house at the time Blackburn disappeared, but I would reserve my questions on that front. Instead, I asked about the house, and he gave his answers without reserve, or so it seemed to me.

The Paradise lodging house was run by Miss Amanda Rickerby and her brother Adam, who was, according to

Vaughan, 'a bit touched'. Their father had bought the place two years since, dying immediately afterwards, his life's aim completed. He'd been a coal miner; he was a drinking man and pretty hard boiled, but evidently a man determined to take his children away from the life of a South Yorkshire pit village. He'd saved all his life, and Paradise was the result. It was now in the hands of his beautiful daughter and her odd brother. There was one other son and another daughter, but they'd 'cleared out entirely', not being able to stand the father.

Vaughan at that moment discovered and swiped away the snot in a way that suggested he was very used to finding the stuff just there, and equally used to dislodging it. Miss Rickerby herself, he went on, 'suffered from lazyitis' and was 'over-fond of port wine'.

'But the house is fairly well kept,' I said.

This, it appeared, was partly on account of the brother, who was a good worker in spite of being a half wit, and had no other interest in life besides cleaning and maintaining the house. He wasn't up to much as a cook and Vaughan believed that the hot supper we had in prospect would be nothing to write home about. But the lad had help every day in the season from a maid called Beth who was quite a peach in her own right apparently. And a Mrs Dawson came in year round. She was a great hand at all housework, and, being an older woman, was practically a mother to the two Rickerbys. In the off-season, Vaughan said, she came in only on Mondays, Wednesdays and Fridays.

'So I'll see her tomorrow?' I enquired, and at this Vaughan stopped and looked up at some clouds riding fast and ghostly through the black sky.

'Yes, Jim, you will,' he said, walking on. 'Sorry about that, I was just thinking about something else that's happening tomorrow.'

'I wouldn't have thought you could buy a house like Paradise on a miner's wages,' I said, 'even if you *did* save all your life.'

'I don't know about that, Jim,' said Vaughan.

'Where was the pit village exactly?' I asked, as we came up to a pub called the Two Mariners.

'Search me,' he said. 'Somewhere near *coal*.' And he fell to thinking hard, and frowning. '. . . Somewhere up Durham way, I believe it was, Jim.' He pushed open the pub door, saying, 'I like it here of a Sunday. It's quiet and you can talk.'

Talk about what? I wondered, as we stepped into a wooden room with pictures of sea-going men all around the walls, both painted and photographed, but not a single live person of any description to be seen. Somebody must have been in the room lately though, for a good fire was burning in the grate and two oil lamps were doing the same on the bar top. There was a door open behind the bar, which was quite promising, and Vaughan was evidently confident that *someone* would turn up and serve us a drink because he placed the paper package on a table near the fire, took off his cape, and pitched it over a chair, removing a pipe and a tin of tobacco from one of the pockets in the process. He left his muffler about his neck, and this in combination with the pipe made him look like a university man, which perhaps he had been.

He walked over to the bar, and shouted, 'Rose!'

A woman came through the door behind the bar: she was small, brown and stout.

'How do, Mr Vaughan?' she said.

'Two pints of the Four X please, Rose,' he said, and only as the pints were being pulled did he call over to me, 'Four X all right for you, Jim?'

He turned back to the barmaid. 'Bit quiet . . . even for a Sunday.'

'All gone to bed,' she said. 'Most of our lot will be at sea come sunrise.'

'*We've* yet to have our supper,' he said.

'Well, that's Miss Amanda Rickerby for you,' said the barmaid.

Theo Vaughan brought over the pints, and placed the package between us. He then lit his pipe, which went out directly, and placed his feet up on a stool, so that he was quite relaxed, only I had the idea that it cost him more effort to keep his feet up on the stool than otherwise.

'Cheers, Jim,' he said, and we clashed glasses.

He was very forward indeed. From the way he acted you'd have thought he knew me of old, but that was quite all right by me.

'I'm bursting to see inside that package,' I said, and he picked it up with his yellowy fingers and took out a quantity of picture post cards. The top one showed trains unloading at a dockside.

'Old Fielding and I are connected through the railways,' said Vaughan. 'We ran a little business: post card publishing. Well, *he* did. The Fielding Picture Post Card Company – had a little office in Leeds. Armoury Road, I don't know if you know it, Jim. I had high hopes that it might one day become "The Fielding and *Vaughan* Picture Post Card Company", but as long as it went on, I was Fielding's employee. Commercial agent, do you know what that means?'

'Not really.'

'It means nothing, Jim. But it was all right. I mean, he *is* all right, old Fielding. Bit stuck-up, bit of an old maid, and a bit weird in some of his tastes, but decent enough to work for and he struck lucky with the business for a while. We'd done a few runs of cards for some of the big hotels up and down the coast, and to make a long story short some of these caught the eye of a bloke called Robinson, who's the publicity manager of your lot: the North Eastern Railway. I expect you know him pretty well?'

'You're wrong there, Theo,' I said.

'I'm pulling your leg, Jim,' he said, sucking on his dead pipe. 'Robinson gave Fielding the contract – I should say one of the contracts – for stocking the automatic picture post card machines you see on the station platforms.'

'Oh,' I said.

He looked again at his pipe.

'You know, I think I prefer cigars, Jim. At least a fellow can get them *lit*.'

'You smoke cigars, do you?'

'On occasion, yes. . . Anyhow, that was me for a year, Jim: third class rail pass in my pocket, and I'd go about re-filling these machines with the cards we'd commissioned.'

I knew the machines. They were in most of the bigger stations. You put in a penny, and pulled out a little drawer that contained a card with ha'penny postage already on it. Some showed North Eastern Railway scenes: interesting spots in the system. Others might show Yorkshire views in general. Vaughan pushed the top-most card across to me.

'Is that Hull?' I said.

'Might be,' he said. 'It was one of the winter series.'

For all his build-up, he didn't seem very interested in it. The card was from a painting, and there was writing across the top of it: *The Industrial Supremacy of North East England. The Secret of Success: Cheap Power, Labour Facilities and Raw Materials.* Then, in smaller type: *For information as to sites and special advantages apply to the commercial agent, North Eastern Railway, York.* It was hard to imagine anyone wanting to receive it through the post. I looked at Vaughan. He seemed to want me to say something about it.

'That artist is coming it a bit,' I said.

'How's that?' asked Vaughan.

'Looks like a Class S, does that engine. But you'd never see one of those on dock duties – not in a million years.'

'Why not, Jim?' asked Vaughan, but I could tell he wasn't really bothered either way.

'Too big,' I said. 'They're hundred mile an hour jobs. The company's not going to waste 'em on loading fish.'

Vaughan nodded as though he was satisfied with this. He slid over another card.

'Summer Series,' he said.

This too was from a painting. It showed a sea cliff in twilight. 'The Yorkshire Coast' read the heading. Then: 'Railway stations within easy reach. For particulars write to the Chief Passenger Agent, Department 'A', North Eastern Railway, York.' Vaughan was eyeing me again. I felt minded to ask what he was playing at, but couldn't quite see my way to doing it. Another card was put down: a photograph of a signal gantry on what looked like a foggy day.

'Where's that?' I said.

'Search me,' said Vaughan.

'That one's crossed,' I said, pointing to one of the signals, which had a wooden cross nailed over the arm. '... Means it's out of commission.'

'That right, Jim?' said Vaughan. 'Interesting is that.'

But he wasn't interested in the least.

Out came another card. A station master and a couple of porters stood on a little country platform somewhere.

'That fellow's managed to get his dog into the picture,' said Vaughan, pointing, and then another card came from the packet and was put down. This showed a flat-bed wagon carrying a great boiler or some such outsized article that overhung the wagon by about six feet. A handful of railway officials stood about grinning foolishly.

'Out-of-gauge load,' I said.

'However would they move a thing like that, Jim?' asked Vaughan, who kept looking over my shoulder, as though expecting someone to come up behind me. But the pub was still quite empty.

'They've to keep the next track clear,' I said.

Vaughan nodded.

'They'd run a breakdown wagon along behind it,' I said. 'A crane, I mean, to lift it clear of any obstacles that might come up trackside. Fancy another?' I said, indicating our empty glasses. Vaughan gave a quick nod; I walked up to the bar, shouted 'Rose!' and the trick worked for me too.

When I came back to the table and handed Vaughan his pint he took down his feet from the stool, and ran his hands through his long hair. He then blew his nose on the blue handkerchief, and I saw that there was another card in my place, and this was a comic one, like a picture out of the funny papers. It showed a baby in a cot, and the words above read: 'A Present from Scarborough'.

'One for the holiday makers,' said Vaughan, who was now

fiddling with his pipe.

'Enough said,' I replied, giving a grin. But then a thought struck me: 'I don't suppose *this* one was sold on the stations.'

'Not likely,' said Vaughan. 'This isn't one of the Fielding lot. I'm a sort of free agent now when it comes to the cards.'

He'd got his pipe going properly at last. Rose had gone away from the bar again. Vaughan said, 'I bring a good many over from France, as a matter of fact, Jim.'

'Oh yes?' I said. 'Pictures of French trains, would that be?'

'Not quite, Jim,' and he put down another card, which showed a lady holding a bicycle.

She had no clothes on.

I looked up at Vaughan, who was frowning slightly and sucking on his pipe in a very thoughtful manner.

PART THREE

Chapter Nineteen

'Do you suppose she means to get on that bike?' I said, handing back the card.

Vaughan took his pipe out of his mouth and gave a grin.

'I think the saddle's set a little too high, Jim,' he said. 'But she looks a game sort, doesn't she? Matter of fact, I *know* she is.'

'You know her?' I said.

'Home grown, she is,' he said, and I didn't quite take his meaning.

He now returned the package to the cape pocket, and I was relieved at that. I wasn't well enough acquainted with Vaughan to talk sex with him.

He said, 'Drink up, Jim, or we'll be late for supper,' and we walked out of the pub, and reversed our steps, with no sound in the Scarborough Old Town but the breathing of the German Sea.

For a while, nothing was said between us. Vaughan seemed to have attained his object in showing me that particular card, and it had done its work – I'd been made to feel rather hot by it, which brought Amanda Rickerby more and more to mind. Not that I hadn't seen plenty of similar ones before. They would do the rounds of any engine shed, and there was an envelope in the police office that was full of them, and marked 'Improper'. Any stuff of that nature discovered on a train (down the back of a seat or folded into a newspaper on the luggage rack) and taken into the lost luggage office would not be collected or enquired after, and would come to us. But the rum thing was that when it was placed in the *left* luggage it wouldn't be called for either. So we had our ever-growing file in the police office containing pictures and little home-made-looking books, and one day the Chief said to me, bold as you like, 'Every man in this office looks at that file when left alone,' a remark that put me on the spot rather, and was no doubt meant to do so. I just coloured up and changed the subject, for I *had* leafed through it from time to time.

No one ever suggested throwing it out, anyhow.

As we walked along Newborough, I noticed a little alleyway going off to the left directly before Bright's Cliff, and this one ran steeply but smoothly down to the Prom, almost like a slip-way for ships, rather than ending in a steep drop. A woman stood shivering halfway down it, and she eyed us directly and took a step towards us as we went past.

'You might form your own opinion as to how she gets her living, Jim,' said Vaughan.

'That would be the quickest way down to the beach, would-n't it?' I said.

'Eh?' he said.

'Where she stood?'

'It would, Jim,' he said, 'but the beach is for summer.'

The woman had retreated into her doorway, and so my gaze shifted to the black, writhing sea beyond. The wind was getting up. As we gained the cobbles of Bright's Cliff, I said, 'What happened to Fielding's post card company?'

'Lost the North Eastern contract,' said Vaughan. '. . . Back end of 1912, hardly a year after we started. Went bust as a con-sequence.'

'Why?'

'The cards weren't liked. I mean, cross-eyed station masters on lonely platforms, busted signals, details of dock working, "Sunderland Station Illuminated and Photographed by Kitson Light". Fielding found all that interesting but you see he's an intellect, is old Howard . . . or so he tells me. He lacks the common touch.'

'Is he in with you as regards the . . .?'

'The continental specialities? He is not. Well, he *wouldn't* be, now would he?'

'You keep it a secret from him, do you?'

Vaughan stopped walking, as if to make a declaration.

'I see nothing shameful in it, Jim,' he said, 'and so it's not kept secret – not from men, anyhow.'

'Does Fielding approve?'

'Not exactly, Jim,' said Vaughan. 'Not exactly.'

'How does he get his living?' I enquired.

'He has private means, Jim. We're both lucky in that way. His old man did well for himself in the law, you know.'

'Barrister?'

'Solicitor,' he said, and he was eyeing me. The word made me turn white as paper at the thought of all that lay ahead.

'Is his old man still alive?'

'Hardly, Jim. Howard's pushing sixty, you know. *My* old man *is* living.'

'Where?'

'Streatham,' he said, taking his key from his pocket as we approached the door of Paradise. 'A very dismal place in London that suits his character to perfection, Jim. But I shouldn't complain really. The old boy puts five pounds in the post every month, which is not riches but better than a poke in the eye with a blunt stick.'

'Miss Rickerby doesn't usually run to a hot tea on Sundays, does she?' I enquired, as Vaughan pushed at the door.

'She does not. Of course, you know why she's laying it on tonight?'

'I've no notion,' I said.

'I'd say it was all on your account, Jim,' he said, and we stepped into the hot hallway and a smell of cooking.

Vaughan darted straight upstairs. I removed my hat and great-coat, then turned and tidied my hair in the hall mirror. I tried to tell myself this was normal behaviour before supper taken in company, but in fact I was only doing it for Miss Rickerby's sake. It must be true, if Vaughan had noticed it, that the lady had taken a shine to me, but that didn't mean she wasn't out to kill me.

This time I did hang my coat in the hall, first checking that my warrant card was stowed safely in my suit-coat. I followed the food smell along the hallway, coming first to what I imagined to be the dining room. It was on the front side of the house: a faded room with a table that could have sat six but had cutlery laid for five, which must mean that Amanda Rickerby and her brother would eat with we three paying guests. The white cloth was a little askew and nearly, but not quite, completely clean. Also, the wallpaper – decorated with a design of roses the colour of dried blood – had come away a little around the two gas lamps that roared softly on the end walls, and there was a black soot smudge above the fireplace, like a permanent shadow.

Two paintings hung from the picture rail that ran round the room. The first was above the fireplace smudge, and rocked a little in the updraught of a moderate, spluttering blaze. It was a painting of a sailing ship, with a rather dusty name plate at the bottom: 'Her Majesty's Wood Framed Iron Frigate "Inconstant", 16 Tons.' Was it any good? It wasn't signed – not that I could see. Perhaps it was signed on the back. As I looked at it, the fire fluttered and the flute note came. Again, the fireplace was small and imperfectly swept. Crouching down, I saw that a fancy pattern was set into the black iron over-mantel, like the badge of a king. It was a museum piece really.

The second painting was on the wall over-opposite, and showed a high, thin, brightly lit house with smaller ones massed below as though combined in a great effort to raise it up. Scarborough from the sea. The harbour stood in the foreground and that gave the clue: it was Paradise of course, and I made out my own room – the top one, and the brightest of the lot.

The kitchen was next to the dining room, and the food cooked in it would have to be carried the half a dozen yards between the two doors. The kitchen door stood open. The gas gave a yellow light, and the walls were of white brick. The place was stifling. There was a great table, bigger than the one in the dining room, and Amanda Rickerby stood at one end of it, her brother at the other. She was singing lightly. I caught the words, 'Why are you lonely, why do you roam?' and I knew the song but couldn't lay name to it. She broke off (not on my account, for she still hadn't seen me) and, pointing at a pot bubbling on the range, said, 'Egg yolk.'

Her brother went to the larder to fetch an egg, and Miss Rickerby carried on singing – 'Have you no sweetheart, have you no home . . .' – and she could sing so very well that I was almost sorry when she saw me and stopped, and smiled, at the same time pushing something behind the knife polisher, which was one of a great mix-up of things on the big table. She knew I'd seen her do it, but this only made her smile the wider, as though it was all part of the game that seemed to be going on between us.

'We're trying a little bit of French cooking, Mr Stringer,' she said, indicating her slow-witted brother at the range.

'Oh,' I said, 'what?'

'Scotch broth,' she said.

I heard a sniff from behind me, and Theo Vaughan was there.

'There's nothing particularly French about Scotch broth,' he said, nodding at me. There was no sign of shame at his late behaviour in the Two Mariners. He had a glass in his hand, and was making for one of the objects on the table – the beer barrel laid in for the guests. The kitchen seemed to be open house for everyone, and Vaughan was now filling his glass from the barrel tap.

'The Scotch broth is just the starter,' Miss Rickerby said, then: 'I thought you didn't care for this beer, Mr Vaughan.'

'Oh, a pint of the Two is fine after a couple of the Four,' he said. 'Ask any beer man.'

'I suppose that, being that bit more drunk, you just stop caring,' said Amanda Rickerby, grinning at me.

The fact was that our trip to the pub had been nothing to do with the beer. Vaughan had wanted to take me out to show me the cards. . . . But why?

The range was set before a recess that might once have been the fireplace. It was too big to fit in, and perhaps accounted for the heat of the house. All the other fireplaces were small, after all. Adam Rickerby stood at the range next to a stew pot. He was holding a knife over an egg, and eyeing his sister with a look of panic.

'Gently now,' she said, with half a glance in his direction.

The knife clattered down on the egg, and all its innards dropped into the broth.

'*That* weren't right,' he said, as though it had all been his sister's fault, at which Amanda Rickerby for once turned away from me, and gave her full attention to her brother.

'It won't hurt to have the whole egg in, Adam,' she said. 'It won't hurt at all.'

'I've to put salt? Pepper?'

'That's right. But go easy, love.'

Vaughan was eyeing the lad with a look of dislike.

'I'm off through,' he said, and he went into the dining room, or so I supposed.

'It's the second course that's the French dish,' said Amanda Rickerby, turning back towards me. 'I can't pronounce it. Mr Fielding found the recipe in one of his books some weeks ago, and we thought we'd try it tonight.'

She slid a bit of paper across the table to me. At the top somebody had written 'Croquette de Boeuf'.

'That's French all right,' I said.

'Can you go through Sunday without a treat of some kind, Mr Stringer?' she enquired. 'Don't tell me: you go to a Morning Service every Sabbath without fail?'

'That's not what I call a treat,' I said.

'Nor me,' she said, and took from behind the knife polisher the object she had hidden: a glass of red wine, and she boldly took a sip, as if to say, 'There's nothing to be ashamed of in a glass of wine.'

Her brother was removing a tin tray from the oven, making the room even hotter. The stuff inside it was red and lumpy – smelled all right though.

'Is it done, our lass?' he said, holding it in the hot cloth and offering it towards his sister.

'It's beautiful, Adam,' she said. 'Mr Stringer,' she ran on, turning back to me, 'supper is about to be served.'

'I'll go into the dining room then,' I said.

'Good *thinking*,' she said. 'And do take a glass of beer with you.'

She indicated a line of glasses on a shelf near the door. I took one and helped myself from the barrel.

'Shall I take one for Mr Fielding?' I enquired.

'No,' said the brother, looking up at me sharply as he put the meat into a serving dish, and then he added, in a somewhat calmer tone, ''E 'as wine.'

I thought how the house was that fellow's life. He was master of all its little details.

Returning to the door of the dining room I clashed with Howard Fielding, who held a wine glass and a bottle of white wine, half full with a cork in it.

'Good evening again, Mr Stringer,' he said, and he made his way towards the head of the table with his twinkling sort of walk. He indicated that I should take the place to his right side. Vaughan was already sitting to his left, looking sadly at his beer glass, already empty in front of him. Miss Amanda Rickerby then entered holding her wine glass and a black album, saying, 'We're all here then – no need to ring the bell,' and sat down at the end of the table opposite to Mr Fielding. Finally, Adam Rickerby came in with a big tray, and began distributing the soup bowls. As he did so, Miss Rickerby eyed me in the most thrilling way. I must be just her sort, I decided.

'Cedar-wood box after supper, Howard?' Vaughan asked Fielding, without looking up from his empty glass.

'Perhaps Mr Stringer would care to join us at the box?' said Fielding, pouring himself a glass of wine, and he turning and looking his mysterious question at me, with head tilted, so I said, 'I'm sure I would, thanks,' and took a drink of my beer.

Everybody had the soup now, and I was just about to fall to, when I saw Fielding close his eyes and sit forwards. I thought for a fraction of time that he'd actually pegged out there and then, but he was saying grace, and the final word of it was hardly out of his mouth when I heard a terrible racket such as is made in a bath when the last of the water goes down the plug. This was Theo Vaughan taking his first mouthful of soup.

'What's in the cedar-wood box?' I enquired, after Theo Vaughan's second mouthful, which was quite as loud as the first had been.

'Cigars,' said Vaughan, and I felt an ass, for what else could have been in it?

I flashed a look at Amanda Rickerby. She was still eyeing me, an amused expression on her face. She was turning the pages of the black album while sipping her soup. Every so often she would exchange a muttered word with her brother, but she hardly left off staring at me throughout the meal, and I felt that she was a temptress in league with the naked bicyclist.

'Mainly Shorts, I'm afraid, Mr Stringer,' said Fielding. 'We've smoked the last of the Coronas from Christmas.'

'Well, even a short cigar is longer than a cigarette,' I said.

'Diplomatically spoken,' said Fielding, which made me feel rather a fool.

Fielding and Vaughan both being cigar smokers, the stub in the top room might have belonged to either of them just as easily as to Blackburn. It was plain that Fielding thought himself superior to Vaughan, but the two seemed to jog along together pretty well in spite of the failure of the business they'd worked in, and in spite of Vaughan's dealing in improper post cards. Fielding's private means must be greater than Vaughan's, for his clothes were not only cleaner but of better quality. His linen cuffs were a *bit* out at the edge, but it was only decent cloth that would fray like that, and the cuff links looked to me to be made of good gold.

I glanced over at Amanda Rickerby. She met my gaze, I looked away quickly; looked back again more slowly to see her smiling.

'This is the guest book for last year, Mr Stringer,' she said, indicating the black album before her.

Was the name of Blackburn in there, and was she teasing me by keeping it from me?

'I put ticks next to the ones I want back, crosses against the ones I don't,' she said.

And she suddenly turned to Fielding.

'Do you remember Mr Armstrong, Mr Fielding?'

Fielding smiled and nodded.

'He was a very strange . . . well, I was about to say gentleman,' Amanda Rickerby continued. 'He collected seaweed, Mr Stringer. It was his hobby. It was left all over the room to dry. He needed pails of fresh water to clean it – and then he had the nerve to complain about Mrs Dawson's cooking. But Mr Fielding took him in hand.'

Fielding nodded graciously again, saying, 'I merely pointed out that sole à la Normande was *supposed* to contain fish. He collected seaweed but did not eat fish – slightly paradoxical, I thought.'

'Howard didn't care for him at all,' Vaughan put in, addressing me. 'He drank beer from the neck of the bottle.'

'He was rather a vulgar young fellow,' Fielding explained. 'He was from Macclesfield. The North Bay of this town would have been more to his liking . . . You'd have thought that a man interested in marine biology would have had more decorum.'

'*I* wouldn't,' said Amanda Rickerby. 'I'm putting a cross by his name.'

And she did so, before turning the page.

'Mr and Mrs Bailey,' she said, looking towards Fielding again, '. . . from Hertfordshire.'

'Rather a pleasant couple, I seem to remember,' said Fielding.

Miss Rickerby made no answer to that but looked down at the book and came over very sad, it seemed to me. I wanted to help her, bring her back to smiling, but after a couple of minutes I was aware of Adam Rickerby standing over me and saying, 'Yer've done, 'ave yer?'

I hadn't quite but I gave him my bowl and he took it away along with all the others. Only after he'd left the room did I think: *Ought I to have eaten that? Perhaps Blackburn had been poisoned?* The soup had seemed quite tasty anyhow, if nothing to write home about. The meat, when it came in, was the cause for a little more in the way of excitement.

'Croquette de boeuf cooked to a turn, Miss R,' said Fielding, when he'd taken his first mouthful, and she seemed to come round from a stupor or a dream.

'I only superintended,' she said. 'It was Adam who cooked it really.'

But there seemed no question of complimenting Adam Rickerby.

'Beef *patty*, I call it,' said Vaughan, who'd already eaten half of his.

'Oh come now, Vaughan,' said Fielding. 'What about the delicious dressing?'

'Beef patty,' repeated Vaughan, 'with *tomato sauce*. Perfectly good though,' he added.

'Certainly is,' I said, trying to direct my remark to both Amanda Rickerby and her brother. '. . . Goes down very nicely.'

But there was something in it I didn't care for, some spice, and the taste of it somehow made me think the dining room fire too hot. Had I been poisoned? No. It took hours to notice if you had been, and what could possibly be the *reason*? About half a minute after, Vaughan pushed his empty plate away and fell to sucking bits of the meat out of his moustache while eyeing me. The meal ended for all shortly after, when Adam Rickerby stood up and reclaimed all the plates. There would be no dessert, evidently. Pudding was for summer only, together with all other good things.

'Will you be joining us for a smoke, Adam?' I enquired, as he approached the door with the pile of plates.

Fact was, I felt a bit sorry for the bloke. His sister was kindly towards him in her speech and expressions, but never lifted a finger to help him in his duties.

'I've t'plates to clear,' he said, the words coming with a fine spray of spittle.

'After that, then?'

'Then, I've t'plates to *wash*.'

I gave it up, and he left the room. Fielding was good enough to wait until he was through the door before leaning towards me and saying, 'The boy is weak in the head, Mr Stringer. An injury to the brain sustained when he was fourteen.'

'He does very well considering,' I said. 'I knew there must have been something of the kind. What happened?'

Silence for an interval; and they all gave me the tale together, as though they'd rehearsed the telling of it.

'My brother was straight down the mine from school,' began Miss Rickerby.

'One of those timbers in a mine ...' said Vaughan, 'that holds up the whatsname.'

'A pit prop,' Fielding put in, 'that holds up the shaft.'

'One of 'em broke,' continued Vaughan, 'and a quantity of coal came down on him.'

'Two and a half tons, Mr Stringer,' said Fielding.

'It rather put him off coal mining,' said Vaughan, who was now staring at the ceiling and stroking his moustache. 'Well ... as you can imagine.'

'So you see,' Amanda Rickerby said to me, 'this house really *is* Paradise to my brother.'

Chapter Twenty

At length, the way became clear for my return to the chart room. The youth led me up in silence; he would not meet my eye. The Captain and Mate waited with chairs pushed back from the table, as though they'd just put away a good supper. The Mate indicated one of the chairs, and the two made no objection when I moved it closer to the stove. This burned too low as before. I asked them to put more coal on from the scuttle that stood alongside, and the Mate did this readily enough as the Captain eyed me. It wasn't as though they lacked fuel on that bloody ship. The pocket revolver was on the table at the Captain's place as before, together with coffee, bread, cold meat of some description and a round cheese. It was all I could do to look at the stuff, let alone eat it.

'Well?' asked the Captain when I'd settled down.

'I'm not at *all* well,' I said. 'I've a terrible headache.'

'Not what I meant,' said the Captain.

'You were not asking after my health?' I said.

'He means carry on with the talking,' said the Mate.

I eyed him. It did not seem likely to me that the common run of collier – of the sort that carried coal from the North of England to the great gas works of London – would have a foreigner as First Mate. But these two were confederates of long standing – *had* to be, since they were together weighing the idea of doing murder.

Most likely it *was* an ordinary collier, and an English one at that. Sometimes, they had funnels that were hinged, like ships in bottles, so that they could go all the way upriver – up the Thames – but the usual trip was to the mighty gas works at Beckton, which came just before the start of the London docks. The colliers were in competition with the coal trains. The North Eastern company carried coal to London over its own metals and those of the Great Northern, but most of the stuff made the long journey by sea. Had I been put on with coal? None was loaded at Scarborough, I knew that for a fact. But this ship would have passed Scarborough on its way south.

The chart room swayed like a tree house in a high wind, and for a moment I was in that tree house, for my mind still wasn't right. I looked down at my hands: the redness was fading somewhat from them, and my memory returning by degrees. I started talking. I did not let the Captain and the Mate see my mind entire as I spoke, and tried to make myself seem cooler towards Amanda Rickerby than I had been in reality. I talked to them about her much as I might have talked to the *wife* about her. I was rehearsing, so to say, the way I might tell the tale of Paradise to Lydia. It was only when, after an hour or so, the Captain once again consulted his watch and nodded towards the Mate – who rose to take me from the chart room – that I wondered whether I would ever have the chance to put the story right, and to make amends.

But make amends for what, exactly?

The Mate was descending the outer bridge-house ladder behind me, and the over-grown kid I'd seen before waited on the deck below. They had entrusted him with a gun, and he continued to look at me as though I was a dead man. It broke in on me that I was a prisoner under escort. It was as though I was the criminal; as though the Captain and the Mate were sitting in judgement on me, the hearings of the trial being conducted in instalments fitted around the performance of their duties in the ship. I supposed they could only hide themselves from the crew for short intervals.

But how long was the run to London from the northern places where the coal was dug? It was roughly four hundred miles' distance, and a ship making about six knots would do the journey in three days and nights at the maximum. By that reckoning there would be only the one more hearing to come.

I descended to the gunwale on the starboard side, facing the land, which ran along with us, rising and falling. The night sky was darker that way; the light rose from behind me. The land, then, lay to the west. I thought I made out bays, hills, perhaps a thin wood on a low stretch of cliff. And now there was a new sound rising on the air, a beating, on-rushing sound, the source of which disturbed the waves of our wake. At the foot of the ladder, a conference was taking place between the Mate and the lad.

I looked back towards the land, and now saw a beautiful, flowing ribbon of lights being drawn over the cliff top. I do not believe that I had ever been happier to see a train, even though I had no hope of catching this one. I then turned my head to the right and saw the source of the new noise: another ship, blazing light on our starboard side, the landward side. It was bigger than us and gaining on us at a great rate. I knew that I had seen this all before, and of course I was now inhabiting the scene shown on the painting in the ship room at Paradise. The very sky was the same colour: a dark blue with a rising pearly light on the horizon.

The Mate had gone aft; the over-grown kid remained. The

mass of the mid-ships blocked my view in that direction, but I hoped that a row was brewing, that the crew had mustered on the after deck, pressing to know why they must keep to one half of the ship, and threatening mutiny.

The kid had evidently had his orders, for he motioned me to come down the ladder, and to move for'ard with him. I did so, with the gun on me. It was a revolver that he held, a biggish one. I could see by the mid-ships lamps that it was clarted in grease, which might mean it had only lately been taken out of storage, which might in turn mean it would be stiff to operate. But if that trigger, with the kid's finger presently upon it, travelled one quarter of an inch I was a goner.

'I hope you know what you're about, son,' I said, as we walked halfway for'ard. 'This is a serious doing: kidnap of a police officer, assault. Twenty-five-year touch if you're run in.'

The boy kept silence.

'And what about that gun?' I said. 'Are you sure you're up to firing it?'

He re-pointed the thing at me, but he was watching the on-coming ship. We both were. It wasn't a collier – too clean, sat too high in the water. It was a superior ship altogether to our own, with two funnels amidships and a high foc's'le, proudly carried. It lagged back not more than a couple of hundred yards now – not close enough to hail, but close enough perhaps to strike out and swim to.

'That gun,' I said. 'Fire it, and the fucking flash'll blind you.'

'Eh?' he said.

'Are you sure you can work it? I mean, is it double or single action?'

'You'll find out soon if you don't shut up,' he said.

The other ship was starting to make us roll in a different

way. I might swim into its path and wait in the water, but would the cold kill me? Would I be spotted, and if so would I be rescued? The ship gave a long, low horn-blow, like the mooing of a giant cow, and the sound threatened to deafen me and I think the kid also, for the look in his eyes was one of shock and fear. He looked down at the gun, then up at me, and something had made him talkative.

'Don't come it about being a copper,' he said. 'You're a bloody stowaway.'

'You're talking through your fucking braces,' I said.

The kid was again eyeing the other ship.

'Stowaway . . .' I said. 'That's what you've been told, is it?'

'And you can't kidnap a dirty stowaway,' said the kid, turning back towards me. 'You're no copper,' he said again. 'You'll be *given* to the coppers at the turnaround.'

'Turnaround?' I said. 'Where?'

We were close to the gunwale, practically leaning on it. I put my left hand on the cold iron, and the kid made no move to stop me. A deck ring bolt was between us, and a pile of rope. The rope might prevent him from making a grab at me, should I attempt the leap. I edged still closer to the gunwale. The sea was – what? – twenty feet below and quite black. It looked like oil; smelt like oil for the matter of that. But then again it seemed to roll almost playfully, with only the occasional wave uncurling itself to make a leap and hitting high against the hull with a slap that set the iron ringing. Now the oncoming ship was blowing its horn again, as if in encouragement, just as if to say: 'What are you waiting for, man? Make the leap!'

Chapter Twenty-One

I stayed behind alone in the dining room after the meal. I was studying the painting opposite to the fireplace because something about it troubled me.

I hung back there about five minutes, and when I came out, I saw Adam Rickerby moving rapidly towards the foot of the stairs with a giant tin of paint or white-wash in each hand. The wife had laid in a couple of similar-sized cans at our new place, all ready for me to start decorating, and it was all *I* could do to lift one of them. Adam Rickerby carried two with ease and was now fairly bounding up the stairs with them. Well, he had evidently washed the pots in double-quick time.

I followed him up to the first landing, where the door of the ship room was closed. Were Fielding and Vaughan already in there? But Rickerby was climbing at the top of his speed to the next landing, and again I followed him up. Coming to the floor that was being decorated I could not see him: the corridor stretched away darkly. But there came a noise from the second door down on the left. That door stood ajar, and I walked in directly to see Rickerby standing by an open window with a shrimp net – very likely the one I'd seen in the cupboard upstairs – in his hand. The low gas showed bare, flaking walls, white-wash brushes and rolls of wallpaper on every hand – and it was the green stripe again. Why did the landlady persist with that? Her colour was grey-violet, the colour of her coat and hat. The sea wind surged fiercely against the frame of the open window like a roll of drums, and I saw that behind Adam Rickerby a hole had been knocked in the wall, showing another, darker room beyond.

'Can I *help* you?' he said.

Of all the questions I might have asked, the one that came out was: 'Why is the window open?'

'Carry off the smoke,' said Rickerby.

'There is no smoke,' I shot back.

'It's been carried off.'

With his wild hair, the smock-like apron and the long-handled shrimp net he held, the lad was halfway to being bloody King Neptune.

'Smoke from what?' I said.

The room had one of the small iron fireplaces but it was not lit. Rickerby's gaze drifted down to an object on the floorboards by his boots, half hidden in scraps of torn wallpaper: a paraffin torch of the sort used for burning off paint. It might have smoked at one time; there might have been something in his tale.

'Why are you holding that shrimp net?'

'I mean to use t'pole.'

'For what?'

'Reaching up.'

'To what?'

'Ceiling.'

'Why do you want to reach up to the ceiling with the pole?'

'I don't.'

And I nearly crowned him just then, which might not have been so clever, given the size of him.

'I mean to reach up wi' t'*brush*,' he said.

'So you'll tie the brush – the white-wash or distemper brush

– onto the pole, is that it?'

He kept silence, watching me. Presently he said, 'Aye,' and I wondered whether there might not have been a note of sarcasm there, and – once again – whether he was brighter than I took him for.

'What's the work going on here?'

' . . . Making an apartment.'

'Why?'

He looked sidelong, looked back.

'Bring in a different sort.'

'A different sort of guest? What sort?'

'The sort that likes apartments.'

Holiday apartments were more expensive than holiday rooms, and I supposed that the difference would repay knocking down walls to create them.

I believed that I had got as much as I would get from Adam Rickerby.

'I'm off downstairs just now,' I said. 'I'm off to smoke a cigar.'

Under the steady gaze of the over-grown schoolboy, and with mind racing, I turned and quit the apartment-to-be.

Approaching the ship room, I fancied for the second time that I heard muttering from behind the door, which stopped directly upon my opening the door and entering. I saw the black sea tracking endlessly past the tall, delicate windows. If Fielding and Vaughan had been speaking, they'd been doing so without looking at each other. Vaughan lay flat on the couch and again smoked towards the ceiling. Fielding sat in his armchair facing the tall windows. In that warped, wide room the fire was too small, the fireplace smaller still, and yet the room was too hot.

The gas was noisy here, as in the rest of the house. It sounded like somebody's last breath, going on for ever. Was it the gas that made the room hot or thoughts of the landlady that made *me* hot in it? Something had changed about the few sticks of furniture in the room. None of these quite belonged. It was as if they'd been meant for a different room, and I fancied that if somebody struck up on the piano, it might crash through the ancient floorboards. I noticed for the first time an alcove set into the wall beside the piano, with two bookshelves fitted into it. Each held half a dozen books, all – at first glance – about ships or the sea, or paintings of same, and I took them all to be Fielding's.

Set between his armchair, and Vaughan's couch, was the second armchair. The small bamboo table had been pushed towards it, and a cigar, already cut, rested on a little saucer that made shift as an ash tray. Beside it was a box of long matches: wind vestas. As I sat down at my chair and took up the cigar, Vaughan rolled a little my way, blowing smoke. His reddish, down-pointed moustache looked odder still when set on its side. Fielding also altered position somewhat, so that his gaze was now midway between me and the sea.

'I'm obliged to you,' I said to Fielding after lighting the cigar and shaking out the match. I was glad to have got my smoke going first time, for there'd only been one match left in the box – which seemed to sum up the whole house. Fielding nodded courteously in my direction, and crossed his legs, which he did tightly, in a fashion rather womanly. Vaughan watched me for a while, then rolled back to his former position.

'It makes a cracking cigar divan does this,' he said.

'And it will be fit for nothing else once you've smothered it in ash,' said Fielding. 'The Lady will not like it.'

No, I thought, but she won't be the one who cleans it.

'You have lots of books on ships,' I said to Fielding.

'*About* ships, I think you mean,' he replied. 'I assure you that none of them are *on* ships. I have many about railways as well, and quite a fair number of novels.'

'He's got enough books to start a bookshop,' said Vaughan, 'and that's just what he means to do.'

An interval of silence, and then Fielding leant a little my way, like a man about to pass on a confidence. 'There's a good lock-up shop on Newborough, Mr Stringer,' he said. 'If it falls into my hands, it will be re-fitted throughout and will indeed become a bookshop as Vaughan says ...'

'Second-hand books,' said Vaughan, nodding at the ceiling, as though he thoroughly approved of the idea.

'*Antiquarian*,' corrected Fielding.

He seemed to have the ability to start and finish businesses just like that; seemed to have the capital to do it as well – and to buy new books.

'Theo ... Mr Vaughan here ... was showing me some of your cards for the platform machines,' I said. 'Just my sort of thing, they were.'

'But you take a close interest in the railways, Mr Stringer,' said Fielding, cocking his head and smiling at me. 'The average passenger does not, or so Mr Robinson of the North Eastern company assured me.'

'Robinson's a pill,' said Vaughan.

'He told me', Fielding ran on, still smiling, 'that as a supplier of images I lacked the common touch.'

'Bloody nerve,' said Vaughan, who'd already mentioned to me this famous saying of Robinson's.

'Told me to my face,' continued Fielding, 'and do you know

'. . . he was putting on a silk top hat at the time.'

It was impossible to tell from his expression how angry he was, if at all.

'You must be pretty mad at the Company,' I said.

'I should just think he *is*,' Vaughan said.

He would keep putting his two bob's worth in. Again, it was hard to work out if Fielding minded very much.

'Pretty mad?' Fielding repeated coolly. 'From their point of view they acted logically. I admit that I rode my own hobby horses a little too hard.'

'The straw that broke the camel's back', Vaughan put in, 'was Sunderland station.'

'I produced a card showing Sunderland station at night,' said Fielding, blowing smoke in the direction of the sea, '. . . illuminated by the new system of oil lighting supplied by the Kitson Company. On the rear of the card was given the number of lamps, also the cost of oil and mantles, installation and maintenance. It came out at three farthings per lamp per hour.'

'Cheap,' I said.

'Decidedly,' said Vaughan, who was trying to blow smoke rings.

'But Robinson didn't care for it,' Fielding continued. 'He told me, "It's meant to be a post card not a company report," and suggested instead a card showing holiday makers at Sunderland. I then made the mistake – as I now see in retrospect – of venturing to suggest that only a certified lunatic would take a holiday in Sunderland, which does not have any beach to speak of.'

'*Factories*,' said Vaughan, 'that's what Sunderland has.'

'Where were the pair of you living when you had the card business?' I enquired.

'Leeds,' said Fielding. 'I was rather shaken after the collapse of the business. I moved here last summer – a sort of convalescence, I suppose.'

'Then he wrote to me saying I might like it,' Vaughan added.

'Where were you in Leeds? If you don't mind my asking?'

'Central,' said Fielding, uncrossing his legs, and I wondered: Is he being short with me?

'Both in the same digs?'

'Howard was at the better part of town,' said Vaughan, blowing smoke.

Blackburn had lived at Roundhay; I wanted to work it in.

'I know a spot called Roundhay,' I said. 'You weren't there by any chance?'

'We were not,' said Fielding, and he cocked his head at me, as if to say: 'Now why ever did you ask that?'

Vaughan was eyeing me too.

'You two must like having this place to yourself in the winter,' I said presently.

No reply from either of them.

'Do you ever come here in summer, Jim?' Vaughan suddenly enquired. 'I mean, do you fire the excursions?'

'I'm usually rostered another way,' I said. 'Half the time I'm running into . . .' And I revolved the towns of Yorkshire for a while: '. . . Hull.'

'Ah, now Hull is the plum,' said Fielding, rising from his chair and carrying his cigar stub towards the fire, where he dropped it carefully into the flames; he then brushed the ash from his fingers and briefly inspected his fingernails. 'One of our cards showed the electric coaling belts on the Riverside Quay,' he added, returning to his seat.

'Shown on a day of heavy rain, they were,' said Vaughan.

'Good job old Robinson never saw that one or he'd have put the mockers on sooner than he did.'

He was examining his own cigar, which, like mine, had a little way to run. 'Sound smoke, wouldn't you say, Howard?'

'A little dry,' said Fielding, speaking as though his mind was elsewhere.

'I wonder why that is?'

'We should keep a little pot of water in the cedar-wood box.'

I was about to try and get the conversation back to the winter visitors, as a way of returning to the subject of Ray Blackburn, when Fielding unexpectedly saved me the bother.

'Yes,' he said with a sigh, 'it was my suggestion that the Lady advertise for railway men. Well, she was in rather low water then as now. But then, you see, the first one we had in went missing.'

'I know,' I said, somewhat alarmed in case I had revealed my true identity, and perhaps too fast, for Vaughan propped himself up on his couch while Fielding rose once more from his seat, and stood before me with arms folded and one little foot tapping away.

'Of course,' I said, 'Ray Blackburn was Leeds and I'm York, so I didn't know the fellow personally. But I know what happened.'

'You *know*!' exclaimed Fielding with half a smile.

'Disappeared in the night,' said Vaughan. 'Spirited away in the dead of bloody *night*, Jim.'

'To obtrude a fact or two, Mr Stringer,' said Fielding, 'Mr Blackburn went to bed at about eleven-thirty, and was nowhere to be seen when the boy went up to him with a cup of tea at seven the next morning.'

I didn't much care for that, since the boy had promised to

bring *me* tea at seven as well. I was certain that I'd been installed in the room Blackburn had occupied, and it was beginning to seem as though I'd stepped into his very boots.

'Were you both in the house when it happened?' I enquired.

'Oh dear,' said Fielding, 'you sound like the gentlemen in blue.'

He was down on the coppers then, and that was unusual for a respectable sort like him.

'Same people in the house then as now,' said Vaughan, 'which is why we've all been on the spot these past weeks. How many police teams would you say we'd had, Howard? Past counting isn't it?'

'Not quite,' said Fielding. 'We've had three visits from the Scarborough men, two from the Leeds. A little potation?' he enquired of me, nodding towards the sideboard.

'But we're right out!' exclaimed Vaughan.

'I took the liberty of replenishing the supply,'

'Spanish sherry?' said Vaughan, rising to his feet.

'It's in the usual place,' said Fielding, and he nodded significantly at Vaughan.

Well, that place was evidently outside the room, for Vaughan went quickly out of the door and returned after a few moments – in which Fielding kept silence while smiling at me – carrying a tray on which stood a bottle and some small glasses. He set this down on the top of the piano and began to pour, slopping the stuff about rather as he did so, perhaps because the piano top was too high for the operation.

'Really, Vaughan,' said Fielding, looking on, 'it will not do; it will not do at all . . . I'm sorry it's not decanted,' he said, turning my way.

'Don't worry on my account,' I said, chalking up another

idiotic remark. *Was* Fielding taking the rise out of me?

'Did nobody hear anything?' I said, extinguishing my cigar on the saucer.

'*We* didn't,' said Vaughan, passing out the drinks. 'We'd been at this stuff all night, one way or another. Absolutely mashed we were, come midnight.'

'I don't care for this "we", Vaughan,' said Fielding.

'Begin at the beginning,' said Vaughan, regaining his couch. 'Blackburn turned up at about the same time you did, Jim. Supper was served directly, and it was a hot supper, then as today. One of Howard's recipes. The Lady happened to have some peculiar sort of chops and some old cheese lying about . . .'

'Veal Parmesan,' Fielding cut in.

'Well, it was the Lady's first railway man,' said Vaughan, 'so I suppose she wanted to pull out all the stops.'

'Who cooked the meal?' I asked.

'The boy of course, Jim,' said Vaughan, draining his glass. 'When supper was over, I asked the fellow if he'd care for a pint, and so we walked over to the Two Mariners, just as you and I did, Jim. Well, it was a bit of a washout in the pub. The fellow hardly said a word, and I came back with him at about ten past ten, barely half an hour after we'd set off. I'd forgotten my key so had to ring the bell. Howard here answered the door and let us in.'

Fielding nodded at me, confirming this.

'Blackburn then went straight up to his room,' said Vaughan, 'and Fielding joined me in here, and we had a bit of a chat about the lad: Adam, I mean. I'd seen him earlier in the day, a little before Blackburn turned up, acting in a rather queer fashion in this room, Jim. It was just as darkness was falling, and he was standing by the window there with no gas lit, and waving . . .'

'A shrimp net?' I put in, and Vaughan frowned.

'No, Jim, not a shrimp net. Why would he be waving a shrimp net? He was waving an oil lamp about.'

'Waving it out to sea?' I said. 'Signalling?'

Vaughan nodded.

'I thought so, Jim.'

'Perhaps the gas had run out, and he'd needed the lamp to see by.'

No answer from Vaughan; he was staring up at the ceiling. Behind Fielding, the wind was getting up, becoming unruly by degrees, and you just knew it would end badly. If that sea had been a bloke in a public bar you'd have moved into the saloon. With head cocked, Fielding watched me watching it, as if to say, 'Why are you surprised? Any man worth his salt ought to know the ways of the sea.'

Chapter Twenty-Two

'Hand over the gun,' I said to the kid.

With the revolver in my hand I would take my chances with the Captain and the Mate, wherever they'd got to. If I couldn't get it off the kid, I'd go over the side. This was the programme. I didn't believe the kid would shoot, and he might not have the chance. The other ship would overhaul us in a couple of minutes' time, which gave me about thirty seconds' leeway – thirty seconds to leap while in full view of their bridge. 'If you hand it over,' I said to the kid, 'I'll see the judge lets you off with a talking-to – got that?'

He shook his head very decidedly, but he was shivering.

'Hold *on* to it, and you'll be lagged for most of your life. Fire it, and you'll fucking swing.'

'Come off it,' said the kid. 'Nobody on land knows you're here.'

That couldn't be right. *Somebody* knew – somebody in the Paradise guest house knew. The kid was facing me, but watching the other ship with the tail of his eye. He was in a funk all right; the gun hand was shaking, but he now cocked the hammer with his thumb. It cost him quite an effort, and he had to steady the thing with his other hand, but now I had the answer to my question: it was a single action revolver, and I was halfway to being dead.

'What *are* you, son?' I asked him. 'Ship's cook? Captain's boy?'

'You fuck off,' he said, and from somewhere aft I heard, floating over the waves and the wind and the engine beat, the voice of the Captain. He was speaking more loudly than he ever had done to me, and with more anger, although this anger was directed more at himself, as I believed, than at any other party. 'I don't see it,' I heard him say. 'I just don't *see* it.'

The kid heard it too, and perhaps he wanted to talk to drown it out.

'You needn't worry about me,' he said. 'You ought to be looking out for yourself.'

'You think I'm a stowaway,' I said to the kid. 'It's customary at sea to shoot stowaways, is it?'

The kid nodded slowly.

'Stowaway,' I repeated. 'What do you think I *am*? Hell bent on a free ride to the bloody gas works? That's it, isn't it, son? We're on a run to Beckton with a load of gas coal. You'll come back empty, will you? Or with a load of coke? Where've we come from, eh, son? The Tyne? Dunston Staithes?'

'You're nuts, you are,' he said, but there wasn't much force behind the words. He was hatless, and his hair blew left and right. In the weak light of the dawn, I could see clear through to his scalp. He'd be quite bald in five years' time; he was wasting his best years at sea.

I pictured the great wooden piers at Dunston where the coal was pitched from railway wagons into the colliers day and night under a black cloud that rolled eternally upwards. That was the main starting point for the coal-carrying vessels. But the ship gaining on us carried a clean cargo; it had a smart red hull. I saw now that two blokes stood on the foc's'le, facing each other and still as statues. Was there a hand signal for 'Come alongside'? I ought to have paid more attention to the super-annuated skipper who had given talks on seamanship to the Baytown Boys' Club.

The kid had one eye in that direction too.

'How do I know you're a copper?' he said.

How *was* I to prove it without my card? My mind raced in a circus.

'Do you know York station?' I said.

'No. And what's that got to do with it?'

I could hear the throbbing engines of the other ship now, quite distinct from the roar of the sea.

' . . . Because I'm a railway copper,' I said, 'and that's where I work. The police office on Platform Four.'

'Come off it,' said the kid.

I tried to recollect the words on my warrant card but could not, perhaps because of whatever had happened to me. There was some stuff on it about the directors of the railway company. It was more about them than it was me, and very wordy and over-blown.

'Just you take my bloody word for it,' I said, and the kid almost laughed. Well, I couldn't blame him for that.

I put my hand out for the gun, saying, 'Give it over,' but he made no move. I'd seen the Chief take a gun off a man. He did it by force of character – *and* by shouting abuse. You could scare a man by shouting even if he was armed and you were not.

I glanced down at the restless waves; a wind blew up from them. The sea was waiting for me to come in – then there'd be some fun. Only you were liable to be killed outright if you jumped straight into freezing water. Your heart would attack you in revenge for the shock. I looked over again to the other ship, where the faces of the blokes on the foc's'le showed white.

They were looking our way. They contemplated us calmly, and their vessel was swinging closer.

The kid watched them too.

'Witnesses,' I said. 'I can read the name of that ship. I can hunt up those blokes later on, and they'll testify to what they saw . . . Hand over the shooter.'

But I *couldn't* read the name. It was something foreign. However, it appeared that one of the two mannequins on the foc's'le was fitted with a moving arm, for he saluted us just then.

'They see us,' I said. 'I reckon they're coming alongside.'

I put my hand out again for the gun.

'You won't like it in gaol, son.'

'It'll be just like here,' he said, and the gun was in my hand.

I tried to look as though I had expected this development. I held the gun; I commanded the ship – the whole of the seas.

Chapter Twenty-Three

I held up my glass of Spanish sherry as though trying to decide whether it agreed with me or not. It looked like cold tea, and tasted like cold, very *sweet* tea.

'Vaughan left me at quarter after eleven, Mr Stringer,' said Fielding, with the black sea boiling behind him. 'I then remained here, reading, until half past, when I decided I'd better take my boots down to the boy. He's generally in the kitchen at that time, and one of his last duties is to clean the boots.'

'And as you were coming back up, you saw Blackburn going down with *his* boots,' Vaughan put in.

'That is correct,' said Fielding slowly, as though not over-keen on the fact having been mentioned. 'We crossed on the bottom stairs.'

'How did he seem?' I asked.

'How did he *seem*?' Fielding repeated, cocking his head. 'Rather morose. He barely gave me good night.'

'So the last person to see him would have been the boy?'

'Or our landlady,' said Vaughan. 'She'd been in the kitchen when you'd taken your boots down, hadn't she, Howard?'

'I believe that she *had* been,' said Fielding, 'but she'd gone up to her room by the time I got there.' He turned to me, explaining: 'It is the Lady's habit, Mr Stringer, to read articles from the newspapers to her brother, last thing.'

'And to drink wine,' added Vaughan.

I felt the urge to defend Amanda Rickerby against this slur, and immediately felt guilty on that account. A man ought to have feelings like that only for his wife. But then again my wife smiled at Robert Henderson, and yet every time *I* met him while walking, the bastard cut me dead.

A strange kind of flat boat was putting out from the harbour. It looked like a brightly lit, floating station platform with three men waiting for trains on it, and it was bucking about pretty wildly. Fielding saw me eyeing it.

'It works in combination with the Scarborough dredger,' he explained. 'They scour out the harbour approach every few weeks.'

'We think we know what happened to Blackburn, Jim,' Vaughan said. 'We think he jumped into the sea.'

'Why would he do that?'

'Well, he was pretty cheesed off about *something*,' said Vaughan, 'and that's fact. I often worry whether it was something I said to him after supper. You see, he'd been quite *bright* at supper.'

'You're advertising for railway men again,' I said, 'or at any rate, Miss Rickerby is.'

'Is she?' said Fielding, and he frowned. It wasn't like him not to know something.

'That's why I'm here,' I said.

'Of course,' said Fielding, with a single rapid nod of the head.

'The house is still on the North Eastern list,' I said. 'Any lodge within five minutes of the station is eligible, although strictly speaking, I don't think this *is* within five minutes.'

'It is if you run like mad,' said Vaughan. 'I'm off to the toilet,' he went on, rising from the couch. '. . . Toilet then bed.'

'Won't do, won't do,' said Fielding, shaking his head. 'You are not "off to the toilet". You are going to the *lavatory*, and we do not wish to know.'

'Please yourself,' said Vaughan, who gave us both good night before quitting the room.

Fielding said, 'I have tried my best to bring that young man on, Mr Stringer, believe me.'

I wondered whether this was how he saw Vaughan, as somebody to be brought on, much as the wife regarded me.

'I'm pleased that the fate of poor Blackburn didn't put you off coming here,' he said.

'I have his same room as well,' I said.

'As well as *what*?' he said, smiling. 'Won't you have another sherry?'

'All right then,' I said. 'I'm obliged to you.'

He twinkled his way over to the piano and brought the tray to the occasional table, where he filled my glass, passing it to me very daintily. I took it from him in the same way.

'In so far as I've known them,' he said, 'I've found engine drivers and firemen rather a rough class, but you conduct yourself in a very gentlemanly way, if I may say so.'

I nodded, thinking: Is he onto me? I touched my pocket book, through the wool of my suit-coat. It was there all right, the warrant card within it. Fielding couldn't possibly have had sight of it. Anyhow, he was smiling at me in a sad sort of way that made me think the compliment genuine.

'Did you find that Blackburn was like that?' I asked him.

'He was rather tongue-tied,' said Fielding, sitting back down in his accustomed seat. 'A big fellow but carried his size well. A dignified man . . . handsome . . .'

'Do you know what he and Vaughan talked about on their walk after supper?'

'Well,' Fielding said, 'I can make a hazard.'

'Rare one for the fair sex, isn't he?' I said. 'Mr Vaughan, I mean.'

'He's a rare one for *pictures* of the fair sex,' said Fielding. 'He showed you some of his samples, I suppose.'

'Yes,' I said. 'One.'

'Was it the naked lady on the trapeze?'

I shook my head.

'It was the naked lady holding the bicycle.'

'It is the same ... *artiste*,' said Fielding with a sigh.

He was evidently pretty well acquainted with the cards himself, even if he didn't approve of them.

'Made out he knew her,' I said.

'He'd *like* to know her,' said Fielding, 'I don't doubt that. He's minded to set himself up as a photographer in that line, you know.' He shook his head for a while. 'It's my fault in a way. I mean, I brought him into the post card world.'

There came a noise from the doorway, and Miss Rickerby was in the corridor with her brother.

'Tell me, Mr Stringer,' Fielding was saying quite loudly, 'how do you manage to spot all the signals while rushing along the line? I believe the North Eastern is the most densely signalled railway in the country. Sixty-seven on one gantry at Newcastle alone.'

He was trying to cover up the subject of our conversation.

'Well,' I said, 'each man has his own pet way of remembering where the signals are. Speaking for myself, I . . .'

'They're like gladioli,' said Amanda Rickerby, coming into the room looking rather pink about the face but none the less fetching for that.

'*How* are they?' I said.

'That's what they look like,' she said. 'When there's more than one, I mean. I find them quite pretty but it frightens me when they change because nobody's near by and suddenly they *move*.'

Her brother came into the room behind her, and I thought: You could say the same for him. He brought the paint smell with him, and there were specks of white-wash on the backs of his hands.

'Boots,' he said.

'Come again?' I said, because he was looking my way.

'Do yer boots,' he said, almost panting.

'We have our boots *on*,' said Fielding, not to the boy but to Miss Rickerby, who was of course eyeing me. 'You can't very well clean them now.'

For the first time I looked back boldly at Amanda Rickerby, and even though both of us were smiling it was obvious in that moment of honesty that neither one of us was exactly what you might call happy.

'It's just gone eleven,' her brother said. 'I clean t'boots from eleven on.'

'But the hot supper has thrown us all late,' said Fielding, and again he was appealing to our landlady rather than addressing the boy.

'The gentlemen will take them down to the kitchen in the next little while if they want them doing, Adam,' said Miss Rickerby. 'And you have something for Mr Fielding, don't you?'

The lad took a note from the front pocket of his apron, marched up to Fielding, and handed it to him.

174

'What's this?' said Fielding.

'If you read it,' said the lad, 'then yer'll *know*.'

'Put through the letter box, just now,' said Miss Rickerby. 'I hope you don't mind, but I had to look at it to see who it was for. It's from your recorded music people.'

'Yes,' said Fielding, now glancing at the note. 'It's just a reminder about the meeting.'

'Mr Fielding is the chairman of the Scarborough Recorded Music Circle,' Miss Rickerby said to me, 'which is pretty good going considering he doesn't have a gramophone.'

'It is a little irregular,' said Fielding, colouring up, 'but . . .'

'He won't tell you that they pleaded with him,' said Miss Rickerby. 'Modesty forbids. He is also in the Rotary, Townsmen's Guild etc., sidesman at St Mary's church, and I half expect him to come in for tea and say he's been made Mayor – only he'd never let on. I'd just find this funny hat and big golden chain while straightening his room.'

Fielding was making a sort of waving away gesture with his right hand, as if to say, 'All this is nonsense', but he'd been fairly dancing about with pleasure at the landlady's compliments. She now leant in the doorway with folded arms, smiling and giving Fielding a sad but very affectionate look which made me a little jealous that for once her eyes were not on me.

'Miss Rickerby,' said Fielding, 'my dear Miss Rickerby, won't you . . .' For a moment I thought he was stuck for words, but he finished: '. . . give us something on the piano.'

'No, Mr Fielding,' she said, smiling, but privately now and looking down at her shoes. 'No, I most certainly will not.'

Chapter Twenty-Four

Fielding said good night, walked along to his bedroom, and closed the door. Standing just outside the sitting room I watched him do it, which was easy enough as his bedroom was on the same floor (and faced the right way to have the sea view). There were two other doors on that floor. One stood open, giving onto a fair-sized bathroom, all white with gas light burning. The other was closed. I walked over to it and knocked, and there was no answer. I was alone on the silent landing. I turned the handle and opened the door a fraction, gaining a view of a large, pale blue room that smelt of talcum powder. I saw a dressing table with triple mirror, and a night-dress was thrown over the bed like a dead body. A low fire burned in the grate, and there was a paraffin heater hard by that was turned up to the maximum judging by the stifling heat. This was Miss Rickerby's room.

She's like a cat, I thought – luxuriates in the heat. I closed the door as gently as possible, and I heard a rattle from behind me. It was Fielding's door opening. He wore a night-shirt, dressing gown, and his hair was all neatly combed; but he was only trip-ping his way across to the bathroom.

I turned and walked up the stairs towards the floor being decorated. My own bathroom was on this landing somewhere. Most of the wallpaper had been stripped from the landing walls but some remained in patches, showing the green stripes that still survived upstairs. The gas jets roared, giving a shaking white light, and I wondered whether they kept going all night. I stopped next to a dangling strand of the green wallpaper and felt minded to pull it away. I was reaching out towards it when the roaring of the gas gave way to the roaring of water – a whole waterfall seemed to have been set in motion somewhere out of sight beyond the walls. A door flew open along the corridor, and Vaughan appeared in shirt sleeves, with braces dangling and the seething din of the flushing lavatory behind him.

'Is that the bathroom?' I said.

'It is, Jim,' he said, 'but I haven't had a bath. When you've had a heavy supper, I always think it's best to . . .'

'I know,' I said, cutting him off.

'I've been twice in the past ten minutes,' he said, which made me worried again about the food we'd eaten, even though I felt all right.

'This is me,' Vaughan said, indicating a closed door. 'Care for a peek?'

He proudly occupied the worst room I'd seen so far in the house. It had the green and less-green wallpaper on three walls, and the dried-blood roses on the fourth. The effect was of two rooms that had crashed into each other. The roses were singed and discoloured behind two copper gas pipes that rose up either side of the fireplace. These ran up to little pale green shades that made the whole room look sickly. On the mantelshelf a pipe stand had spaces for a dozen pipes but held just one. The small fireplace was dead, but Vaughan too had a paraffin heater going. It was directed at the wall, like a child being punished for naughtiness in a school form room.

'A few damp spots there,' he said as I looked at it.

Vaughan had evidently been lying on his bed, and right next to the pillow end was a portmanteau stuffed with clothes, and a pile of copies of *Sporting Life*. The only furniture besides the bed and washstand was a wicker chair and a cabinet with the door open. A black trunk marked, for some reason, 'WELLINBROUGH' in white painted letters stood alongside the cabinet. There were no pictures at all on the walls. The flimsy curtains were drawn, but Vaughan too would have overlooked the sea. He was sitting on the wicker chair and removing his boots. I thought: I've got to get out of here before he takes off his trousers.

'You an early riser, Jim?' he said.

'Do you call seven o'clock early?' I said.

'I call it bloody ridiculous,' he said. 'Have a care tomorrow, will you, old man? I can hear most of what goes on up there.'

I looked up.

'But you heard nothing the night that Blackburn disappeared.'

'I was half cut then, Jim . . . And you know, there might have been something . . . something about two, something again about four. A sort of rumbling.'

'Did you mention it to the coppers?'

He shook his head.

'Not certain of it, Jim . . . not certain. You don't go in for physical jerks, I hope?' he added as I looked at the gas pipes, noting that they continued rising beyond the two shades, disappearing into the ceiling . . . and yet there was no gas plumbed into my room.

Vaughan, having thrown one boot towards the cabinet, now threw the second in a roughly similar direction.

'I should take these downstairs for the lad to clean,' he said.

'And will you?'

'Doubt it,' he said. 'I give that youth a wide berth.'

'Does he ever fly off about anything?' I enquired. 'He always seems liable to.'

Vaughan frowned.

'Shouldn't wonder,' he said. 'He's cracked.'

'But you've never seen him do it?'

'I've seen him on the point of blowing up – then I've made myself scarce.'

'When did you find out about his accident?'

'Oh, that all came out when the police started asking questions. They could see he was nuts, and wanted to know why. Miss Rickerby told them, and then she told us all.'

'You don't suppose he did for Blackburn, do you?'

'Blackburn jumped into the sea, Jim,' said Vaughan, who was now kneeling down and fishing about inside the trunk. '. . . Or that's what we all tell ourselves in this house. I mean, none of us likes to think we're sharing lodgings with a murderer.'

He lifted a book out of the trunk, and rifled through the pages, as if to make sure they were all properly bound in.

'Well,' I said, 'no-one can say what happened.'

Vaughan stowed the book back in the trunk.

'The lad's got a hell of a job on with that decorating,' I said.

'Well, he's making an apartment, Jim. It's Fielding's idea, and he's persuaded the lady of it. Eliminate the rough element.'

I looked upwards again, following the pipes with my eye.

'Where do they go?' I said, indicating them.

'Up into the floorboards. Up into your room, I expect.'

'But there's only an oil lamp in my room.'

'Well,' he said, 'perhaps there was gas once.'

There *had* been. The painting in the dining room showed my room the brightest.

'Why would it be stopped?'

'Economy,' said Vaughan with a shrug, and he was now at my side.

'Here's our little friend again,' he said, and he passed me a post card showing a woman – the bicycling woman. Only now she was painting a picture. You couldn't see it because the easel faced away from the camera but you could see everything *else*. The card came from a new envelope, lately fished from the trunk.

'Who *is* this bloody woman, Theo?' I said.

'Yorkshire lass,' he said, and he passed me another card.

'Told you she was game,' he said, and she was now sitting on a gate before a meadow and dangerously close – I would have thought – to a country road. Vaughan said, 'You can tell it's a windy day, can't you?'

'Why put these sorts of picture on post cards?' I said. 'I mean, it's not as if you can post 'em, is it?'

'For collectors,' he said. 'And you can post 'em in envelopes, Jim.'

I glanced over towards his bed. There was a tin of something there. At first I'd taken it for a tin of lozenges, but I now read 'Oglesby's Pilules', and, underneath, 'Oglesby's Pilules are a Certain Cure for Blind and Bleeding Piles'.

'Do *you* have piles, Jim?' he enquired, seeing where I was looking and holding out another post card. 'Sometimes I can't walk around town. Rather fancy studio shot. I presume that swan is stuffed,' he added, passing me the card.

'Look here,' I said, 'why are you showing me these?'

He stepped back, offended.

'What's the matter, Jim?' he said. 'Has old Fielding warned you off?'

'Warned me off what?'

'Business connection,' he said.

'Eh?'

'You can have the choicest selection from the choicest range. A hundred cards for a quid, Jim.'

'Why would I want a hundred?'

'You can have *two* hundred if you want. To be perfectly honest, I'm keen to sell the whole stock, hence the special rate. Of course, you're a chum as well – that's the other reason.'

He moved over to the fire, leant on the mantel-shelf, and looked shrewdly at me, or at least I supposed that was the idea.

'But maybe you think rather narrowly of me for bringing them out.'

'You mean me to buy them and sell them on?' I said.

He nodded quickly.

'They go like hot cakes in any engine shed,' he said. 'Sixpence a piece. I've blokes on the Great Northern and the Hull and Barnsley, and they're getting rich at this game, Jim. When the samples are first shown there's a bit of a frost, I'll not deny it. Blokes are shy, as I can see you are, Jim; they're married men, and it's on their conscience a little, but I promise you that after a couple of weeks, when they think back to what they've seen, and turned it over a little in their minds, why . . . there's a regular rush, Jim.'

'The cards are not legal though, are they?'

'*Where?*' he demanded, still with the shrewd look. '*Where* are they not legal? They're jolly well legal in France.'

But then he relented a little.

'The coppers can be a nuisance,' he said. 'But it's small

apples to them, Jim. I know that from experience. Would you care for a bottle of beer?'

'Well,' I said, 'what time is it?'

'Quarter to midnight,' he said.

I grinned, for it was a crazy situation. It seemed about a week since I'd come into Scarborough station with Tommy Nugent.

'It's nearly midnight, Jim!' said Theo Vaughan, laying the card package down on the bed. 'I'm not going to mince words! I believe in plain speaking!'

I was curious to see where he'd go for the beer, and in the end – after a bit of head scratching on his part – it was the portmanteau. The bottle opener he found at last in the bottom of the closet.

'I don't run to glasses,' he said, handing over the bottle. 'But you're not the sort to bother. Try giving old Fielding a bottle and no glass and just *see* what happens!'

'What *does* happen?' I said.

'Nothing,' said Vaughan. 'But it's the look he gives you.'

'He'll drink it then?'

'He'll drink it all right.'

Vaughan took a pull on his beer, and fell to eyeing me for a while.

'I should just think he will,' he ran on. 'What's the old devil been saying about me? But go on, Jim, I can see you want to question me. Get straight to it. Honesty and trust and plain-dealing – that's the start of any business connection.'

'Did you show your cards to Blackburn?' I said.

That knocked Vaughan, I could tell, for he asked, '*What* cards?' and went back to his shrewd look.

'Well,' I said, taking a pull of beer, 'the ones presently under discussion. The ones you've just asked me to question you about.'

At this, Vaughan might have nodded, but it was done too fast for me to be certain.

'The coppers want to know every detail of my dealings with the man, which amount to this: sitting next to him at one supper, during which he was more or less silent; going with him to the Two Mariners, beginning in hopes of conversation and ending in *complete* silence.'

'But on the walk – in the pub – you did show him the cards?'

'I *suppose* so.'

Vaughan was pacing now, beer bottle in hand.

'And he didn't take to the cards?'

'You should have seen him when I took 'em out, Jim. Face like bloody yesterday and he said, "I shall be mentioning this to Miss Rickerby."'

'Oh,' I said.

'Next development, Jim,' said Vaughan. 'The coppers – the Scarborough lot – made a search of the house – well, they've made several – and they turned up a few of my choicest cards in one of them. I had them stowed away in two places in this room, and they evidently found both. No action was taken. They just gave me a bit of a rating, you know. They were quite decent about it really. I think they knew it was a bit unsporting, the way they came upon them, and to be honest I think they rather enjoyed the experience. Bit of light relief. Now I knew that Blackburn had threatened to split on me to the Lady, and I didn't know whether he had done, or whether she'd told the coppers. So I thought it best to come right out with it, and let on that I'd shown Blackburn a couple of samples.'

He took a long pull on his beer before continuing:

'But if I thought that would bring an end to the matter I thought wrong, Jim. Three times in the past five months I've been called in to the copper shop on Castle Road.'

'I can't imagine the Lady splitting,' I said. 'She seems pretty free and easy – she'd just think those cards were a bit of a laugh.'

Vaughan seemed quite bucked by the thought. He nodded and said, 'I can just see her in a series of her own, Jim. She'd be shown all day about her normal activities only without a stitch on. You're getting pretty hot at the thought, I can see it, Jim.'

'No, no, I'm just, you know . . . rather *hot*.'

'Mind you,' he continued, 'what you'd end up with would be a lot of photographs of the Lady drinking glasses of wine.'

'If the cards drew the interest of the coppers,' I said, 'and they've been all over this house, how come you've still *got* all the cards?'

'I haven't nearly as many as I once had,' said Vaughan. 'They've had some of the best ones off me, and I generally keep the few I do have in a little hidey hole outside this house.'

'Where's that then?' I asked, taking a pull on my beer.

'Just now, Jim,' he said, 'it's the left luggage office at Scarborough station.'

I finished my beer, and put the bottle on the mantel-shelf.

'I'm off to get my boots cleaned,' I said, 'if the lad's still about.'

'You back at work tomorrow, then?' asked Vaughan.

'If they've fettled the engine,' I said, opening the door, 'then yes. But I've got a feeling I'll be stuck here another night.'

No railway man was ever required to wait two nights for an engine. It made no kind of operating sense, but I had decided that I was on the track of something. Besides, Vaughan showed no sign of thinking anything amiss. I turned in the doorway, and took a last look at the room.

This was the real meaning of the term 'bachelor's lodgings'. The phrase was meant to mean something different but this was it in practice.

'We'll talk about a business connection tomorrow, shall we?' said Vaughan, and I nodded in a vague sort of way.

'You look about ready to move out of here,' I said.

'I've always got an eye out. After all that's gone on here I'm a bit sick, but then everyone's under the gun because of this bloody never-ending investigation.'

'Even Fielding?' I said.

'Him most of all,' said Vaughan.

'How come?'

'I shan't say, Jim. I'm sworn to silence.'

But I didn't doubt that he'd let on eventually, and here was another reason for staying on at Paradise.

''Night then,' I said.

On quitting Vaughan's room I needed a piss, and so stepped into the bathroom he'd earlier come out of.

The cabinet by the side of the toilet stood open. Inside was a mass of razor blades in paper wrappings, a length of elasticated bandage, a big bottle of Batty's Stomach Pills, something called Clarke's Blood Mixture, Owbridge's Lung Tonic, some ointment for puffed-up feet, Eczema Balm ('the worst complaint will disappear before our wonderful skin cure'), and a red paste-board packet with a picture of a dead rat on it. Rat poison in the bathroom cabinet: 'Fletcher's Quick-Acting Rat Poison', to be exact. The ingredients were printed on the back: 'Lampblack, Wheat Flour, Suet, Oil of Aniseed, Arsenious Acid'. This last came from arsenic, and it struck me that there was a whole murder kit in this cabinet. But the investigating officers had obviously not thought so – otherwise they'd have taken the stuff away. I wondered whether it was Vaughan's stuff, or whether it belonged to the household in general. I unbuttoned my fly, and I was just slacking off, playing the yellow jet spiral-wise in the toilet bowl and thinking on when the door opened behind me. It was Vaughan again. It was less than a minute since I'd seen him last.

'I know you won't mind me interrupting, Jim,' he said.

'It could have been worse,' I said, craning about.

'Old Fielding,' he said, as I left off pissing and pulled the chain. '. . . Guess where he was in the three months before he came here?'

The flushing of the toilet was so loud (it was as if the thing was throwing down half the German Sea) that I couldn't hear what came next, and had to ask Vaughan to speak up.

'York gaol!' he repeated, over the dinning of the waters.

Chapter Twenty-Five

With gun in hand, I began to turn about, but stopped to watch the kid. He had backed away from me, and his right hand rested on the gunwale. Behind him, on the other ship, the man who had raised his arm had lowered it, and he had turned a different way, looking for another bit of good to do; his vessel was also bouncing and swinging away from us, taking him on to the next business.

The kid, leaning against the gunwale, turned from me to the departing ship. But I ought not to be bothering about him. I had a decision to make. I could go for'ard with the gun or I could go aft. At present, I was looking aft. I could see clear past the bridge house to the wake our ship was making. I ought first to make for the engine room, stop the blokes who were creating that wake. They were party to a crime as long as they continued their work. I pictured them as small, half deafened and blinded, blackened blokes who never questioned the ringing bells that brought their commands. I would go to the bridge, and work the lever that told them to change direction. Suddenly a great wind came, and the fore-deck behind me went low and the bridge house tilted towards me, as though its illuminated windows were eyes, inspecting me. The ship righted itself, and there came the sound of hammering – a hammering on iron. I turned fully about, facing away from the kid, and I was instantly felled by a giant, flying sailor.

The gun flew from my hand as I collapsed to the deck. The ship made another slow rise as our struggle began. There were not at first any blows; at least, I did not think so at the time. It was more like a kind of wrestling, in which I was ever closer smothered by the sailor's great weight and his wide oilskin. I was under him, and his stinking breath, and then for an instant I was up, seeing the sea from the wrong angle as the ship pitched again – and catching a glimpse of the gunwale, where the kid had been standing, and was no longer. In that moment of distraction, the sailor had caught hold of my ears, one in each hand. They made convenient handles for him as he contemplated me. His great face was in two halves: black beard and the rest – and the rest was mainly nose. *You are ugly*, I thought, and perhaps he meant to say the same to me. He got as far as 'You' before rage over-took his speech, and he dashed my head down onto the iron deck.

The next time I lifted my head, I lay in the iron parlour again, my only companion the mighty slumbering anchor chain. The ship rose and fell, and I slipped in and out of dim dreams. Presently I looked down at my right hand, which lay like a thing defeated. No gun there.

I had been on the deck, and removed in one dark instant from it. The same had happened to the kid, only I was sure he'd gone overboard in hopes of reaching the second ship. Why had he given over the gun? Because he knew he was in queer, and didn't want any part of what was going on or was *about* to go on.

I fancied, over the next long while, that I occasionally heard the ringing of a bell but it was nothing more than a faint tinkling through the iron walls, and I could not keep count of the strokes. My pillow was a link of the anchor chain, and it served as well as goose feathers. My trouble was the cold, and I would ward it off by ordering myself to sleep which I seemed able to do at will. They hadn't drugged my coffee on my first trip to the chart room, I had decided. Instead, I had picked up a sleeping sickness as a result of whatever had happened at Paradise.

The house came and went in my dreams along with all the old familiars: the red-shaded oil lamp, the over-heated blue room, the roaring white gas, the magician with his kettle, the long needle. In addition, a man with puffed-up feet scrambled about on the bathroom floor for blood tonic, and the poor fellow was cutting himself to ribbons in the process, being quite desperate. A voice spoke in my head, a smooth character sent to explain my own thoughts to me said, 'You see, Jim, he was the last man left in Scarborough.'

Nobody walked the Prom; the lighthouse was dark; the two carriages of the funicular railway stood dangling out of reach, neither up nor down; each of the three hundred and sixty-five rooms of the Grand Hotel – one for every day of the year – stood empty, and drifting black smoke had possession of the town. The sea had come all the way up to the railway station. It was exploring the excursion platforms and the engine shed beyond. I saw the wax doll in the lavender room, the blue flame of the paraffin heater, and a paper fan that, when folded out, revealed a painting of a sea-side town that was not Scarborough but showed Scarborough *up*, put it to shame, this one being sunlit, with handsome people walking along a pretty promenade, and a light blue sea beyond.

All at once I was there, with my own wife and my new wife, who chatted away merrily, which I knew to be wrong, and which did cause me anxiety, but I put it from my mind for I was away from Scarborough in an altogether better sea-side

Chapter Twenty-Six

Walking down the stairs towards the comfortable landing with my boots in my hand, I revolved the words of Theo Vaughan. Were they true? He must know that I could hardly check by asking Fielding himself.

He had, according to Vaughan, been lagged for raising funds for a publishing company that didn't exist. It went down as fraud. It hadn't been such a great amount of money, and it had all been repaid so he'd only got three months. Vaughan had once had the newspaper clipping that told the whole tale, but he'd lost it (which went a little way to his credit, I thought, since it seemed to mean he didn't have a plan to use the information, but would just blurt it out as the fancy took him).

The prison sentence explained Fielding's presence in Paradise, according to Vaughan. He'd always been keen on the sea, and had come to Scarborough to catch his breath after the shock. He found the house to his liking, if a little low class, and had taken it in hand; set himself to raising the tone with fancy recipes, a few sea paintings here and there, cigars in the ship room, sherry in the evenings. He'd put some money into the house too, and was largely paying the cost of the redecoration of the second floor, for the prosecution had not finished him financially speaking.

I approached the kitchen, and the door was on the jar, letting me see the long table. All the items upon it were a bit better ordered now, and stood in a row: knife polisher, big tea pot, vegetable boiler, corkscrew, toast rack, two dish covers. The kitchen had been cleaned, and the supper things put away. Adam Rickerby had done it, I knew. He liked things orderly. That youth now sat at one end of the table, applying Melton's Cream to a pair of women's boots – his sister's evidently – and she was reading to him from a newspaper with a glass of red wine at her elbow. She was certainly a little gone with drink, but she spoke very properly.

'Interview with foreign secretary,' she read, and took a sip of the wine. 'Sir Edward Grey had an interview with Mr Asquith at 10 Downing Street this morning . . .'

'*Where?*' her brother asked, quite sharply, as though the matter was of particular importance to him.

'10 Downing Street,' his sister repeated, before carrying on reading. 'The interview was unusually prolonged. Sir Edward Grey remained at 10 Downing Street for just over an hour and a half.'

She turned the page of the paper, and Adam Rickerby sat back and thought about what he'd heard for a moment. He then took up a brush, and began polishing the boot, saying, 'Any railway smashes?'

'*No,*' his sister replied very firmly.

'Runaway trams?' he enquired, with spittle flying.

'Nothing of that kind,' said Amanda Rickerby. 'How lovely to see our Mr Stringer,' she ran on, looking up at me. But as I walked over to her brother and handed him my boots, she turned two pages of the paper in silence.

I heard soft footsteps behind me. They belonged to Fielding, who was approaching in dressing gown and slippers with his own boots in his hand.

'Have you been to Eastbourne, Mr Stringer?' Miss Rickerby asked, looking up from her paper as I gave my boots to the boy.

'Eastbourne in Sussex?' I enquired.

'Well, I don't think there's another.'

'Is there something about it in the paper?'

'Are you avoiding my question?' she asked. She smiled, but looked tired.

'I've never been there,' I said. 'I just wondered why you mentioned it.'

Fielding, having given his boots to the boy, was lifting the kettle that sat on the range, pouring boiling water into a cup and stirring.

'Ovaltine,' he said, seeing me looking on. 'Would you care for a cup, Mr Stringer?'

'Oh, no thanks.'

The stuff was meant to bring on sleep, and Fielding must have made it every night, for Miss Rickerby paid him no mind as he went about it. She said, 'Eastbourne is the one place I prefer to Scarborough, Mr Stringer.'

'Well, I wouldn't know,' I said, and then I thought of something clever to add: 'But this is Paradise. How can there be any advance on that?'

'Oh, I should think there could be,' she said. 'Probably quite easily.'

Adam Rickerby was polishing Fielding's boots, going at them like billy-o.

'Don't denigrate the house, Miss R,' said Fielding, with the cup in his hand. 'Eastbourne *is* fine though.'

'Told you,' Amanda Rickerby said, addressing me.

'Debussy wrote *La Mer* at the Grand Hotel there,' said Fielding, and since he was addressing me particularly I nodded back, in a vague sort of way. 'Then again it's a shingle beach and you can't sit on it . . . Good night all, and batten down the hatches. We're in for a storm, I believe. You should take a look at the size of the waves getting up just now, Mr Stringer.'

He quit the room, and I too made towards the door when Amanda Rickerby spoke.

'It's late, Mr Stringer,' she said, looking sadly down at her wine glass. 'I believe that Sunday has already gone.' And then, in a glorious moment, she raised her eyes to mine: 'Have you had your treat yet?'

'I had a bottle of beer in Mr Vaughan's room. Does that count?'

'I'm not at all sure that it does.'

'Have you had yours?'

'No.'

'Well then,' I said, 'that makes two of us.'

I glanced over at Adam Rickerby, who'd finished my first boot. What he made of this exchange between a near-stranger and his sister I could hardly imagine. He was polishing hard.

'I'm obliged to you for doing that,' I called across to him.

'I'll bring 'em up in t'morning,' he said, not looking up.

I walked through the doorway, and Amanda Rickerby rose from her seat and followed. She wasn't done with me yet, and I knew I was red in the face.

'When you go to bed, Mr Stringer . . .'

'Yes?' I said.

'Oh . . . nothing.'

She wore an expression that I could not understand.

'Why does your brother want to know about railway smash-es?' I whispered, after a space.

'Oh just . . . morbid interest.'

'I could tell him a few tales,' I said.

'You've caused a few smashes yourself, I dare say,' she said, looking up at me and shaking her hair out of her eyes.

'In a roundabout way,' I said.

'You hardly know whether to claim credit for them or not.'

I was for some reason lifting my hand, which might have gone anywhere and done anything at that moment; might have stroked her amazing hair or pressed down on her bosom. But in the end it landed on my collar, and gave a tug for no good reason apart from the fact that the whole house was over-heated.

'Any road . . .' I began, and I heard the wife's voice, saying, 'Don't say that, Jim, it doesn't mean anything.'

'Will you be staying with us tomorrow night?' asked Amanda Rickerby.

'Depends on the engine,' I said. 'But it might come to that.'

'Good,' she said. 'Good *night*, I mean,' she added, with a very fetching smile, and I felt both an excitement and a kind of relief that anything that was going to happen between us had been put forward to another day. When I walked into the hall-way, I saw Fielding, lingering there apparently adjusting the coats on the stand, and I was glad I'd kept my pocket book and warrant card in my suit pocket. He left off as I approached, and climbed the stairs at a lick.

I dawdled up, thinking of the wife and Amanda Rickerby, weighing the two in the balance. Neither was very big on housework but in the wife's case that was because she was too busy doing other things. I couldn't imagine Amanda Rickerby in the suffragettes, as the wife was. She couldn't be bothered. Was she on the marry? She certainly acted like it, and I felt guilty for not letting on that I already had a wife.

Had she been the same with Blackburn? He'd evidently been a good-looking chap . . . But surely a woman who owned a house as big as Paradise would want more than a railway fireman.

. . . And what had she meant to say to me about going to bed?

Had she proposed joining me?

As I came up to the undecorated landing, I thought with anxiety of the wife, calling to mind the Thorpe-on-Ouse fair of the previous summer. It had been held on Henderson's meadow by the river. Robert Henderson and Lydia had coincided more than once there, and he'd as good as forced Jack Silvester, who kept the village grocery, and was a tenant of the Henderson family, to give her a prize at hoop-la even though her hoop had not gone over the wooden base on which the prize – a jar of bath crystals – had stood. Silvester had called out, 'Oh, bad luck!' and then immediately met the hard eye of Henderson. The wife was always going on about the condescension of men to women, and here was a very good example of it, as I had later told her. The crystals were not rightfully hers; she ought not to have taken them. Instead, she would soak for what seemed like hours before the parlour fire in the perfumed baths the crystals made. Lily of the Valley – that was the scent, supposedly. The stopper had come wrapped about with ribbon, and the wife had carefully replaced that ribbon after every use of the crystals.

She'd told me that she couldn't believe she'd gone all these years with un-scented baths, so perhaps it was the crystals themselves and not a matter of who had been responsible for her getting them. Her plan was to get on, and I believed on balance that she was determined to pull me up with her, and not run off with Henderson. She surely wouldn't have made such a great effort into making a trainee lawyer of me if she meant to clear off.

I always knew what the wife wanted, and sometimes our marriage came down to nothing *but* the question of what she wanted. But what did Amanda Rickerby want? On all available evidence, me in her bed or her in mine, but I could hardly believe that was right. Her approaches were too direct. Women went round the houses when they wanted to fuck someone.

Chapter Twenty-Seven

I lay on my own narrow bed at the top of the house. I'd kept the window open, and the scene beyond was now illuminated by the flashing of the lighthouse, which seemed to light up the whole empty horizon for hundreds of miles, the light then dying away raggedly like a guttering candle. With each successive flash, the sea seemed to boil more violently.

The fire – lit, as I supposed, by Adam Rickerby – burned two feet away from my bed and it made the room too hot like the rest of the house. I turned on my side and watched the line of white light under the closed door – for the gas in the little hallway still burned – and I thought of Fielding. Well, it stood to *reason* that he was an ex-convict. An apparent gent living permanently in a Scarborough boarding house would have to be in queer somehow even if he wasn't broke, and he certainly didn't seem to be that. He was one of those free-floating businessmen who lived by a series of schemes, and that sort often did pretty well even though the schemes never came to anything.

I ran through some motives for murder – with which the house was fairly bursting. Adam Rickerby was generally nuts, and would defend the house at all costs. Fielding's post card company had been given the chuck by the North Eastern Railway, and he was a man with a past. Had Blackburn known him in Leeds, and been threatening to talk out of turn about him? Fielding wouldn't want the Recorded Music Circle to know he was a convicted fraudster – that'd put a crimp into his social life, all right.

Vaughan was a dirty dog in all respects, and was either honest and open with it, or a splitter who had something to hide. He paid lip service to the idea that Blackburn had made away with himself. But he also seemed to keep trying to drop Fielding in it, and he'd begun pointing the finger at Adam Rickerby into the bargain. The business of the signalling out to sea: why would Rickerby do that? His chief concern as far as I could see was sticking to the bloody meal times. Was Vaughan really trying to put the knock on Adam Rickerby? But he'd as good as put himself on the spot at the same time. By letting on that he'd shown the special range of cards to Blackburn, he was admitting to acting in a way that a sober-sided man like that could easily take against.

Amanda Rickerby? She was mysterious all-round, and she too might well have something to keep from the world at large. She drank, for starters; she was anti-religious where Blackburn had been a bible thumper, and she was funny about the rent. She was, or had been, short of money. She was up to something, anyhow.

I rolled over to the other side and looked at the fire, noticing that it was starting to smoke a little. I climbed out of bed, picked up the water jug that stood by the wash stand, and dashed a pint or so onto the red coals. The sound was tremendous. How a fire protested when you did that! I was replacing the water jug when my toe scraped against something in the floorboards. Looking down, I could make nothing out, so I edged along by the bed until I came to the table where the oil lamp and matches sat. I lit the lamp, carried it back over, and set it down. A short length of lead tube – about a quarter inch worth – stuck up. It was the top of one of the two gas pipes that rose up beyond the lamps in the room of Theo Vaughan: the stub that had remained after the gas pipe (and gas *light*) in my own room had been removed. Gas would naturally rise to the top of any vertical pipe, but this stub had been nipped tightly shut with a pair of pliers to stop any escape and, leaning closer, I could detect no gas smell from it. Lead, being soft, is easy to nip in that way and I was satisfied that a perfect seal had been made.

I lifted the lamp to the other side of the hearth, and there was the second outcropping of pipe. It too was tightly sealed and gave off no smell. I returned the lamp to the table, blew it out, lay back in my bed, and listened for footsteps on the stairs. I heard the chimney flute note at one o'clock by my watch, and again at four, and I don't believe I slept in all that time but just revolved endlessly the mysteries of Paradise while trying to anticipate the surges of the sea wind against the window. As I lay on the bed I had mostly faced the door but, on hearing the chimes of five rise up from the Old Town, I decided the worst of the night was finished, turned over to face the wall rather than the door, and fell asleep amid the dawn cries of seagulls.

Chapter Twenty-Eight

I awoke and lifted my hand to the back of my head. A delicate sea shell, a fine crab shell perhaps, seemed to hang in my hair. I could not quite trust my hand, for it was made nerveless by cold, but the thing seemed to be at the same time part of me, and not part of me. I tried to tug at the thing, and it both cracked and melted. I brought my hand down, and there was a sticky dampness to it. I could not make out its colour but I knew it to be blood; when dampness comes out of nowhere it is generally safe to assume the worst – to assume that it is blood.

My headache was no worse, anyhow. If anything, I fancied that it was easing, and it had been a while since I'd had one of the electrical flashes. But I wanted badly to get warm. I sat up and put the oilskin more tightly around me. The rise and fall of the ship had become a gentle rocking, a soft swinging, nursery-like. I thought of the wife. Was it true, as I suspected, that she would no longer carry her basket down the main street of Thorpe-on-Ouse in case Robert Henderson should see her about her marketing, and think her low class for not having a servant to do it for her? I could picture Lydia very clearly both with and without basket in the middle of Thorpe, which was proof that my memory was returning. It also seemed to me that there was nothing to choose between the two mental pictures. I had been a fool to fret about Henderson – my anxiety had come from having no graver matter to worry about. I would go back to Thorpe and I would have it all out with Lydia, and if it came to it I would go up to his big house with the stone owl sitting over the door, and I would clout Henderson. Furthermore, I would not be a solicitor, because I did not want to *be* a solicitor. Even at thirty I was too old and the change of life was too great, and the lawyers were at the shameful end of railway work. It seemed to me, as I sat in that rolling black iron prison, that I had gone to Paradise looking for trouble and hardly wanting to come back because my future, although apparently promising, had been taken out of my own hands. But I *would* return to York and I *would* reclaim my future, and if I didn't then I would take a bullet, and there would be nothing between these two outcomes of my present fix.

. . . Yet while the image of Lydia in Thorpe was clear in my mind, I could still not recall the end of my time in Paradise; and how could my future be contemplated until I had done that? My memory of the final events was lost in a jumble of over-heated rooms propped high above a black sea – a sea that was never still, but that came on in a way somehow un-natural, like a crawling black field.

I lay still; began once more to shiver. I might have slept again in spite of the shivering, and presently, there came a disturbance in the iron room. I could not say what had caused it, but something had changed. All was still again, and I kicked out at the nearest chain link, and it was as though the thing had nerves and had taken umbrage at this, for the part that ran up through the hole shivered for a second, and then the great snake began racing upwards through that hole, making a breakaway with a tremendous, deafening roar that forced me to clap my hands to my ears and move to the furthest corner of my cell.

Chapter Twenty-Nine

When I awoke the lighthouse beam was off, and all was grey along the front. Throwing the bed clothes aside and moving rapidly towards the window I thought some calamity had occurred, but it was just an early winter's morning in Scarborough. There came a knock at the door.

'Yes,' I said.

'Yer tea,' said Adam Rickerby.

'Morning,' I said, opening the door – and he passed me an enamel tray with tea things set out on it. My boots, highly polished, were strung by the laces about his neck. These he set down just inside the door, together with a big jug of hot water for shaving. He'd carried the tray in one hand, and the jug in the other. He was dressed as before, in the long apron, but his hair had grown a little wilder in the night.

'Do you know what time it is?' I enquired.

'I bring t'tea at seven o'clock.'

I had forgotten our arrangement.

'You bring the tea at seven, therefore it *is* seven o'clock,' I said, putting the tray down on the bed.

'Put it on t'table,' he said, and just for a quiet life I did so.

'Did *you* sleep well?' I enquired, because I was determined to discover more about this queer bloke.

'I've ter be off down now,' he said. 'I've t'breakfasts to do.'

'*I* had a topping sleep,' I said, '. . . only the fire smoked a little.'

'I'll tek a broom 'andle ter t'chimney,' he said.

'Do you know why it smoked?'

'Gulls,' he said. 'They nest in chimneys.'

'But it's only March,' I said.

' . . . Don't follow yer,' he said.

'Gulls don't nest until April or so. I was born in a sea-side town so I know.'

He eyed me for a while.

'Could be last year's,' he said, very rapidly.

'But has no-one else complained of a smoking chimney in this room? Did the fellow Blackburn not complain?'

'Who?'

'Blackburn. You might remember him. He was the one that vanished into thin air while staying here.'

''E did not.'

'Didn't vanish?'

Adam Rickerby took a deep sigh, for all the world as though I was the simpleton and not him.

''E med no *complaint*.'

I took a sip of the tea. It was perfectly good.

'I'm obliged to you,' I said.

'Are yer after a reduction in t'rent?' he enquired anxiously. '. . . Want yer money back, like?'

'No, why ever do you ask that?'

'I asked yer,' he said, more slowly, and once again giving that flash of unexpected intelligence, 'because I wanted ter *know*.'

So saying he turned about and marched back down to the kitchen. I then moved the jug over to the wash stand, and I had all on to lift it with two hands let alone one. After a shave and sluice-down, I went down to breakfast, which was taken at the kitchen table – apparently this was how it was done in winter.

Amanda Rickerby was there, which surprised me at that early hour. Then again she was reading a novel and sipping tea rather than doing any of the breakfast chores. These had evidently all been left to Adam Rickerby, who was moving plenty of pots and pans about at the range. The landlady glanced up and gave a sly smile by way of saying good morning. She was more beautiful than was needful at breakfast. Over-opposite her – and with his back to me – was Fielding, wearing a fairly smart black suit and very carefully finishing a kipper.

'Morning!' he said, taking a bit of bread to the few remaining specks. 'Sleep well, Mr Stringer?'

'Yes thanks,' I said. 'You?'

'Very well indeed.'

'I didn't notice the storm, if there was one.'

'Hardly anyone's out from the harbour,' he said, dabbing his mouth with a napkin, 'so I think it's still in prospect.'

'Where's Mr Vaughan?' I asked, and the answer came from Adam Rickerby, who was eyeing me steadily from the range.

''E gets up late,' he said.

'His money came this morning,' Amanda Rickerby put in, 'so I don't think we'll be seeing much of him today.'

She indicated a letter propped up against the knife sharpener. It was addressed to Theodore Vaughan.

'You'll be for the Scarborough engine shed then,' Fielding said, 'and the run back to York.'

'Dare say. If the loco's fixed we'll run it back light engine. That means . . .'

'I know,' Fielding put in. 'Without carriages.'

I didn't like it that he knew.

'If I know those gentry, they won't want to keep an engine idle for more than a day,' he said.

205

'Those gentry?'

'The engineers of the North Eastern Railway.'

'No,' I said, 'but there was only one fitter at the shed and . . . Well, if it comes to it, I might have to stop here another night.'

'Why not?' he said. 'Make a holiday of it!'

Amanda Rickerby read on, but then none of this was news to her.

'If you do come back, you'll have the infinite pleasure of meeting Mrs Dawson,' said Fielding, passing his plate to Adam Rickerby.

I remembered about the daily woman.

'She's due at ten,' said Amanda Rickerby, still with her eyes on her book, 'thank God.'

I thought again of the wife who, being the religious sort of suffragette, never said 'thank God', and who only read books in bed, being always on the go when she was *not* in bed.

'Porridge,' said Adam Rickerby, and it was by way of being a statement of fact.

As I stared at the porridge that had been put before me, Fielding gave a general 'Morning!' and quit the room.

I began to eat; Amanda Rickerby read, and sipped her tea.

I'd almost finished my porridge when she looked up, and said, 'I hear you've been asking about Mr Blackburn.'

Silence for a space. I watched her brother at the range. Who'd told her of my questions? She was not smiling.

'We believe it was a case of suicide,' she said.

'Yes,' I said.

'Some event seemed to have thrown a great strain on him.'

'Kipper,' said Adam Rickerby, putting it next to my porridge. He retreated to the range, from where he enquired: 'Kipper all right?'

'I haven't started it yet,' I said.

'What a time that was,' said Amanda Rickerby. 'The police all over the house – it does nothing for business, you know.'

There was a hardness in her eyes for the first time, and I thought: This is what you'd see perhaps quite often if you were married to her. She was still beautiful, but in spite of rather than because of her eyes.

'I thought it would be a miracle if we ever got another railway man in,' she said.

'Yes,' I said, contemplating the kipper, 'I can quite see that.'

And when I looked up she was smiling and her eyes were shining again: 'You are that miracle, Mr Stringer.'

PART FOUR

Chapter Thirty

On the lower level of the Promenade, a man at a road works was making hot gas, seemingly for his own amusement. No-one was about. The beach was like black glass. I could make out a couple of dog walkers on the sand, a few hundred yards in the direction of the Spa. They minded the sleeting rain; the dogs didn't. It was nine-thirty, and I had half an hour to kill before I met Tommy Nugent at the station. Facing the sea on the lower Prom was the iron gate leading into the Underground Palace and Aquarium. It was padlocked, and there was a poster half slumped in a frame alongside it. 'Great Attractions of the Season', I could just make out: 'Voorzanger's Cosmopolitan Ladies & Gentlemen's Orchestra, 21 in number including Eminent Soloists, will give a Grand Concert Every Sunday at 8'.

But not in winter, they wouldn't.

'Swimming Exhibitions', I read lower down: 'In Large Swimming Bath by Miss Ada Webb and Troupe of Lady Swimmers, and High Divers at Intervals'.

I walked on towards the harbour: the sea water baths were closed, and never likely to re-open by the looks of it. I climbed the wet stone steps to the higher Prom. The ships in the harbour were huddled tight at all angles. A fishing boat approached, bucking about like mad, and I was surprised the blokes walking the harbour walls weren't looking on anxiously. But I soon saw the value of those walls, for the boat steadied the instant it came between them.

I wound my way up towards the shopping streets. The Scarborough citizens had the sea, the cliffs, the great sky and the Castle to themselves, but all was black. I saw a broken bathing machine in a back yard. Because Scarborough was a happier place than most in summer, it was a more miserable one come winter. I walked up Newborough, heading the opposite way to most of the trams, which thundered down the road from the railway station as though they meant to hurl themselves into the sea when they reached the bottom.

According to the station clock tower it was dead on ten when I walked through the booking office and onto Platform One. The station was still guarded by the moody coal trains. It was biding its time until summer, and there was hardly a soul about. The station bookstall stood like a little paper encampment, and the magazines hanging by clothes pegs from it fluttered in the wind that blew along Platform One. Tommy Nugent was buying a paper – *The Scarborough Mercury*. He hadn't seen me yet. The two kit bags were at his feet, and he was having a laugh with the bloke who ran the stall.

'Bloody hell,' he said, when I walked up to him, 'I'm surprised to see you. I thought you'd be dead.'

'Well, you didn't seem too upset about it,' I said, as we walked away from the bookstall. 'Where did you put up?'

'Place called the Rookery or the Nookery, or something.'

'Did you have a sea view?'

'Did I fuck. Anyhow, I was hardly in the room. I came by your place twice in the night, you know. First at midnight, then at five.'

'Five o'clock? Not with the guns?'

'Of course.'

'I appreciate that, Tommy. But there was no need.'

'The house was all right then, was it?'

He seemed quite disappointed.

'It was very interesting,' I said. 'Now I'd better see if the Chief's sent the case papers.'

'I have 'em here,' said Tommy.

He'd evidently collected the envelope from the station master just before I'd arrived. It had come up in the guard's van on the first train of the day from York, and the Chief had marked it, 'For the Attention of Nugent and Stringer, York Engine Men'. It was better than seeing 'Detective Stringer' written there, but then again the Chief hadn't troubled to seal the envelope, and it turned out that it held no case report but just witness statements from the residents of Paradise. This was the Chief all over: rough and ready, not letting a fellow relax.

'I'll have a read of these later,' I said.

'Aye,' said Tommy, 'we've to collect our engine. It's all ready according to the SM.'

'It might be,' I said, 'but I'm staying on.'

'But you said the house was all right.'

'Well, it is and it isn't.'

'I'm coming back with you, then.'

'No, Tommy.'

'Why not?'

'They've no more rooms going today than they had yesterday,' I said, and he began protesting and questioning me over the sound of a train that was materialising out of the rain beyond Platform One. Behind Tommy, pasted onto the station building that housed the ladies' and gents' lavatories, was a poster showing what had been on at the Floral Hall six months before. Alongside it was a post card machine. I must've seen it dozens of times before but I'd never remarked it until now. Was it one of the ones filled by the firm of Fielding and Vaughan? The words 'Post Cards' went diagonally up the front of it; underneath was written '2d, including ℋd postage'. You put the coins in a slot and I said, 'pulled out a little drawer indicated by a picture of a pointing finger. You couldn't *select* your card but had to take pot luck. I fished in my pocket for a couple of pennies.

'You can get yourself a relief fireman and run the engine back,' I told Tommy. 'But I'm not coming.'

'*You* were meant to be a relief, if you remember, Jim,' he replied. 'They'll think I'm poisoning my bloody firemen . . . Who are you sending a post card to?'

'Nobody,' I said, dropping in the coins and telling myself that whatever was on the card would be a clue to the goings-on at Paradise. I pulled the drawer and the card showed a country station scene, hand coloured. All that was written on it was 'Complicated Shunting'. A tank engine, running bunker-first, was pulling a rake of coaches away from one side of an island platform; another two carriages waited on the other side. This activity was being watched by a schoolboy. A few feet beyond the rear end of the engine, a man who carried his hat in one hand and a bunch of bright red flowers in the other, and whose hair had been coloured a greenish shade, was crossing the line by barrow boards. Nobody looked out from the engine, so the bloke appeared to be in mortal peril.

The picture made me think of Mr Buckingham: 'While crossing the tracks at a country station, Mr Buckingham was run over by a reversing tank engine. He survived the accident, but it was necessary to amputate his legs . . .'

A flicker of an idea about the Paradise mysteries came to me but it was lost beyond recall when Tommy said, 'You're buying a card for no reason? It's turned you a bit bloody nuts, this bloody business.'

The train had come in, and stopped with the sound of a great sneeze from the engine. I looked to my right, and saw the guard stepping down. It was Les White, with his leather bag over his shoulder and his glasses in his hand. He was polishing the lenses with his handkerchief, and he looked lost without them on, but when he set them back on his nose and swivelled in our direction . . . well, it was like the beam of the bloody Scarborough lighthouse. He nodded at Tommy, who said a few words about the state of our engine. White then set off along Platform One. I was glad he hadn't been the guard who'd brought in the witness statements; glad that a fellow could only come in from York to Scarborough *once* in a morning. As I watched him go through the ticket gate, another idea about the case broke in on me, and it made me very keen to get to the engine shed.

'Come on, Tommy,' I said, and a couple of passengers who'd stepped down from the York train looked on amazed as we went beyond the end of the guard's van, and jumped onto the tracks. You could do that if you were a Company man and to ordinary folk watching, it was as though you'd stepped off a harbour wall into the sea.

Chapter Thirty-One

The engine simmered outside the Scarborough shed like a prize exhibit, freshly cleaned and with not a whiff of steam coming from the injector overflow. The tall fitter, who stood by it with the Shed Super alongside *him*, explained that he'd left the steam pressure from yesterday's run to decline overnight and then, first thing in the morning, he'd replaced the valve, having by a miracle had exactly the right part lying about in the shed. Steam had then been raised again; the Super had telephoned through to Control, who'd told the signalmen along the line to expect to see the engine running back light to York very shortly, and meanwhile some lad had gone at the engine with rape oil so that the boiler fairly gleamed.

'But we can't take it back today,' I said.

The Super had a white flower in his top pocket; the fitter had a mucky rag in his. The fitter was twice the size of the Shed Super and half the thickness, but they both now folded their arms and looked knives at me. Tommy was up on the footplate. On the way over to the engine shed, I'd told him all about the goings-on at Paradise and he'd accepted that he couldn't come into the house himself but he still held out against finding a relief fireman and running back to York on the J Class. He wanted to stay in Scarborough for as long as I did.

Suddenly, I'd had enough of the pantomime; I decided to

get down to cases with the two blokes.

'Look here,' I said, 'the fact is, I'm a copper.'

'You *sure*?' asked the Super, and I produced my warrant card from my suit-coat pocket.

He inspected it closely, and the fitter had a good look as well.

'You're not a fireman then?' the Shed Super enquired presently.

'I'm on a bit of secret police work,' I said, returning the card to my pocket, 'or at any rate, I *was*. If you want the chapter and verse, you can telephone through to Chief Inspector Saul Weatherill at the York railway police office – and your opposite number at York North Shed's in on it as well. Best thing is if you ask them to send a new crew.'

'Here,' shouted Tommy, who'd now climbed up onto the footplate, 'you've sorted out this fire hole door!'

'Cylinder oil!' the fitter called up, then he went back to eyeing me.

'Can I have a read of your ledgers?' I asked the Shed Super.

He looked dazed as I explained: 'I want to know how many times a Leeds bloke called Ray Blackburn fired engines into Scarborough.'

'Name rings a bell,' said the Shed Super.

But it did more than that with the fitter.

'Blackburn?' he said. 'He's dead.'

'He is,' I said, 'but how do you know?'

'*Scarborough Mercury*,' he said, as we turned and entered the shed.

Scarborough being a terminus, every engine that came in had to go on the turntable before heading out, and the turntable was in the shed. The number, make and point of origin of all the engines that came through would be recorded in

217

a ledger, together with the names of the crew, and those ledgers were kept in the Super's office, which was in the back of the shed. We exchanged the falling rain for the shouts, clanging and smoke smell as we made towards those ledgers. But it turned out that the big fitter had all the vital entries in his head.

As we stood in the Super's office, supping tea from metal cups, the fitter explained that the name of any crew man who came into the shed more than half a dozen times would get about, and Blackburn had been through on just about that many occasions. He then related the fact I already knew: at the time of his last turn, Blackburn had been running Leeds–York, and had volunteered to fire his train on the extra leg to Scarborough, the York fireman booked for the job having been ill. I'd assumed this Scarborough trip to be a one-off until the sight of Les White had reminded me that very few railway men go into any station just once.

In fact, according to the fitter, Blackburn had done half a dozen Leeds–Scarborough turns before his final run. These were always on a Saturday, and they'd been Saturdays in the season when extra Scarborough trains were laid on from all the main towns of Yorkshire. The ledgers – when the Super handed them to me – confirmed the fitter's recollections, much to his own quiet satisfaction: Blackburn had fired into Scarborough on the final two Saturdays of August, and on all four in September. He hadn't worked into the town again until Sunday, 19 October, which had proved his final trip. The other coppers who'd investigated his disappearance must have known about these earlier trips, but had evidently thought them of no account. Had the Chief known of them? If so, why had he not told me? To my way of thinking, these earlier trips changed the whole picture.

In that little office, which was like something between an office and a coal bunker, the fitter and the Shed Super had gone back to eyeing me with arms folded, as if to say, 'Now what do you mean to do with this data?'

I put them off, for I didn't quite know, as I told Tommy when we came out of the shed. I would just keep it in mind when I went back to Paradise that someone in the house might have had dealings with Blackburn before he pitched up on that final Sunday.

It was raining hard now and sea, town and sky seemed in the process of merging. We came off the Scarborough railway lands by a new route that took us through a black yard full of wagon bogies and out onto a street of biggish villas, getting on for half of which were guest houses. The window sign 'Vacancies' came up over and again, and I imagined dozens of lonely landladies watching Tommy and me from behind their net curtains and hoping we'd turn in at the gate. How did they last from back-end of one year to May of the next?

There came the long scream of an engine whistle as we walked down the street, and it sounded like a cry of alarm on behalf of the whole town. I'd meant to get shot of Tommy as soon as possible and head directly back to the house, but it was still only eleven, and the sight of him limping in the rain while carrying the two kit bags made me think I ought to find a gentler way to put him off.

We came out onto a wide road that curved down towards the Prom between two great walls. It was as though the real purpose of this road was to channel tons of water into the sea. Huge, rusted iron plates were set into the bricks, and they too seemed part of a secret drainage system. We followed it down, and when we hit the Prom the wind hit *us*. The sea was black and white and crazed, with the waves all smashing into each other, and exploding against the sea wall. A tram came up, and passed by with clanging bell, and it seemed to be floating along, such was the quantity of water swirling over the lines.

There was a refuge close to hand, however, in the shape of a very pretty little ale house. The name 'Mallinson's' was written in a curve on the window, going over lace curtains that blocked out the lower part of the glass. How thick was the glass of that window? Quarter of an inch, but once Tommy and I were inside, we found that it held off the German Sea very nicely.

It was a cosy little place – dainty for a pub, with lace curtains, upholstered chairs, tables covered with white cloths, and knick-knacks on the mantel-shelves of the two fireplaces. It was the sort of sea-side place that ought not to be open in winter, and ghostly somehow as a result, but there were a fair few in. The drill was that you were served ale from jugs by good-looking serving girls who toured the room carrying trays. I bought glasses of beer for Tommy and myself, and then left him to warm himself by the fire as I stood steaming in my great-coat while reading the Paradise witness statements, stopping only to look at the water falling against the windows, which was now coming more like silent waves than rain.

On the top-most piece of paper, someone had written the word 'Blackburn' and underlined it twice. The other papers, attached by a pin, were the statements. Everyone in Paradise sounded different – higher class – in their statements. All save Fielding.

Amanda Rickerby's was first. She said: *I make it my business to see that my guests are not only well catered for in their ordinary wants, but also that they should be happy and really enjoy their time in Paradise. However, I can only go so far as regards the latter. Mr Blackburn seemed to me shy and reserved. He was perhaps rather low about something. He was what I call 'deep'.*

He had apparently knocked on the door of the house at eight o'clock, and enquired about a room, having seen the advertisement for the house at what Amanda Rickerby called 'the engine hall' at Scarborough station. Miss Rickerby herself had answered the door to him. He had by her account 'preferred' the small room at the very top of the house: *I think on account of the sea view from there, which is a particularly charming one, and you have the benefit even at night, the harbour being so prettily lit up.* He had remained in the room until Adam Rickerby had rung the hand bell for supper at 'about eight-twenty or so'.

She said that he'd sat quietly at supper, gone for a walk with 'one of our residents, Mr Vaughan – I think to a public house.' While sitting in the kitchen, she'd heard them return: *They were admitted to the house by Mr Fielding, I believe, but I only heard them coming in. I did not see them.* To the best of her knowledge, Vaughan and Fielding had then sat talking in the sitting room, and Ray Blackburn had gone up to his room at the top, which was now mine. She understood that he'd later brought his boots down to the kitchen, but she'd *left* the kitchen by then, and had gone to bed. She had not seen him again; she had nothing further to add.

Howard Fielding 'had found Mr Blackburn a very thoughtful and pleasant gentleman, but no conversationalist'. He went on: *Having lately had a business connection with the North Eastern Railway, and having some knowledge of the Company, I tried to draw him out over supper on railway topics. We touched, as I remember, on locomotive boiler capacities, the role of the fire-*

man as compared to that of the driver, and the railway speed records. But Mr Blackburn only responded to the degree compatible with ordinary politeness. After supper, at about nine-thirty, my friend and fellow resident, Mr Vaughan, then invited Mr Blackburn to take a stroll with him. I believe they walked to a public house. They returned to the boarding house perhaps forty-five minutes later – I admitted them myself – and Mr Blackburn, looking perhaps rather out-of-sorts, went directly upstairs. Mr Vaughan and I then took a nightcap in the sitting room.

I thought: That's quaint – 'nightcap'.

Fielding's statement continued: At eleven-thirty, I took my boots downstairs to the kitchen for cleaning. Adam Rickerby is generally on hand to clean boots between eleven and midnight. After giving my boots to the boy, I returned to my room, passing Mr Blackburn on the stairs. He was taking his boots down. I said, 'Good night', and he merely grunted by way of reply. I never saw Mr Blackburn again.

I turned over the leaf, and came to the words: 'Adam Rickerby, co-proprietor of Paradise Guest House, saith . . .' and saw that the lad had been magically given the powers of speech by the Leeds coppers: Mr Blackburn was at all times a quiet gentleman. I noticed he was quiet when he first came into the house, and he continued in that way. Quiet, I mean. I cooked the supper on the evening in question, as I generally do in the winter time. It was a hot supper. Mr Blackburn ate all his food. He went for a drink with Mr Vaughan. These gentlemen came back at I don't know what time. At half past eleven or so I was cleaning the boots in the kitchen, and sitting with my sister. She was reading to me from the papers. I am not educated up to reading. Mr Fielding came in, late on, with his boots. Mr Blackburn came after with his. I cleaned the boots and went to bed. I sleep on the ground

222

floor, in the room that used to be the wash room next to the scullery. I heard nothing in the night. On waking, at half past five, I did my early chores until six-thirty. No-one else was about. I then took Mr Fielding up his boots and early cup of tea. I returned to the kitchen, and collected Mr Blackburn's boots and tea. I took these up to his room with hot water. He was not there.

I turned over the page, and read, 'Theodore Vaughan, resident of Paradise Guest House, saith . . .' And there were two pages for him as against one for everyone else: *I found him a pleasant enough chap, rather thoughtful. Over supper, I formed the distinct idea that he was happy with his own company. But it is my custom of a Sunday evening to take a walk; I was putting my cape on in the hall when Mr Blackburn happened to come by. I asked whether he would like to come along with me, and he agreed. In the course of our strolling we passed the Two Mariners, a pleasant public house. I suggested that we take a glass of beer. Again, Mr Blackburn agreed. I can't recall our conversation in detail – something of Scarborough history, something of railways. We were back at the house soon after ten o'clock, less than an hour after our departure. Mr Fielding let us in, since I'd forgotten my key. Mr Blackburn then went up to his room, and I went into the sitting room, where I smoked a cigar and drank some sherry with Mr Fielding. I went up to bed not long after eleven. I believe that Mr Fielding went up later. I occupy the room directly beneath the one used by Mr Blackburn. At first I was busy about my own preparations for sleep and going between my room and the bathroom on the landing opposite, and so was not paying attention to the noises from overhead. I am led to believe that Mr Blackburn carried his boots downstairs before midnight, and there were perhaps some noises that indicated that activity, but I could not say for certain. I was very tired, and fell asleep shortly after.*

Blackburn came down with his boots . . . But what significance could that have either way?

I drank my beer and looked about the pub. The more booze that went down, the more I was looking forward to going back to Paradise and seeing Amanda Rickerby. I wanted to take her on, one way or another.

'What about those cards?' I asked Tommy after a while. 'Why do you suppose Vaughan showed them to me when he'd already got into bother for showing them to Blackburn?'

'I've an idea about that,' said Tommy.

'Same here,' I said, and as Tommy stopped one of the serving girls and bought us another couple of glasses of ale, I gave him the benefit of my idea:

'I reckon Vaughan showed me the cards for a reason, and it was nothing to do with selling them on to me and making money. He knew he was on the spot. He knew there was suspicion about what had happened as a result of him showing them to Blackburn, who was a very straight bit of goods, remember. Vaughan wanted to make out that he was free and easy with the cards; that he might show them to anyone and nothing would come of it – that it really *was* all a bit of a laugh.'

(I suddenly recalled Mr Ellis, the old boy who'd sold galoshes, and had just quit the guest house. Vaughan had perhaps held off from showing him the cards on account of his age, and the fact that he was never likely to be interested.)

Tommy Nugent was nodding his head.

'That's it,' he said. 'If the coppers came at him again, he'd be able to say, "I showed this other bloke the cards as well. Why would I do that if it had caused any trouble with the first one?"'

'Right,' I said, stepping aside to let a bloke come by. 'That's exactly . . .'

Theo Vaughan was standing immediately to my right. He had his cape over his arm, and held a glass of ale half drunk and a cigar half smoked, which meant he'd been in for a while. Cramming the witness statements into my suit-coat pocket, I turned towards him. He gave a start when he saw me, then he grinned and I thought: Either he's a bloody good actor or he's only just this minute clocked me, in which case he would not have heard what I'd said.

He said, 'How do, Jim!'

I introduced Tommy Nugent as my driver and Vaughan shook his hand warmly.

'Where've you been?' I asked him, and he looked at me as if, just for once, *I'd* been over-familiar instead of him.

'Around and about,' he said. 'Errands,' he added, swaying slightly on his boot heels. 'Meant to tell you about this place, Jim . . . Pub run entirely by women, and you don't see that often. Decent looking fillies into the bargain,' and he practically winked at us both. 'What about your engine?'

'It isn't quite right,' I said, 'so it looks like I'll be staying another night.'

'Good-o,' he said.

Tommy Nugent didn't know where to look, for of course he'd only just been reading about Vaughan and his very particular line of business. I think it was to cover up his embarrassment that he muttered something about fetching some more beers and wandered off in search of a waitress. I too was feeling rather knocked, so I said, 'I'm just off to the gents, Theo.'

But he said, 'I'll come with you, Jim.'

He set down his glass and followed me, cigar in hand, out into a white-washed back yard – where the rain flew, and the roaring sea echoed – and into a tiny gentlemen's lavatories with two stalls for pissing. Vaughan stood close enough for me to hear his breathing, which he did loudly, through both his nose and his moustache. I wondered what he'd been doing all morning. Evidently, he'd been drinking for a good part of it. Well, his money had arrived by the post from Streatham; he was in funds. As he started to piss, he had the cigar in his mouth; he then lowered the cigar and when he turned away from the stall I saw that it was extinguished. He was stowing the remnant of it in his waistcoat pocket as I asked, 'How d'you put that cigar out?'

'Private method, Jim,' he said.

'All right then,' I said. '*Why* did you put it out?'

'Can't smoke in the rain, and I'm off back to the house, Jim,' he said. 'Shall I tell them you're expected for luncheon?'

I did not answer immediately. My life, I knew, would be a good deal simpler if I did not go back, and it might be a good deal longer.

'All right,' I said. 'What time?'

'It's generally about one-ish, Jim.'

'Right you are,' I said, in as light a tone as I could. 'Yes,' I said, 'tell Miss Rickerby I'll be in for one.'

I looked at my watch: midday. I did not care for the constant march of the second hand. It wouldn't take Vaughan an hour to reach Paradise, but he went off directly, and when I regained the bar I found out from Tommy that he'd done it in double quick time as well – hadn't even finished his drink. None of this was at all like him, and his behaviour had increased my state of nerves, so that I was fairly short with Tommy as he quizzed me about Vaughan: short to the point that he gave up talking, and just fell to watching the rain and the serving girls with a hopeless sort of expression that made me feel guilty.

It was Amanda Rickerby – she brought out the worst in me. Half the reason I wanted rid of Tommy was so that I could have her glances to myself. I couldn't help thinking that I had a clear run at Paradise, what with Vaughan being such an off-putting sort of bloke, and Fielding being . . . well, was he queer? What was my intention? I did not mean to try and ride the lady exactly, but I certainly meant to do something with her: to arrest her, for instance; have it out with her about Blackburn. I would tangle with her somehow, and I wondered whether my real intention was to get revenge for the way Lydia had tried to push me about. But I knew that I ought not to think this way. If my wife pushed me about, it was because I let her.

I said to Tommy, 'When I go off, will you send a wire to my wife? You might go back to the station, or do it anywhere. The address is the post office, Thorpe-on-Ouse.'

'Saying what?' he asked, and I thought: Saying kind things in general.

'Tell her I'll see her tomorrow,' I said.

He nodded.

'I'm off, Tommy,' I said, and it was surprisingly easy to get away from him, and without even making an arrangement for the next day. Or perhaps not exactly *surprising*, I thought, as I walked along the Prom, with head down and coat collar up, trying hard to keep a straight course against the battering of the wind. After all, he'd seen that the situation at Paradise was pretty involved, and he was back there, warm and dry in the women's pub with a glass of beer in his hand and the guns at his feet should any trouble arise. But it didn't seem likely to – not where Tommy was, anyhow.

Chapter Thirty-Two

The iron wall of the chain locker cracked and the grey Mate stood in the gloom of the companionway holding the pocket revolver.

'How are you, my friend?'

'We've anchored,' I said.

'Come along with me,' he said, and he was holding the outer door open.

'What became of the kid?' I asked. 'Did he jump?'

'Nothing,' said the Mate '. . . He got wet,' he added, at length.

'*Why* did he jump?'

'Yes,' said the Mate. 'Why? I would like to know too.'

Stumbling onto the deck, I saw that our ship had arrived at its rightful home, for it was now one of hundreds or so it appeared. Under the dark blue, roaring night sky, I had the impression of ships in lines stretching fore and aft; some were on the wide channel in which we were anchored – the Thames Estuary, of course – while others appeared to have been picked up and set down amid the streets. I saw a ship that had interrupted a line of street lamps; a ship at close quarters with a church. I had the impression of many smaller vessels patrolling the lines of the big ones like prison guards, and I had the idea that this was also a city of one-armed men, a city of cranes that were all lit by small white lights like Christmas trees. Most were still but every so often one would stir, as though it wanted to confer with its neighbour, or couldn't stand the *sight* of its neighbour, and so must turn aside. The fore-deck of our collier seemed to command the whole of the great docks but I knew I saw only a fraction of the mass; that Beckton stood only on the fringes of the London docks proper and that I had imagined beyond the limits of my vision.

'Where's the gas works?' I asked the Mate, who was eyeing me with his chin sunk into the up-turned collar of his brass-buttoned coat. He shifted his grey-bearded chin so that it came clear of the collar, and indicated an expanse that shone moon-like a little way for'ard on our starboard side – it was perhaps a quarter of a mile off. I saw a jetty crowded with cranes, and two colliers docked there. All was silent and still on the jetties, but you could see the way things would go on come first light. High-level railway lines ran back from the jetties and these penetrated the factory buildings set down amid the great fields of pale blue dust; the lines smashed through the front walls, came out through the backs and ran on to the next, like lions jumping through hoops in the circus, only these were not factories but retort houses, where the coal was taken to be burnt and the gas made. The York gas works, at Layerthorpe, ran to one retort house but here were dozens, all tied together by the railway lines and set in the wide expanse together with their companions the gas holders, which were perfectly round, like great iron pies.

'Have we made the turnaround?' I asked the Mate, and he didn't answer but indicated with the revolver that we were to walk along to the bridge house once more. As we made our way, there came one repeated clanging noise, echoing through the night, the beating heart of the London docks, as I imagined.

Once again, there was nobody about on the fore-deck, and I saw nobody but the Mate prior to being sat down before the Captain in the chart room. The chart lay on the table as before, the oil lamp and the coffee pot on top of the chart. I doubted that the Captain had given it as much as a single glance on our way from the north. He and the Mate evidently navigated by second nature or force of habit. Running the ship was something they did casually, while attending to other business.

The Mate gave the revolver to the Captain. Behind the Captain's chair, the door leading to the bridge was closed and there was no man out there. For the first time since waking, I noticed the silence of the ship.

The Captain sat with arms folded, and his eyes never left me. I would have said he was a handsome man, although he looked a little like a marionette. There was something neat, cat-like about him.

'Coffee?' he said, and he leant forward and poured me a cup.

'Do you want some carbolic?'

He knew his man had crowned me. I shook my head.

'Food?'

'Later,' I said, and the Captain flashed a look at the Mate that I didn't much care for.

'Do you want to go to the heads?' enquired the Captain.

'Come again?' I said.

'For a piss,' the Mate put in, '. . . or the other.'

He wouldn't say the word. They were quite gentlemanly, this pair, after their own fashion. I thought about the Captain's question: going by the state of my trousers I must have pissed myself at some earlier stage in the proceedings, but I was not going to boast about the fact if the stink coming off me hadn't made it evident. As for the other business – that had all somehow gone by the board. I shook my head.

'Then carry on with your story,' said the Captain.

'I'll start it if you tell me what happened to the kid.'

No answer.

'I reckon he was scared half to death,' I ran on. '. . . Now have we unloaded the coal? No, don't reckon so, because we're still sitting low in the water, and the ship'd be even filthier if we had done. When's the turnaround?'

'For you,' said the Captain, 'it could be quicker than you think.'

We eyed each other for a good while.

'Well,' I said, '. . . where was I?'

'Paradise guest house,' said the Captain.

'I know, but where had I got up to?'

It was the Mate who answered.

'Your engine was all fixed, but you did not take it home with you.'

He made me sound like a schoolboy with a broken toy. Still, it was no fault of his own that he was bloody foreign.

'You should have taken it, you know,' said the Captain, suddenly leaning forwards over his sea chart. 'You *should* have done it.'

Chapter Thirty-Three

Adam Rickerby let me into Paradise without a word. It was midday. I could hear laughter from the kitchen, but made directly for my own room at the top of the house. Climbing the stairs, I realised that Rickerby was following me, and when we came to the floor being decorated I turned and said, 'I'm staying another night.'

'I know,' he said, in his blank-faced way.

I turned and climbed the final staircase, and he climbed it two steps behind. On the attic landing, I turned again and he suddenly seemed enormous, the roof being lower there. I asked his habitual question back at him:

'Can I help you?'

'Aye,' he said, and he was lighting the gas on the little landing.

When the jet was roaring, he turned and held out his hand, saying, 'Two shilling.'

'Don't worry,' I said, 'I'm not going to make off.'

'Who said you were?'

Again, the flash of intelligence.

I paid the money over, and once again he dropped it in his apron pocket. I took my great-coat off, walked into the little room, and put it on the bed. Rickerby looked on from the doorway.

'You've ter put that in t'closet,' he said.

I turned and eyed him. I was minded to tell him to clear off.

'*Why?*' I said.

'It's damp.'

'What of it?'

'Wants airing . . . You might take a chill.'

'That's my look-out, isn't it? Why are you so interested in trains, Adam?'

'Why are *you*?' he said, and he stepped into the room. He was bigger than he ought to've been. Something had gone wrong in the making of him. He took another step towards me. I said, 'Go steady now,' but he still came on, and I damn near told him I was a copper, and that he'd better quit the room. But he went right by me, picked up my coat and put it into the closet, threatening to have the whole thing over and setting all the hangers jangling.

'Why do you like train *smashes*, Adam?' I called after him, as he left the room.

'Because I don't care for *trains*,' he replied, and I'd broken through at last . . .

'How do you mean, you'd broken through?' enquired the Captain, as the rattling of the swinging coat hangers was replaced by the sound of the Mate running his hand over his grey beard, the coldness of the chart room, and the gas smell put out day and night by the Gas, Light and Coke Company.

The Captain had brought me up short. I'd barely started again with my recollections. I'd been pleased to have them returning so clear and complete, and I was forgetting that I might have to answer for them; forgetting about the gun that lay on the table, which was not two feet away from me, but it was only six *inches* from the Captain's right hand. It was a tiny piece, but it would do the job. What was it that Tommy Nugent had said? 'How big a hole do you want to make in their heads, Jim?'

'I don't know,' I said to the Captain.

The Mate smoked a cigar from the tin with the picture of the church on it. He also had before him a plain glass bottle containing a brown spirit of some sort – whisky or rum, not Spanish sherry – and a small glass, which he filled from the bottle pretty regularly. It seemed to be his reward for the ship having reached its destination. But the Captain did not take a drink.

'It was the first obvious connection,' I said. 'The two follow on, do you not see? *Why* and then *because*. It proved he wasn't such a blockhead as all that.'

'You thought that he had been making a show?' the Dutchman put in, but it was the Captain who came up with the right word:

'Shamming?' he said.

'I'm not sure.'

'What happened next?'

'I went to down to the kitchen.'

'And?'

Chapter Thirty-Four

In the kitchen, Amanda Rickerby had her hair down (which made her a different kind of beauty) and was brushing it while she sat at the kitchen table, which was crowded with new-bought groceries. Instead of 'hello', she said, 'Mr Fielding is very chivalrously peeling the potatoes,' and he *was* most unexpectedly working at the sink with his suit-coat off and shirt sleeves very carefully rolled.

'It is extremely unhygienic of me to brush my hair in the kitchen,' Miss Rickerby added, and I saw there was pen and paper in front of her.

'Don't worry on my account,' I said.

'I'm most awfully sorry. I'll stop just as soon as I've finished.'

Vaughan was not present. Adam Rickerby stood by the range, and paid me no mind. He was gazing at his boots, as he was being quizzed by a round, jolly looking woman – evidently Mrs Dawson the daily help.

'How are we off for tinned rhubarb?' she was asking him.

'We've none in,' said Rickerby.

'Prunes?'

'None in.'

'Vanilla essence.'

'Eh?'

'Never mind. Rice?'

'We've none in . . . I reckon.'

'Ah now, I detected a flicker of hope there, Mrs Dawson,' Howard Fielding said from the sink, moving a quantity of peeled potatoes onto the draining board.

'There,' said Amanda Rickerby, who'd finished brushing her hair, and was putting it up. 'What do you think, Mr Stringer?'

Being so curly, it didn't look much different; but it did look beautiful.

'Good,' I said, thinking: As you know very well.

'*Good,*' she repeated. 'But I wish there was a looking glass in here.'

'It's not your boudoir, love,' said Mrs Dawson, who was now in the larder. 'And I wish you wouldn't move everything about from one week to the next. I know it's you and not Adam. *He's* perfectly neat-handed.'

'We should put up a notice,' said Fielding from the sink. '"A place for everything, and everything in its place."'

He'd turned around now, and was smiling at me, drying his hands on a tea towel and giving me that questioning look of his.

'Yes,' said Amanda Rickerby, 'but where would we put it?'

It was then that I saw the glass of wine – white this time – at her elbow, and not only the glass but the bottle. 'But where would we *put* it?' she repeated, in a dreamy sort of way. Looking at me, she picked up her pen, and said, 'How about "excellent in quality"?'

But it seemed that she was speaking to Fielding, even though she had her back to him, for he replied, '*Superior* in quality,' and Amanda Rickerby wrote that down. 'No tinned meat,' he added. 'You have that down?'

Miss Rickerby nodded, more or less to herself. She then said, 'Tariff furnished on application,' and she gave me a lovely, mysterious smile at that. She'd seen that I'd noticed the bottle. It said 'Chablis' on the label, and I could not have pronounced that word but I knew it signified good wine.

'Now I need fresh cheese,' said Mrs Dawson.

'Can you *have* fresh cheese?' asked Amanda Rickerby. 'Mr Fielding's special reserve,' she said to me, indicating the bottle.

'Help yourself to a glass of wine, Mr Stringer,' Fielding called out from the sink. 'It's a rare event to find the Burgundy whites in Scarborough.'

'And he should know,' put in Miss Rickerby.

She found a glass, and poured me some wine.

'It's been standing in cold water since breakfast time,' she said, regaining her seat, 'and what do you think? Mr Fielding sent Adam with a sovereign to buy some lovely fish from the harbour.'

Vaughan now entered in his cape, looking flushed and damp but in good spirits. I wondered where he'd been since the women's pub. Seeing the fish lying in white paper on the kitchen table, he said: 'Good-o, I like a bit of cod.'

'It's haddock,' Fielding called out. He had now acquired his own glass of the Chablis, and it appeared that a regular party was in the making.

'We're going to have it with cheese sauce,' said Amanda Rickerby, '. . . and creamed potatoes.'

But of course she was not lifting a finger to help her brother, who was doing all the work with some assistance from Mrs Dawson.

'Is this normal?' I said. 'For a Monday in Paradise?'

'It is not, Jim,' said Vaughan. 'Potted shrimps and stewed fruit would be near the mark for normal. What are we having for pudding, Mrs Dawson? I fancy treacle tart.'

'All right, Mr Vaughan,' she said, 'I'll just immediately make that for you.'

'Hang about,' he said, 'I'll give you a hand.'

And he walked into the larder and came out with a tin of Golden Syrup, which he passed to Mrs Dawson before sitting back down again and taking a copy of *Sporting Life* from the pocket of his cape. Mrs Dawson took the lid off the tin, saying, 'That's no earthly use,' and passed it to Amanda Rickerby, who peered in before handing it in turn back to Vaughan.

'It's more like *olden* syrup,' she said, but the crack was for my benefit. She seemed most anxious for my approval of all her remarks, and so I grinned back at her – but were the smiles of a woman who was half cut worth the same as those from a sober one? And whenever I see someone drinking heavily in the daytime I wonder *why* they're about it, whereas evening drinking is only to be expected and quite above board.

'Seems all right to me,' said Vaughan, inspecting the treacle and receiving a glass of wine from Fielding. He dipped his finger into the tin, and started licking the stuff.

'It's just because we're all always so blue on Monday,' said Amanda Rickerby, 'and today we're going to be different, and you and I are going to have a lovely long talk, Mr Stringer.'

I thought: At this rate, we're going to have a fuck, and that's all there is to it. All I had to do was let on I was married and that'd put an end to it, and I knew I *should* do it because if you fucked one woman who wasn't your wife, then where would it end? You might as well fuck hundreds, or at least try, and your whole life would be taken up with it.

I saw that Fielding was eyeing me from his post at the sink.

'Just at present, Miss Rickerby is composing an advertisement for the *Yorkshire Evening Press*,' he said.

'You mean *you're* composing it,' Vaughan interrupted. 'Old Howard's a great hand at writing adverts,' he added, turning to me. 'He advertised in the Leeds paper for a promising young man interested in post cards, and I thought: That's me on both counts! You see, I'd worked for a while on one of the travelling post offices, Jim.'

'Which ones?' I enquired.

'The Night Mail "Down".'

I was impressed, for the Night Mail 'Down', with carriages supplied by the Great Northern and staff by the General Post Office, was *the* TPO.

'You must have lived in London at that time,' I said, 'since you'd have worked out of Euston?'

'Born in London, Jim,' said Vaughan, and I wondered whether that alone accounted for his appearing to be of a slightly superior class. I tried to picture him walking every morning through the great arch in front of Euston station.

'Did three years on that,' he said, 'clerking in the sorting carriages and ... well, I saw the quantity of cards being sent.'

'As a misprint in *The Times* once had it, Mr Stringer,' Fielding put in, 'the down postal leaves London every evening with two unsorted letters and five thousand engines.'

I grinned at him.

'Did you quit?' I enquired, turning back to Vaughan.

'Chucked it up, yes. Didn't care for the motion of the train, Jim; gave me a sort of sea sickness.'

'*Mal de mer*,' said Fielding, and everything stopped, as though we were all listening for the sound of the sea coming from just yards beyond the wall of the kitchen. Everything stopped, that is, save for Adam Rickerby, who had been put to chopping parsley with a very small knife, and was evidently making a poor fist of it. Mrs Dawson was eyeing him. I knew she was going to step in, and I wondered whether he'd really fly into rage this time – and with knife in hand. But there was something very kindly about the way she took the knife from the lad, saying, 'Let's do the job properly. You're worse than me, love.'

With Mrs Dawson looking on, and the parsley chopped, Adam Rickerby then lowered the haddock into a big pot, poured in some milk, and set it on the range. At length, the room began to be filled with a sort of fishy fog. Theo Vaughan had finished his wine, and was now helping himself from the beer barrel on the table, saying 'You sticking with the wine, Jim?'

In-between doing bits of cooking in consultation with Mrs Dawson, Adam Rickerby was trying to make things orderly in the kitchen. He was forever shifting the knife polisher about on the table, and presently took it away to the sideboard. Amanda Rickerby, disregarding her pen and paper, was now sipping wine at a great rate and saying things such as, 'I do like it when we're all in, and it's raining outside.' She then turned to me, enquiring, 'Tell us all about trains, Mr Stringer. Have you ever eaten a meal on one?'

Adam Rickerby eyed me as I revolved the question. As a copper, I'd quite often taken dinner or luncheon in a restaurant car, usually with the Chief and at his expense. Would an ordinary fireman do it? Had I ever done it when I'd *been* an ordinary fireman, leaving aside sandwiches and bottled tea on the footplate? No.

'Do you count light refreshments in a tea car?' I said.

'Yes!' Amanda Rickerby said, very excited. 'Is there one running into Scarborough?'

'In summer there is,' I said.

'And might they do a little more than a tea? Not a joint but a chop or a steak?'

'I think so.'

'And a nice glass of wine? When does the first one run?'

'May sort of time,' I said, and she shut her eyes for a space, contemplating the idea.

'Cedar-wood box after luncheon, Mr Stringer?' Fielding called over to me.

I nodded back. 'Obliged to you,' I said.

Miss Rickerby was standing, leaning forward to pour me more wine, and she threatened to over-topple onto me, which I wished she *would* do.

'Care for another glass?' she enquired, sitting back down.

Vaughan gave a mighty sniff, and said, 'You ought to have asked that *before* you filled it, Miss R . . . strictly speaking.'

But she ignored him in favour of eyeing me.

'Well, it goes down a treat,' I said.

'Just so!' said Fielding, and Amanda Rickerby turned sharply about and looked at him.

'Are you married, Mr Stringer?' she said, facing me again – and I knew I'd failed to keep the look of panic from my face.

'Well . . .' I said again.

'Three wells make a river and you in the river make it bigger,' said Mrs Dawson from the pantry, where she was making a list. It was an old Yorkshire saying, but what did it mean, and what did *she* mean by it?

'You either are or you aren't,' said Amanda Rickerby. 'I mean, it ought not to require thought.'

I was fairly burning up with embarrassment. But Mrs Dawson had hardly looked up from her pencil and note pad while making her remark; Fielding was taking the corkscrew to another bottle; Adam Rickerby was stirring a pot; Theo Vaughan was biting his long thumbnail while reading, and the one little pointer on the gas meter that moved around fast was moving around just as fast as ever.

'No,' I said, 'I'm not,' and the cork came out as Fielding said, 'Oh dear.'

'What's up?' said Vaughan, looking up.

'It's corked,' said Fielding.

'It *was*,' said Vaughan, 'but now you've taken the cork *out*.'

'No, I mean the cork has crumbled,' said Fielding.

'What's the harm?' said Vaughan, turning the page of the paper. 'You weren't thinking of putting it back *in*, were you?'

'You don't seem to understand,' said Fielding.

I had betrayed Lydia my wife: our eleven years together, our children . . . I told myself I'd done it in order to keep in with Miss Amanda Rickerby. I had done it for the sake of the investigation, and no other reason. She was on the marry and it was important for me to keep her interest in me alive in order to acquire more data. Amanda Rickerby was grinning at me, and I believed she knew. Yes, *she* knew all right.

I drained my glass, sat back and said, 'You say that Blackburn jumped into the sea, but would that really have killed him? Just to jump in off the harbour wall?'

'I'll tell you what it wouldn't have done, Jim,' said Vaughan, still looking over *Sporting Life*. 'It wouldn't have warmed him up.'

'Lucifer matches, Mr Stringer,' said Amanda Rickerby. 'You can suck the ends and then you'll die. Perhaps he did that.'

'While he was bobbing about in the sea, you mean?' asked Vaughan. 'And you have to suck every match in the box, you know.'

'My dad', said Miss Rickerby, 'did it by drinking a bottle of spirits every day for forty years.'

'Yes, and you think *on* about that, Amanda dear,' said Mrs Dawson. 'I don't like to see wine on the table so early in the day.'

'It's a special occasion, Mrs Dawson,' said Amanda Rickerby, and she rose to her feet. With a special smile in my direction, she said, 'Won't be a minute,' and quit the room.

Theo Vaughan was still sticking his finger into the tin of Golden Syrup.

'I like treacle,' he said.

'Evidently,' Fielding put in.

'I like it on porridge,' said Vaughan.

'That would be sacrilege to the Scots,' said Fielding.

'If you put it into porridge,' said Vaughan, 'it allows you to see *into* the porridge.'

'Very useful I'm sure,' said Fielding.

'It goes like the muslin dresses of the ladies on the beach when the sun is low. They're sort of . . .'

'They are *transparent*, Vaughan,' said Fielding.

'Noticed it yourself, have you?'

'I have *not*.'

'Mr Vaughan, please remember there are ladies present,' said Mrs Dawson. But in fact she herself was the only one in the room at that moment, and she was putting on her coat and gloves, at which I saw my opportunity.

'I'll show you to the door, Mrs Dawson,' I said. Once out in the hallway, I said, 'Very good house, this. It's a credit to you – and to the boy.'

'He's a bit mental, the poor lamb,' Mrs Rickerby said, fixing her wrap, 'but he does his best.'

'I'm thinking of trying to help him in some way. I know he has a strong interest in railways . . .'

She eyed me. The clock ticked. I couldn't keep her long, since she was evidently over-heating in her coat and wrap.

'I know he likes to read about them,' I said, 'or to be read *to* about them.'

'*I've* read to him on occasion,' said Mrs Dawson, 'when we've done our chores of a morning.'

'About what exactly?'

She kept silence for a moment, reaching for the latch of the door. I opened the door for her.

'Youth cut to death by express train,' she said. 'Collision in station, engine on platform. Driver killed, fireman scalded. Car dashes onto level crossing as train approaches . . . He knows his letters well enough to spot a railway item in the newspaper, and then everything has to stop while you read it out.'

'Why?'

'Why? It's just how he is. It's how his condition takes him. He's a very simple lad, is Adam. He has this house, which he tries to keep up. He *did* have Peter . . .'

'Peter?'

'His cat that died.'

The rain made a cold wind as it fell onto Bright's Cliff.

' . . . And he has his little boat,' Mrs Dawson added.

'Oh? Where's that?'

'Sometimes in the stables over the road, sometimes on the beach, sometimes in the harbour.'

'How does he move it about?'

'On a cart.'

'He goes in for a bit of sailing, does he?'

'It's a rowing boat.'

In the kitchen I'd thought Mrs Dawson a kindly woman, which perhaps she was, but she didn't seem to have taken to me and I wondered whether she was the first person in Paradise to have guessed that I was a spy. Or was it just that – being married herself and a woman experienced in the ways of men – she'd somehow known I was lying about not having a wife?

As Mrs Dawson stepped out into the rain, I heard a footfall on the dark stairs. Amanda Rickerby was coming down, and I returned with her in silence to the kitchen, which was a less homely place without Mrs Dawson. It was too hot and everyone looked red. Vaughan was moving some pots and pans aside so that he could get at the beer barrel again; Fielding remained with his back to the sink with arms folded and head down, evidently lost in a dream, but he looked up as we walked in, and Adam Rickerby approached his sister, carrying the fish in its baking pan.

She said, 'Oh dear, Adam love, it's over-cooked.'

She drew towards her another dish.

'The only thing for it,' she said, 'is to break it up, put it in this, and make a pie.'

'A *pie*?' he fairly gasped, and he looked all about in desperation. As he did so, it was Fielding's turn to quit the room. In the interval of his absence, Amanda Rickerby played with a salt cellar, completely self-absorbed, as it seemed to me; Vaughan pulled at his 'tache and read his paper, and Adam Rickerby fell to tidying the kitchen with a great clattering of crockery and ironmongery. When Fielding returned a few minutes later, the lad was arranging the objects on the table: he wanted the knife polisher in a line with the vegetable boiler, the toast rack, the big tea pot, and so on.

'Adam, love,' said his sister, 'don't take on. I'm just going to ask Mr Stringer about summer trains, I'll see to the cooking in a moment.'

'It's too late,' he said. 'It'll be tea time any minute.'

'Well, stop moving things about, anyhow.'

'I en't movin' things *about*,' said Adam Rickerby. 'I'm movin' 'em *back*.'

So saying, he walked directly through the door that gave onto the scullery, and I heard the opening and closing of a further door, indicating that he had gone into his own quarters at the back of the house.

'If luncheon is off then so am I,' said Vaughan, rising to his feet.

'Mr Stringer,' Fielding enquired from his post at the sink, 'will you come upstairs now for that cigar?'

And I somehow couldn't refuse him.

Chapter Thirty-Five

In the ship room the gas had not been lit, and the fire was low. Fielding, who entered in advance of me, was stirring it as I walked up to the left hand window and watched the storm. The wine and the earlier beer had made my head bad, and I had a half a mind to lift the sash and let in the wind and flying rain. I was in no mood for smoking a dry cigar but it would be a way of getting at Fielding. Or did *he* want to get at *me*?

He set down the poker and brought the cedar-wood box over. There were just two short cigars rolling about inside. The Spanish sherry, I noticed, was waiting on the small bamboo table. He poured two glasses, and we both drank. I saw for the first time that he wore a signet ring on his right little finger.

'Quite a panorama,' he said, indicating the window, 'as the post card people say.'

Has he brought me up to show me the view? I didn't want the sherry, but I drank the stuff anyway, as if doing so would bring the truth closer. But Fielding was only smiling politely. He seemed to have no topic for conversation in his mind.

'What ships do you see from here?' I asked, presently.

'Only this morning,' he said, 'one of Mr Churchill's destroyers.'

A noise came from the doorway, and Vaughan stood there in his Inverness cape, grinning with eyes half closed. He was thoroughly drunk by now and breathing noisily through his drooping moustache. He had not been invited, and I fancied that Fielding did not look too pleased to see him, although of course he kept up a show of politeness.

Vaughan closed on me with a post card held out. It might have been the woman earlier shown on the trapeze, only she now lounged under a tree, wearing no clothes as usual but holding a parasol, which would not have made her decent even if she'd chosen to use it for the purpose of *keeping* decent, which she had not done. Vaughan showed it only to me. There was evidently no question either of showing it to Fielding or of hiding it from him, but he could see it from where he stood, anyhow.

'Class A,' breathed Vaughan. 'Quite a naturalist, this one.'

'*Naturist*,' said Fielding, 'and be so good as to take her away.'

Vaughan grinned, turned on his heel, and quit the room. Where was he going? Off to waste more of his allowance?

'I'm used to Vaughan's bohemian ways,' said Fielding, now pouring us out another glass each of the sherry. 'But it does you credit, Mr Stringer, the way that you take him in your stride.'

He sat down in his favourite chair, and I took the couch.

'I suppose they're only the Old Masters brought up to date,' I said, thinking of Vaughan's witness statement.

'It's not the *highest* sort of indecency,' said Fielding.

'The railway cards I liked though,' I said. 'It's not often you see a crossed signal or an out-of-gauge load on a card.'

'Something that might have appealed to a footplate man such as yourself', said Fielding, 'was our series of pictures of double headed trains.'

He was going round the houses; this surely was not meant to be the subject of our talk, but I said:

'You know there are *triple*-headed trains working in some places . . . Up the bank to Ravenscar.'

'I shouldn't wonder,' said Fielding. 'What is it there? Six hundred feet above sea level?'

'Getting on for,' I said. 'They're very *short* trains too.'

'So you've a train with almost as many engines as carriages?' said Fielding, blowing smoke, and tipping his head to one side. He was full of little cracks like that. He moved his little glass from one hand to another, as though practising receiving a glass daintily with both hands. I wondered whether he'd worn that ring of his in York gaol. He'd have been asking for trouble if he had done. I was bursting to ask him whether he really had been lagged, because I could scarcely believe it.

'Vaughan's money came today, of course,' I said, after an interval of silence.

'Yes,' said Fielding. 'It's just enough to keep him idle. Some people might say that a modest allowance has promoted lethargy in my case as well, but I think I'm a *little* more industrious than friend Vaughan.'

'You've carried on various businesses,' I said.

'Yes,' said Fielding, exhaling smoke, 'but who was it said that the key to success is consistency to purpose?'

And he tipped his head, as though really expecting me to supply the answer.

'I don't know,' I said.

'Disraeli?' he said, and he smiled, adding, 'I should have stuck at my original plan.'

'Oh. What was that?'

'In my youth, I trained as a lawyer.'

'A solicitor?

He nodded again.

'I have it in mind to take articles myself,' I said, and he tipped his head. He did not believe me for a minute, or did not credit that it was possible.

'It's a hard road,' he said, and he left too long a silence before adding, '. . . but the work ought to be well within the capacities of a man like yourself.'

Fielding set out to be mannerly at all times, but occasionally he did not come up to the mark. I glanced over to see Amanda Rickerby in the doorway. She stood swaying somewhat, and said, 'There's a person to see you downstairs, Mr Fielding.'

He rose, half bowed at her, and went off through the open door of the ship room.

'Who was it?' I enquired of the landlady. But she walked to one of the two windows without replying.

'What a day,' she said, after a space. And then, remembering my question, 'It was someone from the gramophone society.'

She continued to stare out at the German Sea. Here was another of her silent goes; there'd been one during breakfast, and one in the kitchen not half an hour since. Was it the same thought every time that kept her silent? A ship putting out black smoke was stationary on the horizon. It might as well have been a factory at sea. Miss Rickerby turned and saw the decanter of Spanish sherry.

'Do you want a glass?' she said, moving fast towards it. 'Not that it's mine to offer.'

'Better not,' I said. 'I've just had two.'

She returned to the window with her glass, looking out to sea again. I stood by the next window, so that we were about three feet apart. I did not know what would happen, or what I would do. I was in fact paralysed by indecision, and so it was strange to see, down on the Prom, a tall, thin man moving with great purpose. He wore a Macintosh and a bowler, and was running at the top of his speed through the rain. He skidded up to the beach steps, half stumbled down them in his haste, and continued running over the black beach, going full pelt, heading straight for the waves, where he came to a sudden halt. Amanda Rickerby turned to me and smiled sadly.

'Well, I thought he was going to do ... *something*,' she said.

We faced each other now, and she took a step towards me, with face downturned. She was a head smaller than me, and I could see the top of her curls, and then, when she tilted her face upwards, the powder on her cheekbones, the blueness and greyness that made the overall greenness of her wide-set eyes.

'I am quite drunk, Mr Stringer,' she said.

She appeared to be looking at my North Eastern Railway badge again, really concentrating on it. She took my right hand in hers. Her hand was dry, and she moved it about over mine in a way that was somehow not restless but very calming – the right thing. I could hear footsteps on the stairs.

'You had better lock your room tonight,' she said, quickly.

'Why?'

'Probably no reason,' she said, withdrawing her hand, and giving me a smile that was natural, quick, charming, and just about the most mysterious thing I've ever seen.

Adam Rickerby stood in the doorway.

'Gas 'as run out,' he said. 'Meter wants feeding.'

Amanda Rickerby smiled brightly and much more straight-forwardly at me. 'Do you have sixpence, Mr Stringer? I'll pay you back later.'

Chapter Thirty-Six

Amanda Rickerby went downstairs in the company of her brother.

Events were now rushing on faster than my thoughts and faster also than my morals. What had she meant by advising me to lock my room? Did she mean that otherwise she would come to visit me in the night, and that she needed to be saved from herself? What was Vaughan up to? Mysterious and glooming in the seafront pub . . . in better spirits during luncheon . . . but now making off again. And for what purpose had Fielding taken me up to the ship room? But as I stepped out of that room, one thing was certain: I was alone on the first floor of the house, and both Fielding's and Miss Rickerby's bedroom doors stood open.

I walked into Fielding's first; I hardly cared if I was discovered. In fact being discovered might save me from *myself*. It was a big room, papered in plain green with a red border, better kept than the rest of the house, and very calm and neat, and made more so by the sight of the lashing rain and wild dark sea beyond the two windows. There were red rugs on wide black boards of the kind seen in inns, bookshelves in alcoves. You had to look hard to see the blisters in the wallpaper and the fraying in the carpet, for the gas was not lit, nor was the fire. There were two closets, a tall chest of drawers, a folded table and a smaller table by the bed head with a little drawer set into it. Over the fancy ironwork of the fireplace was a painting of a ship foundering. I fixed my eye on the chest of drawers, and I marched over the carpet towards it, feeling sure they must have heard the drumming of my boot heels on the floor below.

On the top of the chest of drawers lay an ebony tray with hair brushes and a shoe horn. I reached out with two hands, and pulled open the top drawer to its fullest extent. A smell of coal tar soap came up. The drawer contained a quantity of Howard Fielding's under-clothes neatly folded, and many little boxes. With Fielding, it seemed that almost everything came in boxes. There were several round collar boxes, and I quickly lifted the lids of two. They contained collars. I then lifted the lid of a green velvet-lined one. The inside of the lid was white silk, and the words 'Best Quality' were written there. It held solitaires and cuff links. A tortoiseshell one held more cuff links and Fielding's collection of stick pins and tie clips.

I shut the drawer and opened the next one down: comforters, socks, under-shirts, ties . . . and more boxes. I opened the biggest box, made of wood. It held candles and matches. Another wooden one held a tangle of alberts. Next to this was a felt bag with a drawstring. I pulled at the string with two hands, and looked down on half a dozen straight razors with pearl handles. The biggest box was leather covered. I opened it and saw a vanity set, with scissors, nail-shaper, toothbrush all held in place on red velvet – and two twenty pound notes folded in half on top. I shut the drawer, and stood still, listening to the house. Did I hear a door slam downstairs?

I marched up to the sea picture: 'Wreck of a Brig off Whitby', it was called. It showed a ship being rolled over in high seas; two men looked at the brig from the beach, and they were evidently a gormless pair. Why didn't they do something about it?

But I felt the same. I had discovered nothing. Well, nothing except the money, and what did that signify? It was a good amount, but a fellow was entitled to keep forty pounds cash in his bedroom after all. I was still half drunk, and my head was pounding as I inspected the rest of the room. I threw open the first of the closets, releasing a smell of mothballs. Fielding hung *his* coats up all right – Adam Rickerby would have approved. The two had neatness in common, although they'd hardly exchanged a word since I'd been in the house. I moved over to the bookshelves. Novels, collected numbers of *Notes and Queries*, a digest of *The Railway Magazine*, *Famous Sea Tales*, *Marine Painters of Britain*, *A Catalogue for the Collectors of Post Cards*, *The Literary Antiquary*; some volumes on book collecting, some guides to Scarborough. I walked to the little bedside table, opened the drawer set into it, and here was not a box but an envelope. On the front was written: 'Railway Selection – Line-side Curiosities & C'. The flap of the envelope was tucked into place but not sealed. I lifted it up, and there were two post cards: the first showed a woman in a riding hat sitting side saddle on a white horse; the second showed her sitting astride the horse. She was quite naked in both.

I froze, listened to the house; watched the door. There came faint voices from below, nothing besides.

The overall picture was now composing, but the light of day was also fading, and Fielding's room was half enclosed in darkness as I replaced the cards – for there'd been half a dozen in the envelope, all of the same sort – and walked smartly out of his room and into the corridor. Here, I listened again before I approached the opened door of Miss Rickerby's bedroom.

It was not exactly blue but lavender – her colour. The paraffin heater roared faintly as before. In combination with the low burning fire, this made the room too hot, also as before. I made first for the dressing table and opening the top-most drawer I did not care for the look of my face in the triple mirror (which seemed to give all the angles of the photographs in a criminal record card). The drawer held a great mix-up of buttons, buckles, beads, chains, lockets. I pricked my finger on the pin of a butterfly brooch. The stones on the brooch and on the chains and pendants were not precious as far as I could judge, and it made me feel sorry for the owner.

There was some silver there however – just pitched in any-how with everything else. I saw a decorated paper fan. I caught it up, and opened it out, bringing to life a sea-side scene: a long promenade with happy bicyclists, and strollers with parasols and sun hats. I could not make out the words at the top, so I held it towards the seething blue flame of the paraffin heater and read: 'Eastbourne, Sussex'. She liked Eastbourne. I knew that already.

I tried the second drawer. It held some mysterious bundles of cotton and muslin that I knew I ought not to look at, two folded corsets; also a pair of small binoculars, another jumble of jewellery and some documents pinned together. I removed the pin. The first paper was a clipping from a magazine: 'Are You Troubled by Poor Eyesight?' An optician's advertisement – and I felt a surge of love for Miss Rickerby. The next paper was a handwritten letter, and I could hardly read a word of it; there were a couple more in the same shocking hand. I stared at the final page of the final one, and swung it in the direction of the blue light. At length, I made out 'a compass – only a trinket but it works'. The document that came after was type-written, per-fectly clear . . . and all the breath stopped on my lips as I read the heading that had been underlined at the top: *Re: Your*

Claim Against The North Eastern Railway Company. The letter began:

> *Dear Mr Rickerby, please find enclosed a letter we received on the 5th inst. from Parker and Wilkinson of York, the solicitors acting for the North Eastern Railway Company in this matter.*
>
> *The letter offers compensation in the sum of one hundred and twenty pounds and payment of your costs in full and final settlement of your claim. We believe this offer to be reasonable in view of the danger of a finding of contributory negligence against you should the case be pursued and taken into court.*
>
> *As you will see from the letter, this offer stands for the next sixty days . . .*

I returned to the top of the letter. The address was that of Messrs Robinson, Farmery and Farmery of Middlesbrough, and carried the date 11 March, 1910. I supposed they would have known that Adam Rickerby was unable to read, and that the business would be dealt with on his behalf by his sister. She, at any rate, had been the one who'd kept the letter, and it proved that Adam Rickerby had not been made strange by the collapse of a pit prop. He'd tangled with a train, and it was odds-on that the money paid over as a consequence – and paid through the agency of the firm that I would shortly be working for – had bought the Paradise guest house.

I could make nothing of the other papers. I replaced the pin, and my eye fell on the one box in the drawer. It was about three inches square, the lid decorated with sea shells. I lifted the lid, and saw a small silver compass set into a miniature replica of a ship's wheel. But it was the object lying alongside it that I picked up. In the half light I saw the crest of the City of York, the Leeds crest, the sheep, the ears of corn. Here was the badge of the North Eastern Railway, and I was quite certain that it had once belonged to Ray Blackburn.

Stringer,' he added with great weariness as he opened the door and contemplated the wind and the rain. Then he stepped through it and was gone.

I cannot say for certain why, but in the next moment I dashed down the stairs and entered the dining room, kitchen and scullery in turn. Only in the scullery, where the walls were of white-glazed brick, did a gas light burn. The rough wooden door beside the mangle must be the entry to Adam Rickerby's room. I knocked – no answer. I lifted the latch, pushed the door, and the light from the scullery fell on another scullery, or so it appeared, but this with a truckle bed in it. A good-sized barrel stood in the room, an old washing dolly, a quantity of carefully folded sacks, and a bicycle with the front wheel smaller than the back so as to make way for a great basket. There was no carpet on the stone floor, and no fireplace but many thick blankets on the bed, which was neatly made up with hardly a crease in the pillow. A trunk stood by the side of the bed. I lifted the lid, and saw rough clothes, neatly folded. Many objects hung from nails on the wall: a bike tyre, an oilcloth, a sou'wester, an apron, and a cork lifejacket. Well, Adam Rickerby lived by the sea, so it was not surprising that he owned a boat. Most who owned boats owned lifejackets. None of this was out of the common, except that I couldn't quite imagine him in charge of a boat, at large on the seas without his sister to encourage him and set him right when he went wrong.

I stepped out of the room, closed the door behind me, and returned to the gloomy kitchen, where something drew me over towards the knife polisher. It looked like a round wooden wheel, the rim of which had been repeatedly stabbed by knives, although in fact they rested in slots. One of the holes accommodated several long, thin items: three skewers of some sort, and a nine inch needle with an eye, which was perhaps for trussing up meat prior to roasting. In the centre of the polisher was a handle connected to a circular brush: you wound it and the blades inside were cleaned.

I climbed the steps, which were all in darkness; had a piss in the gloomy bathroom on the half decorated floor and wandered along towards the door of the apartment-in-the-making. I turned the handle, and stepped through to see amid the shadows the rags of half stripped paper hanging from the walls, the bare boards and the parade of paint tins. The window stood open as before, and I watched for a while the waves hitting the harbour wall a quarter of a mile off. I knew what I was doing: I was putting off looking through the hole in the wall. I watched the sea make three attempts to send spray to the top of the lighthouse, and then I approached the hole, which was about man-sized.

The shreds of faded green-stripe wallpaper made a kind of curtain over it. I pushed them aside, stepped through, and my boots came down silently – I was on carpet, which was a turn-up. I could *feel* the carpet but not see it, for this second room was darker than the first. But this room too had a window over-looking the front, and objects began to appear by the phosphorous light of the sea beyond: a small sofa, an armchair, a clock on the wall, a high bed with mattress and covers still on and neatly made. There had been some attempt to clear the room: the dwarf bookcase held only one volume, and there were no ornaments to be seen, save for a clock that rested on a tasselled cloth spread over the mantel-shelf. A sheet of paper rested on the counterpane of the bed. I meant to read it, but as I took a step forwards, the flute note came from the fireplace, and I nearly bolted from the room as the paper jumped off the bed, and floated, swinging gently, to the ground. It was the wind coming through the chimney. I walked over, and was relieved to read only the words 'Trips by Steamer' and a list of timings. My hand was shaking as I held it though; I'd had a bad turn, and did not care to stay in the room. I stepped back through the hole, and in a moment I was climbing the topmost staircase under the eyes of old man Rickerby who gave me the evil eye from each of the three photographs in turn.

In the half landing outside my own quarters I fumbled for some matches, pushed open the door, and lit the oil lamp in my little room. It glowed red and the redness made the little room seem the most welcoming of all, and it made me immediately sleepy into the bargain. But I would not sleep. I sat at the end of the bed and removed the piece of paste-board that kept the small window from rattling. I lifted the sash and leant forward, looking down at the Prom below, letting the sea wind move my hair about and breathing deep, cold breaths. I then filled my water glass from the jug by the wash stand and took a drink. I lay down on the bed, and pulled aside the tab rug that lay half underneath the bedstead. The little copper stubs marking the tops of the gas pipes remained tightly sealed. I put the rug back, and listened to the little window shaking. Every small gust caused a fearful din, and the bigger ones seemed set fair to break the glass. I leant forward and lowered the window. It rattled less when closed. I ought really to put back the paste-board, but I could hardly be bothered. I lay still, listened to the waves, and revolved a hundred bad thoughts: Amanda Rickerby had lied about her brother's accident because it might be seen to have given him a grievance against railway men; Fielding was not queer – or he was a strange sort of queer if he went to bed with pictures of naked ladies. I called to mind the pictures. Lucky horse! But I hadn't the energy to make use of the memory – I was tired out, having hardly slept for three nights. I thought of the wife, and how she'd say, 'You're over-strung, Stringer', and brush my hair right back, for she thought it should go that way rather than the parting at the side, and I was sure that it therefore *would* do in time.

. . . But how I liked it when she brushed it back. You'd have thought she'd have better things to do, just because she gener-ally had so much on, what with the Co-operative ladies and the women's cause and the new house and all the rest of it.

I closed my eyes, and I don't believe that I slept, but when I opened them again I saw that there was an intruder in the room, in the shape of a twist of black smoke rising up from the red lamp. As I looked on the redness flared, causing everything in the room to lean away from the window, and then it died away to nothing. The oil had run out. I had the manual for the lamp but no more oil, and I must have light, so I dragged myself to my feet, found my matches in my pocket, and walked out onto the little landing. Reaching up to the gas bracket I turned the tap, breathed the hot coal breath, and lit it, where-upon I was instantly joined on the landing by my own shadow. I had not had sixpence about me, but Miss Rickerby, or her brother, must have fed the meter before going out.

I moved back into the little room, kicked the door shut, and fell onto the bed, where I turned on my side and contemplated the line of white light under the door. The bad thoughts came back: *Robert Henderson's* hair was brushed directly back. In order to have a fraction of his money I must work all the hours God gave at a job I didn't want to do. Five years of articled clerkship, and for what? So that I might offer a kid a hundred and twenty pounds in exchange for half his brain. My thoughts flew to Tommy Nugent, and I hoped he was back in York, courting his girl from the Overcoat Depot on Parliament Street. I pictured the wife again, wearing my third best suit-coat as she showed her friend Lillian Backhouse about the new garden. That was all right: Lillian Backhouse was another feminist, and the suit-coat looked better on Lydia than on me, in spite of it being twice her size.

Amanda Rickerby came to mind once more . . . How had she come by the badge and why had she kept it? My head was fairly spinning. Had she asked me to lock my door in order to protect me from the boy? From Fielding? From Vaughan? (Surely not from Vaughan?) Or did she mean to come up and sit astride me as the woman on the post card had sat astride the horse? I did not believe she would do, but I decided that the moment we'd shared in the ship room ought to mark the end of our relations. I was a married man after all. I stood up, locked the door, fell back onto the bed, and even though it was hardly more than late afternoon, I was asleep in an instant, my boots still on my feet.

Chapter Thirty-Eight

'You were dead wrong about Adam Rickerby,' said the Captain, pushing back his chair and rising to his feet with the pocket revolver in his hand.

If he didn't mean to shoot me, then he might be on the point of quitting the chart room, and I wanted him to stay, firstly because I knew he had secrets of his own touching this matter and secondly because I wanted to talk on. I wanted to get behind the mist, and I now knew I could do it. The recollection of my exchange with Miss Rickerby in the ship room came with many complications, and the best thing was to talk on because my speech brought back my memory of what came next and remembering, at least, was something I could be proud of.

The Mate was eyeing the Captain, and so was I – had been for some little while. It was the difference that made the similarity so plain: the Captain's face never smiling, hers almost always; his hair short, curls not given time to begin, hers abundant. But there was a strength to the Captain's close-cut hair, a sort of possibility in it. How could I not have noticed before that they had only the one face between them: wide, symmetrical, cat-like? The boy had the same face again, but the accident or some earlier event had made mockery of it, stretching it too wide and piling on the curls. He had been over-done. Anyhow, I knew that this was Captain Rickerby sitting before me, and that he had once sent a silver compass set in a miniature ship's wheel to his sister.

'I'll tell you what happened,' I said to him, just as though he was Peter Backhouse, sitting over-opposite me in the public bar of the Fortune of War in Thorpe-on-Ouse with more than a few pints taken; and I *did* feel a kind of drunken happiness, for I could now see the whole thing clear.

'It was the light under the door,' I said to the Captain, who'd now sat back down. 'It was not there – the line of white light – and I was half glad of it, because I knew it would have hurt my eyes if it had been. That was part of my affliction . . . You see, I believe that what happened to me – what was done to me – impaired my memory, but I have now *recovered* my memory. I can go on from here and tell you the whole thing. I have the solution to the mystery.'

I made my play:

'The woman in the post cards,' I said, '. . . not the one on the horse, but the one that Vaughan had liked particularly . . . You see, she was Blackburn's fiancée, and when Blackburn was shown the cards in the Two Mariners he attacked Vaughan, really laid into him . . .'

'They came to blows over this?' enquired the Mate, blowing smoke.

'Very likely,' I said. 'At any rate they were set at odds. Perhaps Blackburn had threatened to go to the police. In the night, Vaughan must have gone up to him, perhaps to try and settle the matter. They must have fought again. Vaughan killed Blackburn, perhaps not intentionally. He hauled the body downstairs, put it on the cart over the road, took it to the Promenade or the harbour wall, and pitched it into the sea. Vaughan knew I was onto him. He'd over-heard me talking to

Tommy Nugent in Mallinson's, and so he tried to do me in by the method of . . .'

'It is nonsense,' said the Mate, lighting a new cigar.

'If you don't tell the truth,' said the Captain, 'you'll never leave this ship.'

I had made an attempt to disentangle myself from the Rickerby family, and failed utterly. Even the bloody foreigner could see the lie for what it was. To cover my embarrassment, I asked the Mate for a cigar, which he passed over together with matches.

Blowing smoke, I began again. 'The light', I said, 'was not there . . .'

I had known straight away the meaning. The pain in my head made movement nigh impossible, but I had to find different air. Each inhalation carried the taste of coal into me, and these breaths could not be released. My breathing was all one way, which was no sort of breathing at all. I rolled off the bed, but was now in a worse position than before with more work to do in order to stand upright. I believe the hardest thing I ever did was to rise from that floor, and unlock that door, whereupon I saw the gas bracket on the little landing, which seemed to be saying: *Don't mind me; I'm nothing in this; I'm not even burning*. But it was on at the tap, and invisible death poured from it. I tried to close the tap, but my hands were not up to the job. I half fell down the first stairs, where I saw in the darkness the first gas lamp of the half-decorated landing. I saw it in the *darkness*, and proper breathing was not permitted here either. I would shortly burst; I was a human bomb. I crashed against Vaughan's door; it flew open, and his room was empty, the bed still made up.

In falling, I rolled underneath another gas bracket that

played its part in the relay of death-dealing. I regained my feet, but my feet were treacherous, might have belonged to another man altogether. I did not know my hands either, which were stained red by all the coal gas in me. I pushed at Amanda Rickerby's door and she rose instantly from her pillow – instantly and yet drowsily. A bottle and a glass stood on the floor by her bed, but she looked beautiful in her night-dress as she made her strange, dazed enquiry: 'How are you?'

She was not rightly awake; she had taken in a quantity of the gas, and I was not in my right mind, which is why I replied, 'I'm in great shape,' and I may have vomited there and then onto her bedroom carpet, which was not very gentlemanly of me. I took the stool from before her dressing table and pitched it through her window, marvelling that my red hands were up to the job. I came out of the room revolving, and struck Adam Rickerby, who was there in long johns and no shirt. He looked like the strong man at the fair, or the Creature from the Jungle. But he did not look to have been gassed – or not badly. Had the poison reached downstairs? I would consult the man who had laid it on for my benefit.

I pushed at Fielding's door, and entered his room for the second time. He sat on his bed; it was all *I* could do to stand. I felt tiredness as a great weight pressing me down to the floor. The room was in darkness, and I could not see the gas brackets, but I knew that here too the coal vapour streamed. He wore a suit, and sat on his bed.

'You locked your door, Mr Stringer,' he said, and I somehow gasped out:

'You sound . . . put-out.'

'No, that was Blackburn,' said Fielding. 'His eye, I mean,' and he gave a little private smile, indicating an object that lay beside him on the bed: the nine inch needle that had been kept in the knife polisher.

He'd done for Blackburn by stabbing into his eye as he slept, no doubt after observing, or over-hearing, whatever creeping about had gone on earlier in the night. The long needle put swiftly into the closed eye – that way there'd be little blood and no noise. He'd meant to do me the same way. But on finding the door locked he'd fixed on a method that took no account of doors, and would bring an end to everything and everyone.

'The gas', he said, from the bed, 'will spare you a deal of trouble even if you don't quite see it. For one thing, you would have been forever buying the lady wine, and she likes the good stuff you know. You would have had to learn all about the best vintages to keep her happy, and you would be starting as far as I can judge, Mr Stringer, from a position of complete ignorance ...'

With every new remark that he made more of the truth – which was not quite as Fielding saw it – came home to me. He too was now breathing wrongly, fighting for it, and rocking on the bed as he did so. His dainty feet were raised from the floor, so that he looked like a child too short for the school form. He had put on a soft-tasselled hat for his own death; a species of indoor hat – a smoking hat, as I believed it was called. He was not smoking but held some long implement – not the needle, which was by his side – but some other long implement, which he passed constantly from left to right hand. If I might lay my own hands on either it or the other ... But that was impossible without air, and I found myself dreaming – and it *was* a kind of floating dreaminess – about a gun. That would be so much faster, and I heard myself wasting air by saying, 'I ought to shoot you down.'

How had he carted Blackburn, a big fellow, down the stairs? The window. The bed in the small room was level with it. Fielding might have fed the body through, and it would then have dropped directly to the Prom; Fielding would have sent the suit down after. He himself, in that different world in which everyone could walk, would have descended by the stairs and the streets, and dragged Blackburn into the water.

. . . But I couldn't believe I had that quite right. It was odds-on that a body dropped into the harbour would turn up again. I stumbled a little way forward.

'Spooning, you would call it,' Fielding was saying. 'He was the first at it, and then you. She spoons with you in the presence of the man who pays the bills. Well, I am sparing you a good deal of expense . . .'

And he seemed to concentrate hard on taking a breath, as though he might out-think the gas, then the word burst out of him:

'*Distemper* . . . costlier than you might think when bought in bulk . . . wallpaper at a shilling a roll . . .'

With great effort he took another breath; he was better at it than me. But I could see that it did not come easily, and he now had to pause and fall silent every few words.

' . . . And the Lady forever changing her mind about the colour.'

It came to me that I was now nearer to him, to the dangerous implement in his hand, and the other one beside him on the bed.

'No!' I said, and I could not say any more, *and* it was a wasted word into the bargain. But I had meant to say that the Lady's colour was lavender.

Two paces to go before I was at Fielding and the bed. But

why kill a man who was dying anyway? I looked to the windows: the first one – closed. To the second one – closed. I should have smashed the glass. I had wasted my time in not doing it, and accordingly I had wasted my life. The room was whirling at lightning speed; my legs were buckling under me and I wanted to be on the floor, stretched right across it; I could not support the weight of my own head. I tried to take a breath but nothing came. I saw bookshelves, a bed, fireplace, Fielding himself, but there was no air in-between any of these objects. I was drowning on dry land, drowning on the first floor but I was not ignorant. Rather, *Fielding* was. I recalled those late silences of the Lady, which were the true indication of her feelings towards me, which were no feelings at all.

'You tell me . . . that you have hopes of becoming a . . . *solicitor*,' Fielding seemed to be saying, and his voice had gone very high on that last word; he'd fairly squeaked it out. 'But there is no royal road to the acquisition of knowledge . . . Mr Stringer, you were born to a world of dirt . . . dirt and dust and coal . . . and that . . .'

I managed another step forwards as he unfolded the jewelled implement in his hand.

'Your presumption,' he said, rocking faster now, his face pink, far, far too pink. 'It scarcely . . . It takes one's breath . . . It takes the breath . . .'

I first thought that the implement might be for the fine adjustment of shirt cuffs, for he held it positioned over his left wrist. He made a smooth, practised movement.

'This gas . . . too . . . slow,' he said, and he breathed in, making a fearful dry squeaking, before swiftly transferring the implement to his other hand, and moving it over the other wrist. He raised it to his neck, and for an instant I thought: The

Chapter Thirty-Nine

'And you believe that he'd killed Blackburn?' enquired the Captain.

I had the idea that the question was asked out of duty, that he was now restless, his mind elsewhere. I believed that I had understood most things in the seconds before Fielding's death, and now that I could recall that understanding, I gave my theory in outline to the Captain. And while speaking I thought the thing through in a different way.

All the trinkets in those drawers of Fielding's, too neatly stored in boxes: they signified a lack of love. Oh, he had the friendship of Vaughan all right, and I pictured the two of them in the ship room, smoking silently: Vaughan lying flat on the couch, Fielding sitting daintily, periodically crossing his legs in a different way. But anyone could have the friendship of Vaughan: he was like a spaniel, and about equally given to cocking his leg in public. The love of Amanda Rickerby was a different matter. Ray Blackburn, a handsome, well set-up man of marriage-able age, had been the beneficiary of her love, and she had kept the company badge as a token of it. He had been to Scarborough several times before the fatal night, although never before to Paradise. I saw the two of them about the town, falling into conversation in the railway station perhaps. She sees him coming along the platform, his dark face further darkened and made more impressive by coal dust, and she chooses to ask him, rather than the funny-looking little platform guard, the time of the train. Where would she want to go to? Hull, Stockton, York, Leeds? It did not matter; the trip would only be a vague plan, anyhow. They would find that they had walked and talked for the entire length of the platform, that they had gone together through the station gates . . . and then they had the whole of Scarborough in which to walk and talk. I did not put it past her to have been drawn by his sober character, which came out of his strong religion. He might keep her on the straight path.

Later on, Blackburn would have been torn. He could not resist the opportunity to travel to Scarborough and to stay at Paradise when the chance arose in the course of his work. I supposed that he'd passed some of the night in Amanda Rickerby's bed. I saw the two of them there, sweating under the sheets in the hot talcum smell of the lavender room, and Fielding lying in his own bed just across the landing and *knowing*. Why? Because he had been listening for it. Had he seen them about the town beforehand?

It would make a married man feel strange to be in that lavender room, at least in the moments before and after the event, the prospect of which had drawn him there. Blackburn had gloomed about the house throughout his stay, which was down to guilt, and his own serious-minded nature.

Earlier on, Vaughan had showed him the special cards, which was just exactly the wrong thing to do to a man of Blackburn's mind. I pictured the two of them walking through the Old Town in the evening: the lobster pots rocking in the wind; the flashing of the lighthouse showing by modern means all the oldness of the Old Town. Blackburn would wonder what he was doing there, with this strange, unmannerly fellow loping along too close-by his side.

Blackburn *had* no doubt blown up at Vaughan, who had taken stick from the coppers ever since for an act he was only now beginning to think of as shameful. But it might become less shameful every time it was repeated. I believed he half hoped I would walk into the copper shop on Castle Road to say he'd shown me the cards as well, but that it had only been in fun and nothing had come of it.

As to Vaughan's whereabouts on that Monday . . . Well, he was a man under pressure and he was in funds. It would not have surprised me if, between Mallinson's and the luncheon-that-never-was, he had paid for something different from what the cards brought him to – some advance on that action. He certainly knew where the accommodating ladies were to be found. I pictured him walking down the alleyways – those alleyways in the shadow of the Grand Hotel, the ones that echoed to the sound of rushing rainwater – and looking in at every doorway in turn. Or were those women to be found on the main streets, above the shops selling trinkets for trippers? It was a sea-side town after all, a place of pleasure. As he stood next to me in the gentlemen's he might have been nerving himself up to asking me to accompany him. I supposed that he often resorted to the Scarborough night houses – resorted to them even during the day – for Vaughan was not an attractive fellow and this was his usefulness as far as Fielding was concerned. He was no rival for the affections of Amanda Rickerby. Fielding made no objection to ugly or old men staying in the house – or families, hence the push to make family apartments. He objected to single young men, such as Armstrong, the fellow who'd collected seaweed.

You might think Fielding a nancy but once you knew different it was obvious that he loved Miss Rickerby. I saw him fairly springing about with pleasure when she had complimented him in the ship room, the whole black sea behind him, utterly forgotten. He coloured up when she addressed him; and he never made any of his little cracks at her expense. But he did not stand an earthly with her, being twice her age and nothing to look at, and while he was not a pauper he was a failure in business and a gaol bird into the bargain. But for a while he'd tried. You *might* say that he'd tried bribery. He was paying for the redecoration of the house; he hung his pictures about the place; laid in cigars and Spanish sherry, and he gave her the benefit of his business advice. The more profit the house turned, the less chance of Miss Rickerby selling up and leaving. But he mustn't have been thinking straight when he recommended that she bring in railway men, for the law of averages said that a marriage-able one would land on the doorstep eventually. Having dealt with one, he had another on his hands directly. But he had read the signs wrongly in my case.

At first, she had given me her smiles and flirtatious glances wholesale, especially in the company of Fielding. But they had been replaced by thoughtful silences when she'd discovered what she needed to know: that he was jealous. I recalled the ways he had tried to take me away from her when she was being over-friendly. At dinner, he had lured me to the ship room with the promise of a cigar; he had done the same at the luncheon that never was, practically ordering me from her presence on that occasion. Late at night in the kitchen he had urged me to go up and look at the waves. The following morning he'd been keen that I should go off to the station to reclaim my engine. And I believed that his hatred of me – and his jealousy – were made plain to Amanda Rickerby when I'd said that the white wine 'went down a treat', and he'd exclaimed, 'Just so!' in a sarcastic way, unable to keep his feelings in check. I saw Amanda Rickerby's face turning quickly, the sight of her face in profile – the sudden sharpness of it. She would have seen him then for the murderer of Blackburn, and known he might try something similar on me.

'I do not say that your sister is a party to murder,' I said to the Captain, 'or complicit in any way. No charge against her would stand. Her behaviour was . . .' And a convenient phrase came to me from my law studies: '. . . It was too *remote* from the crime. She couldn't know for certain that Fielding would try anything. It might have seemed tantamount to slander to have confided her suspicions, you know. In the end she settled for telling me to lock my room.'

The Captain eyed me for a while, perhaps not keen on the sight of a fellow trying to get himself off the hook. At the same time, he was weighing some further plan, I knew.

'And he just dropped the body into the harbour?' he enquired. 'That would be a risk, wouldn't it?'

'I believe your brother, Adam, may have helped him get rid of the body,' I said, and the Captain did not flinch but just glanced sidelong to the Mate, who enquired, '*How*, would you say?'

'I don't mean the lad was involved in murder. It would be just tidying up to him. He was neat-handed, and he had a boat. He was also clever enough to know that this business might bring the house down, so to say. Paradise was everything to him, so he perhaps did Fielding's clearing-up for him. Whether he believed that Blackburn had been killed or made away with himself I don't know. Fielding might have told him anything, threatened him with God knows what. They never spoke again, anyhow.'

'You think they brought Blackburn to us?' the Mate cut in.

'No,' I said, 'Adam brought *me* to you knowing the movements of your ship, and knowing the times it passed Scarborough at no great distance from the shore. But Blackburn . . . what would be the point? The boy would just pitch him into the sea a good way out.'

'You're dead wrong,' said the Captain, eyeing me. 'Fielding killed Blackburn, but Adam Rickerby was not involved in any way.'

He continued to use the surname when speaking of his brother, as though the youth was a stranger to him.

'Well,' I said, 'that's as maybe.'

I had to admit that I could not imagine Adam Rickerby lying to the police, or to anyone. It was his sister who'd invented the story of the mining accident. All he had to do was keep quiet on the subject. Amanda Rickerby had done it for the boy's own protection: it would not do to seem to have a grievance against the North Eastern Railway Company in light of what had happened to Blackburn, as Fielding had no doubt discovered for himself when questioned.

'I'd give a lot to know how you brought me up on board without the rest of the crew seeing,' I said. '. . . Hauled the boat up on the windlass, I suppose, and if anyone asked you'd say your brother was paying a visit, bringing a present of a sack of potatoes perhaps.'

'You think you know everything, don't you?' said the Captain, rising to his feet.

I eyed him levelly. I knew a good deal but I had not fully understood the actions of Amanda Rickerby when we'd stood alone in the ship room. Why had she taken my hand? Where did that fit in with the game she was playing? Had she heard the approaching steps of her brother, and mistaken them for the approach of Fielding, wishing to test him further, to really bring him to the point of murder? Well, she'd been half drunk, and was perhaps more than that later in the evening – knocked out by the stuff – which, I preferred to think, was why she'd let me take my chances against Fielding with the protection only of a locked door. She hadn't even bothered to protect *herself* – not that she could have known he'd go for the whole bloody house.

As I spoke – giving something of this to the Captain and the Mate – a voice in my head said, 'Leave off, Jim. Face facts, man: she ran rings around you.' And I fell silent.

'We now show you something you don't know,' the grey Mate said. 'Come and follow me.'

Chapter Forty

The Captain came too, with pistol in hand. We descended to the room below the chart room, and then we were out on the mid-ships ladder. Again I could see no crew, and could not get a good view of the rear of the ship.

'What's aft?' I enquired, as we descended.

'A red flag,' said the Mate, setting foot on the deck. 'Some coal. Nothing for you.'

'Where are the crew?'

'Mostly ashore,' said the Captain. 'So think on.'

He meant that he had a free hand with me; might do what he liked. I supposed that an unloading gang of some sort remained on board, since it seemed likely that we were about to put off the coal at the gas works.

It was still dark. I still saw the lights on the cranes before the cranes themselves. But the world was stirring. More cranes turned and talked to their neighbours; a train wound through the streets before the flat, moon-like gas works. Every wagon was covered with white sheeting, and the sheets were numbered at the sides – giant black numbers, but they were not in order, so that it looked as though the train had been put together in a hurry. The gas works still seemed to slumber, and the line of dark, sleeping ships of which we were a part remained as before waiting patiently. Yet the factories that commanded the streets were gamely pumping out smoke, making the black sky blacker, keeping it just the way they liked it; and the air was filled with a constant clanking noise, as though great chains were being dragged in all directions.

'Your sister's in the clear and so is your brother,' I said to the Captain as we descended onto the deck, 'even though he rowed me out to this bloody tub. But I'll tell you this for nothing: you'll be in lumber if you don't put me off directly.'

No answer from the Captain; he had collected a lamp from the railing at the foot of the ladder.

'Young Adam would have been banking on you doing the sensible thing,' I said. 'You've still the chance to come right – just about.'

We had remained in the shadow of the mid-ships, and we now stood before the hatchway of a locker new to me. The Captain held up his lamp for the benefit of the Mate, who was removing a padlock from the catch of the iron door. The door swung open, and the Captain stepped forward, holding the lamp to show me a quantity of brushes of all descriptions: long-handled paint brushes, brooms and mops, buckets made of wood and iron, paint tins, a quantity of ropes, a stack of folded oilskins, a hand pump of some sort, a length of rubber hose, and Tommy Nugent in his shirt sleeves. He sat against the far wall, with legs outstretched before him and crossed in a civilised way, as he might once have crossed his legs while lean-ing against a tree trunk and eating a picnic.

From boot soles to neck Tommy looked normal, but his face had the dead whiteness of a fungus and the same horrifying lack of shape. It was *in* at the left cheek, and *out* at the right temple. All his hair had moved to the right side, as though to cover the great lump that had grown there, and his eyes, which were wide open, were no longer level, no longer a pair, the

281

right one having wandered off to have a look for once around the back of his head. I looked again at his legs, and I was ashamed not to be able to remember which one had been crocked. His right hand rested on one of his kit bags, as though to keep it safe no matter what. The mercy was that Tommy did not breathe – and I did not breathe either. The Captain lowered the lamp, so that Tommy seemed to retreat into the locker, and he kept silence.

It was the Mate who said, 'Your friend Tom.'

'Tommy,' I said. 'His name is Tommy.'

Well, he might have been carrying any number of papers that would have given away his identity, but of course I'd told them all about him. I thought of Tommy's fiancée, Joan, wandering alone in her father's shop, the Overcoat Depot on Parliament Street. I pictured the giant overcoat hanging outside like a man on a gibbet. Joan would no longer need to go to the Electric Theatre on Fossgate; she would no longer need to book an aisle seat on account of Tommy's leg, and so could go to the City Picture Palace on Fishergate, where the seats were more comfortable, but . . . *The Romance of a Jockey*, *A Sheriff and a Rustler*, *The Water-Soaked Hero* . . . nobody saw those films alone; it just wouldn't be right.

'He shot at my brother,' said the Captain.

'We have his guns,' the Mate put in. 'We took them from his bag.'

'Adam was bringing you out of the house,' said the Captain. 'He didn't know whether you were dead or alive. He wanted to get you into the fresh air. This . . .' said the Captain, gesturing at the corpse, '. . . he loosed off a shot the moment my brother stepped out of the door of the house. He's at least two ribs broken. How he rowed out to me I've no idea . . .' He indicated the corpse again, saying, 'He was re-loading for a second shot. My brother walked up and hit him.'

'He hit him only once,' the Mate put in.

'And he doesn't know his own strength,' I said. 'Is that it?'

'*He* knew it,' said the Captain. 'It was this idiot that didn't.'

And he nodded in the direction of Tommy.

'He was alive when my brother brought him. He and . . . the two of them thought I'd know what to do.'

'And do you?' I said.

No reply.

Had it been Miss Rickerby's idea to send Tommy and me out to the boat? Had she been in any fit state to make that decision, having been poisoned by the gas? And ought I to count it a kindness that she had sent me out? I pictured her waiting on the harbour wall for her brother's return, and I thought of her and her brother as two children, whereas the Captain was definitely grown-up, or so they might think.

'Your brother made you a present of *two* sacks of potatoes,' I said. 'You must have been chuffed to bits.'

Again, no answer. I wondered whether it had been left to the Captain and the Mate to discover that I was a copper, or whether the two other Rickerbys had made the discovery for themselves. They had evidently put my suit-coat on me before rowing me out, and the warrant card had been in there.

'Your brother might argue self-defence, when taken in charge . . . *if* what you say is true.'

'It's true,' said the Captain, '. . . and he will argue *nothing*.'

He raised the lantern again, making Tommy come into full view once more.

'Go in,' said the Mate.

I stepped into the locker, and the door clanged shut behind me.

Chapter Forty-One

As the smell of Tommy Nugent competed with the smell of paint I sat beside Tommy – there was no help for it, the locker being so small – and watched, over the course of perhaps an hour or so, a rectangle of light form around the hatchway, which was evidently imperfectly sealed. When the rising dawn made the outline completely clear I began to pound at the door with my boot heels, and must have carried on doing so for a clear five minutes.

My fury was directed partly at the door and partly at the Chief. I had been a fool in the Paradise guest house, but I blamed the Chief for Tommy's death. I ought to have been free to make an ass of myself alone. I had not wanted Tommy along and had made that perfectly clear, but the Chief had insisted, knowing very well that Tommy would go armed and that he was trigger happy. Why had the Chief done it? Simply to make mischief? He was pushing seventy but that particular flame never burned out in a man, as far as I could see. Had he sent Tommy to lay on a bit of adventure for a fellow shootist? Or had he wanted to make trouble for me because I'd told him I meant to take articles?

After a long interval of my pounding on the door the whole locker about me began to vibrate, and at first I thought this was my doing, but then the ship seemed to lift, Tommy fell softly against me, and my head was filled with the vibration of the engines. I pushed Tommy off, in an apologetic sort of way, marvelling that I might lately have been carted about in a sack with him; then the tree-house motion came back and I knew that we were moving. Beckton gas works had stirred itself for the day, and we were making for the jetty ready for the unloading of our cargo.

My particular fear, ever since the word 'Beckton' had crossed my mind, was that the Captain would put me off with the coal. Once dead I would be taken up by the mighty steel claw of a crane, swung into a wagon, and carried along the high-level line into one of the retort houses where I would be dropped and burned, becoming who knew how many cubic feet of gas, for the benefit of some ungrateful London householder. A better way of disposing of a body could scarcely be imagined.

It was not that the Captain was evil natured, but I believed him to be weak. This was why he had fled from his own father; it was why he'd heard me out, letting me tell the full tale as he tried to make up his mind what to do with me; it was why he'd showed me the body of Tommy Nugent, letting me see his dilemma in hopes of gaining my sympathy; in hopes I would understand better his reason for killing me. Then again his determination to keep his mentally defective brother out of the arms of the law perhaps went to his credit. The lad had suffered enough – Captain Rickerby might be thinking – at the hands of North Eastern Railway Company employees. Anyhow, he was judge and jury in my case, and I was quite sure it was a role he would have given anything to avoid taking on.

What would the weak man do? He would put a bullet in me and toss me in the hold ready for burning. But the accusing finger then began to point in my own direction. Who was I to charge anyone with weakness? I had lingered in the Paradise guest house half in hopes of fucking the landlady. My mind had been only partly on the case as a result; and why had I wanted to ride the lady? Because she was beautiful, yes. But also to get revenge on the wife, who had taken advantage of my own weakness to gain her own ends.

It came to this: I needed some fire in me; I needed to play a man's part; I needed a gun. I turned to Tommy and, in the light that came from the halo around the door, my eye wandered down from his broken head to his right shoulder, along his right arm and up to his right hand which rested on his kit bag. At first Tommy had had two bags, and where the other one had got to I had no notion. But I was sure that Captain Rickerby and the Mate had been through it with a fine toothed comb. They must have been through this one as well – only for some reason they'd left it in the locker. From one or both of the kit bags they'd removed Tommy's guns – that was the word the Mate had used: 'guns' in the plural. Accordingly there was no prospect of finding a gun in the bag. But it just so happened that when I opened it, I laid my hand directly upon the two-two pistol.

In fact, it was partly wrapped in a towel, but I hadn't had to fish for it. The Captain and the Mate must have been in a panic and no doubt a tearing hurry as they went through the bag. I put my hand into the lucky dip again and found nothing but clothes . . . only something somewhere rattled. I pulled out a cloth bag, and here were the two-two cartridges. The pistol seemed to me – as someone more familiar with revolvers – very primitive: hardly more than a length of pipe with handle, trigger and lever forming three short outgrowths. I pressed the lever; it was very accommodating and the gun broke. I stuffed a cartridge in the general direction of the barrel, and whether

I'd done it right or not I had no idea.

I found out less than a minute later when the door opened and the Captain, holding both his revolver and a coal black sack, appeared before me with the mighty mechanical hand of the Beckton gas works crane descending into the opened hold behind him.

I pulled the trigger; the gun flashed orange; the Captain fell back, and I was quite deafened. In that deafened state I took up the cloth bag, and re-loaded the gun. I stepped out of the locker and over the Captain, who still moved, and who might have been screaming. I saw the Mate, who held no gun and looked at me in a different way; alongside him stood – perhaps – the big man who had floored me. The claw of the crane was rising behind them, and Beckton gas works was far too close on the starboard side. I looked towards the foc's'le and saw two crewmen I did not know, had not seen before, but my surprise was nothing to theirs. I walked over to the port side with the shooter in my hand and there, running fast alongside, was a launch with a rough looking sailor at the wheel and an evident gent in a long, smart, official-looking great-coat standing very upright beside him.

Behind the two was a funnel hardly bigger than either of them, and the top of it was ringed with red paint. They were not quite coppers, I decided, but were somehow in authority. I looked down at them from the gunwale on the port side, and that did no good at all. So I raised my two-two pistol and fired, making not the least effect on the generality of the sailors and crane operators and wharf men. But the two fellows in the launch looked up.

PART FIVE

Chapter Forty-Two

Forty minutes south of York, I looked through the compartment window at the town of Retford: red bricks in the morning sunshine, and a smoking chimney that I believed to be the brickworks, and which I always thought of as a sort of factory for *making* Retford.

I'd run through the place on the main line many times, and had passed through it going the other way only a little under a month before, on my return from London and my imprisonment aboard the steam collier *Lambent Lady*, owned and operated by the firm of Hawthorn and Bruce of West Hartlepool, and contracted to the Gas, Light and Coke Company for the Beckton run. The Captain *was* a Rickerby: John, brother of Adam and Amanda; and the First Mate was Gus Klaason. The great-coated fellow I'd alerted by firing Tommy's pistol was Wharf Master of the Gas, Light and Coke Company who'd quickly alerted the Port of London Authority, an outfit that ran its own police force, and it was those boys who'd taken in Klaason and Rickerby (whose shoulder my bullet had broken). The two had been left unguarded for a minute before a remand hearing at Greenwich Magistrates Court; they'd done a push and were no doubt steaming fast to the far side of the world very soon after. An enquiry was to be held into the matter and a Chief Inspector Baxter of the Port of London Authority Police had written me a letter of apology. But I hardly cared about the escape. Yes, Captain Rickerby had meant to kill me at the last, but his intention had been to save his family from disaster, and he'd certainly put off the moment as long as he could. He had also saved that petrified lad – name of Edward Crozier – from drowning by going about to collect him after he'd tried to swim to the foreign ship that came alongside. (Crozier had by chance seen me brought aboard, and then been roped into the job of guarding me.)

The PLA coppers had been decent sorts, and they'd made me a present of the blue serge suit they'd given me after my rescue. I'd had my choice of any number of suits or sports coats and flannels, since they'd seemed to have an entire tailoring department on the strength. They also had a first class police doctor, who'd told me that carbon monoxide (as from coal gas) combines with haemoglobin in the blood to make carboxyhaemoglobin.

He wrote the name down in my pocket book as a kind of souvenir, saying that this was a very stable compound – and this stability was not a good thing. The poison prevented the lungs sending oxygen to the bodily cells that need it, and it might stop heart, lungs or brain. When it took over half your blood, then you were done for one way or another. I might have been saved, the doctor said, by not having jammed the paste-board into the window frame of my room on my second night – that small amount of ventilation might have been all-important. The doctor did not believe I had taken any permanent injury from my experience, but he did fret about my loss of memory. He asked me questions to test the membranes of my brain, and seemed quite satisfied with the results of this quiz, which ran to enquiries such as 'What is the name of the

Prime Minister?' But I had been testing *myself* ever since. I would run through all the railway companies that ran into York station, or try to put a name and rank to every man in the police office, and do it fast. I would hit a sticking point every so often. For instance, the name of the painting that had been attacked could not have been the *Rickerby Venus*, could it? I asked myself the name of the oldest pub in York and could not recall whether it was the Three Cranes on St Sampson's Square, the Three Crowns on Coney Street or, for the matter of that, the Three *Cups* on Coney Street. I had certainly known the answer once, and I wondered whether the forgetting might not be down to the gas.

Beyond the window, Retford had been replaced by flying fields. I stretched out my legs, loosened my tie, and thought about doing a spot of reading. Beside me on the seat was a copy of the previous day's *Yorkshire Evening Press*, which struck a happy, holiday note in some of its articles, the Easter week-end being in prospect: 'Great Rush to the Sea-side Predicted'; 'Everybody on Pleasure Bent'. All the regiments of the York garrison would be marching through the streets in aid of a recruitment drive, and there would be the showing of a film, *The British Army Film*, at the Victoria Hall in Goodramgate. It promised 'some very wonderful pictures of bursting shrapnel, of quick-firing guns springing out shells at the rate of thirty a minute'. Also, Constable Flower had arrested a 'drunk and incapable' on one of the far platforms of the station. He'd taken him into the cells in the police office by means of a luggage trolley, and this news had caused laughter when, later on in the day, it was announced in the police court.

Beside the *Press* was the latest number of the *Railway*

Magazine opened towards the back of the paper with the page headed 'What the Railways Are Doing' uppermost. This was the classified section of the magazine, and always carried the notices announcing meetings of the Railway Club, who were really a London lot, but whose meetings were open to anyone taking the trouble to write to the secretary for a ticket. At seven o'clock that day – the announcement was circled in my copy of the magazine – Mr A. K. Chambers would be reading a paper entitled 'The New Atlantics with Special Mention of the North Eastern Class Z', and I had the ticket for it in my pocket.

In the office, old man Wright, who distributed the post, had handed me the letter in which it came and I had made a point of satisfying his curiosity by opening the envelope in his presence and letting him see the ticket for himself. The meeting was to be held at the Railway Club's premises: 92 Victoria Street, London SW, and Wright had said, 'You've booked a day of leave for *that*?' Then, later, when he'd thought about it a bit more, 'Seems a long way to go just to hear about trains,' at which I'd reminded him that he was in fact in the *railway* police and so ought not be taking that tone.

It was quite in order to josh with Wright. His wife, Jane, would not be coming back to him as she had made plain both to Wright and to my own wife during a meeting of the Co-operative ladies. But he had developed a plan in response: firstly, he would no longer buy his groceries from any of the Co-operative stores, his wife and her new man, Terry Dawson, being employees of the Movement. This went hard with Wright because the Co-operative stores were much the cheapest, and he was a right old skinflint, but it was the principle of the thing. (The Co-operative slogan, 'The Friendly Store', now rang very hollow in his ears, he told me.) Second of all, he would leave work early twice a week to attend the dancing classes given in the room over the Big Coach public house on Nessgate. Once up to snuff with the two-step and the waltz and whatnot, he would go along to the Saturday afternoon tea dances that were held in many of the hotels of central York, and were known to attract the widows of the City.

'The best one's at the Danby Lodge on Minster Walk,' Wright told me one day in the police office. 'I'm going to try my luck there first.' 'You'll need a *lot* of luck,' Constable Flower had said, in an under-breath, and whether Wright heard it or not, he certainly wasn't put off. He seemed very confident about his plan, and I wondered whether the end of his marriage might not be the making of him.

Of course Wright, being so nosey, had had a field day on my delayed return from Scarborough. Lydia had been into the office twice to ask where I'd got to, the second time in tears. His fixed opinion, he told me later, was that I'd been done in. 'Of course, I didn't say that to her,' he told me, 'or not in so many words', and I dreaded to think what he *had* said for he was not the sort to play down any drama.

On the Thursday morning, three days after Adam Rickerby put me onto the *Lambent Lady*, the Chief himself had gone to Scarborough, making straight to Bright's Cliff to see what had become of me. There he'd found a bloke from the council sent to board over the window I'd smashed when I'd pitched the chair through it. That had been quick work. Someone else in the street had gone into the council offices to complain that the house, having evidently been abandoned, was now a magnet for vagrants and burglars. The Chief told me that the bloke from the council had posted a bill for the work through the letter box before leaving.

It seemed very unlikely to me that the bill would ever be paid.

The Chief had broken into Paradise in company with some of the Scarborough coppers. There were signs of people having left in a great hurry, although the gas had been turned off. It was the Chief himself who'd come upon the body of Fielding, which was just as well since he was well equipped to stand that kind of shock.

I'd returned to Bright's Cliff a few days after with the Chief, some coppers from Scarborough and Leeds, and the Scarborough coroner, a Mr Clegg. By then Theo Vaughan had turned up, having walked into the Scarborough copper shop to make a clean breast of ... well, not much. He'd staggered back to the house at three in the morning on Tuesday, 17 March, and found it empty. The smashed window and the gas reek had terrified him, and – knowing that he was still under suspicion over the last bit of bad business in the house – he'd taken a few of his belongings (including, I didn't doubt, the remainder of his Continental Specialities) and fled the scene.

I'd talked to Vaughan in the coroner's court and had given him the whole tale over a cup of tea during an adjournment in the inquiry. I asked him whether he'd known that Fielding was sweet on the lady of the house.

'Not in that way, Jim,' he said, 'not in that way.'

He was every bit as familiar as he had been before, despite the fact that he now knew me for a policeman. When I told him how I'd come upon the special post cards in Fielding's bedside drawer, he said, 'He must have had 'em away from my room, Jim. I tell you ... no man can resist.'

He then leant towards me, with droplets of cold tea dangling from his 'tache, and might have been on the point of again offering to sell me some at a knockdown price. I believe he was only put off by the clerk of the court coming up to me at that moment and addressing me as 'Detective Sergeant Stringer'.

Mr Clegg had praised me before his court, and the Leeds and Scarborough coppers also seemed to think I'd done a good job. It came down to this: I'd made myself the mark, and I'd cracked the mystery – and it *was* cracked all right, papers amounting to a confession to the killing of Blackburn having been discovered amongst Fielding's belongings. He'd known Blackburn as soon as he turned up at the house; had seen him about in Scarborough on earlier occasions with the Lady. He had observed them buying oysters on the harbour wall, later walking in Clarence Gardens. It was perhaps there that Blackburn had made her a present of the North Eastern badge that she so much admired.

In exposing Fielding I *had* left two dead bodies in my wake, but this seemed to be taken quite lightly by everyone in authority: one of the dead was a man who would have swung anyway, and that went down as quick and violent justice of the sort the Chief and many another favoured. But as regards the death of Tommy Nugent, I *blamed* the Chief. He'd been too reckless from start to finish, and I meant to have it out with him.

During the visit to the house in company with the Leeds and Scarborough men, I saw a different side to the man. He knew he'd made a bloomer over sending Tommy Nugent with me, and he acted accordingly. I believe that 'chastened' is the word. He'd liked Tommy Nugent, was saddened by his death, and seemed to take the responsibility for it, but that wasn't enough for me.

We'd all (the Leeds and Scarborough coppers, the Chief and

me) gone off to the Two Mariners after inspecting the house, and I'd given the story, which was fast becoming a party piece, over a few pints. As when addressing Captain Rickerby, I'd played down my infatuation with the Lady of the House, although I think one of the Scarborough coppers guessed at it; he'd questioned her over the disappearance of Blackburn and had evidently half fallen in love with her himself. When we coincided in the gentlemen's halfway through our session in the Mariners, he congratulated me on saving her life by the smashing of the window, for that was the supposition – theirs and mine: that she had survived the gas, and made off with her brother to avoid being taken in charge over the killing of Tommy.

'She was a peach, wasn't she, that one?' the Scarborough copper said. 'I wouldn't have minded tomming her myself.'

He told me that he was circulating her and Adam's descriptions in the *Police Gazette* as being wanted for questioning over the death of Tommy Nugent. 'But I'll tell you this,' he added, buttoning up his flies, 'I half hope we never find her.'

'I don't suppose you ever will,' I said, which might have been taken as rather rude, but I was the star turn that day and could have got away with anything. As I told my tale, one of the Leeds blokes kept saying, 'Well, who'd have thought it?' and 'What a turn-up'. He might have been a stooge, paid to boost me.

The Chief had kept silence as I gave my account, even when, towards the end – and made brave by my three pints – I'd eyed him and said in front of everyone, 'Tommy Nugent ought not to have been sent. He was gun crazy – out for any opportunity to loose off a bullet.'

Later, on the train back to York, as I sat with the Chief in a smoking compartment we hardly spoke a word, and I knew that for the first time in our acquaintance this was *my* silence rather than one of his. I'd been stirred up by my success in the pub, and I now felt I had the measure of the Chief. I would let him stew before I said my piece.

He smoked and I sat over-opposite, looking sidelong.

'Will you have a cigar?' he enquired, just after we'd come out of Seamer.

'I reckon not,' I said.

'It *is* a smoking compartment, you know.'

'Yes,' I said, 'but that doesn't mean it's obligatory, does it . . . sir?'

'Obligatory,' he muttered under his breath.

A silence of twenty minutes followed that exchange.

'I want to say something about this case,' I said, as we flew through Rillington.

'Fire away,' he said.

'You sent me into that house unprepared.'

'Correct.'

I was a bit knocked by that but I ploughed on: 'Unprepared in the following ways: number one . . .'

'No,' said the Chief, who had now turned and was looking through the window.

'Eh?'

'Don't put numbers to it. I'm liable to get a bit cross if you do that. Put it shortly.'

'I had no sight of the case papers,' I said. 'Well, I had the witness statements, but none of the reports. I had no account of the personalities in the house.'

The Chief was still looking through the window.

'Firstly,' he said, '. . . Christ, you've got me at it now . . . you had all the papers that were to hand. The others were missing and have never turned up since.'

'That's a bit funny, isn't it?'

'Well, you don't seem to be laughing about it. And even if more papers had been to hand, do you think those Leeds and Scarborough blokes are up to writing an account of anyone's *personality*?' He fairly spat that word out. 'What do you think they are? A bunch of fucking novelists?'

' . . . And you gave me no advance warning of the job,' I said. 'Well, one day – not enough.'

'I didn't want you shitting yourself for a whole week, did I? It might have been bad for your health.'

'I wouldn't have been shitting myself . . . sir. I would have been developing a plan of action.'

'I didn't want you to develop a plan of action.'

'Why not?'

'Because it would have been crap.'

'Thanks,' I said, and the Chief stood up. He suddenly looked big – too big for Malton station, which we were just then pulling into.

'Where are you off to?' I said.

'The next carriage,' said the Chief, blowing smoke.

The chief said 'carriage' when he meant 'compartment'. He was old-fashioned in that way.

'I don't care for the smell in this one,' he continued, as he pulled open the door.

'And what smell is that?'

'*Lawyer*,' he said, and he disappeared along the corridor.

I sat alone until Kirkham Abbey came up – a good twenty minutes. Then I too stood up and walked along to the next compartment. From the corridor, I looked through the window at the Chief, who was sitting there with the gas lamps turned up full. He hardly ever read on a train, but would always sit under bright light. The lamp immediately above him illuminated his head in such a way that I could count the hairs. There were not more than a dozen. I shoved open the door, and entered the compartment. I sat down facing the Chief. He met my gaze while exhaling smoke, at which my gaze shifted somewhat to the left – to the 'No Smoking' sign pasted on the window.

'I'm not complaining on my own account,' I said. 'It's my job to go into dangerous places.'

'Congratulations,' said the Chief. 'It's only taken you ten fucking years to work that one out.'

'But you shouldn't have sent Tommy Nugent. *Why* did you send him?'

'He wanted to go,' said the Chief. 'He was bored. There's a lot of it about, you know. *I'm* bored listening to you.'

I watched the dark fields roll by the window. There was absolutely nothing at all between bloody Barton Hill and Strensall.

'Who was the man you were speaking to in the station when we came back from the Beeswing?' I said. 'It seems an age since, but it was only Friday. You weren't over-keen that I saw you.'

'None of your fucking business,' said the Chief, and just at that moment I *knew*.

'Do you want me to stay on the force?' I said.

'It's not obligatory,' replied the Chief, and now we were in *his* silence, and we remained in it all the way back to York.

On arrival at the station, I walked through the arch in the Bar Walls to Toft Green, where the Grapes public house was dwarfed by the new railway offices. It was a perfect little jewel box of a pub, with the name spelled out in the stained glass of the window. The name of the landlord – the new landlord – appeared over the door: John Mitchell, licensed to sell beers, wines and all the rest of it. He was holding a cheerful conversation at the bar, and I broke in on it directly by asking whether Chief Inspector Saul Weatherill of the railway police had wanted to hold a 'do' in the pub.

'Aye,' said Mitchell, a bit dazed.

'You spoke to him about it at the station on Friday, didn't you?'

Mitchell nodded.

'What was it in aid of?' I enquired.

'Leaving 'do' for a fellow call Stringer. Why?'

The Chief, then, had *not* bargained on me dying in Scarborough, and not only had he come to terms with my leaving the force, but he was willing to make a party of it. It was this that decided me.

'You may as well forget about it,' I said. 'I'm Stringer, and I en't leaving.'

Chapter Forty-Three

At King's Cross station, a succession of pointing-finger signs directed me to: 'King's Cross for St Pancras', which was the Underground station; the booking office of same, where I bought a penny ticket; and the southbound platform of the Hampstead Tube.

Charing Cross Underground station was being rebuilt, I discovered on arrival, but the pointing fingers were there as well, directing me past the men hammering, sawing, mixing cement – and onto the platforms of the District Railway, where I waited for a westbound train while figuring in my mind a particular bench in the Museum Gardens at York, the one set just before the ruins of St Mary's Abbey. It was there – on the day of my return from the London docks – that I had told the tale of Paradise to the wife, taking care to put a quantity of rouge and kohl onto Amanda Rickerby's face and a good ten years onto her age.

'She was a scarlet woman,' the wife had said, in an amused sort of voice, as though to save me the trouble of going to any further lengths.

Naturally, I also left out my own blushes and faltering speech, my own keenness to be in the company of the lady. But I did admit that she had taken my hand in the ship room on the second, fatal evening.

'And what did you do then?' the wife asked.

'Nothing,' I said, and the wife had kept silence.

'Don't you believe me?' I said.

'I know you did nothing, Jim,' she said, and it seemed to me that she sounded almost disappointed, as though I'd failed her own sex. She also sounded distracted, and it struck me that I ought to have predicted that she would be. Whenever you have some important matter to relate and you've taken a time working yourself up to doing it, you invariably find that the person you're telling it to is thinking of something else entirely – something much more important, or at least more closely touching upon their own lives, which comes to the same thing.

'Have you seen Robert Henderson lately?' I asked, when I'd come to the end of my tale.

'Yes,' she said, and in that moment everything hung in the balance. The white stones of the ruined abbey were no longer beautiful; instead they were just so many tombstones, a representation of death.

'He came over to see me yesterday,' said Lydia.

'To do what?' I said, eyeing her.

'To make love to me.'

'Hold on a minute,' I said, turning to her on the bench.

'I told him to kindly leave the house immediately,' said the wife, and the abbey and the gardens, with the crocuses and daffodils and speckless blue sky were all beautiful again.

'But there was a difficulty, of course,' said the wife.

'I'll say there is,' I said. 'It's *his* bloody house.'

The wife nodded and stood up, startling the peacock that had wandered up to our bench.

'You've to come with me, Jim,' she said.

'Where are we off to?' I asked, as she set off at a lick.

'He told me', Lydia said, as we tore past the observatory,

through the gates of the gardens and out into Museum Street where a trotting pony with trap behind nearly did for us both, 'that there would be a general rent increase across the estate, and that he would let me know about it shortly.'

'Christ,' I said, trotting myself to keep up with the wife as she turned a corner. 'That's going some. He's a bigger bastard than I thought.'

'Don't use that language, Jim,' said the wife, as we marched diagonally across St Helen's Square with very little regard for the folks in the way.

'I told him', the wife said, addressing me over her shoulder, 'that he had better let me buy this house immediately on the terms mentioned when we rented it.'

'And what were they?' I asked, shouting over the barrel organ played by the bloke who stood every day at the start of Davygate. (Wanting to limit my dealings with Henderson, I'd kept out of the detailed negotiations about the house.)

'He'd said we could have it for a hundred and fifty,' the wife called back.

'Well,' I said, dodging one bicyclist and nearly running into another as a result, 'he'll just go back on that, won't he?'

'Oh no,' said the wife, 'he agreed to it there and then. He was very shamefaced. I think he knew he'd done wrong.'

'Well, he'll know for certain when I go round tomorrow and smash his face in,' I said.

'You won't, Jim.'

'I bloody will.'

'You won't, Jim, because he's off to India. Sailing first thing in the morning – looking after his father's interests out there.'

'It's about time he got a job,' I said. 'I suppose that's why he tried it on.'

'Very likely,' said the wife, and we were now outside the door of the Yorkshire Penny Bank on Feasgate. It was where the wife kept her inheritance from her mysterious, very Victorian father who'd died, extremely ancient, shortly after our marriage and who'd owned more than one London property.

'You've not enough to buy the house,' I said.

'Have you never heard of a mortgage, Jim?' said the wife, pushing open the door; and I saw that she'd brought all sorts of household papers in her basket.

An hour later we were at our other favourite bench – in the little park next to the Minster. The wife had arranged the mortgage in record time but even so we'd missed the start of Evensong in the great cathedral, about which I was secretly quite pleased – and the wife hadn't minded too much. She was happier than I'd seen her in a good while.

'What's the medieval word for what he was proposing, Jim?'

'Same one as today,' I said. 'A fuck.'

The wife frowned at me, for a pair of respectable ladies happened to be passing by our bench at just that point.

'I don't think those blokes with the broad swords and the boiling oil were too particular about polite language,' I said.

'*Droit de seigneur*,' said the wife, 'that's it,' and she shook her head. '. . . Incredible in this day and age.'

'We might go in after the first reading, if you like,' I said, nodding towards the Minster.

'All right, let's,' she said, and she took my hand.

'By the way,' I said, rising from the bench, 'I'm not going into that solicitor's office.'

I had been expecting an explosion; instead we kissed.

'I'm so relieved, Jim,' she said. 'I could hardly bear to bring it up after all the work you've put in. But now that we've a mortgage to repay you've got to be earning, and the wages of an articled clerk just wouldn't have been enough.'

We walked over to the east entrance of the Minster, and an usher in a red robe came up to us just inside the door, whispering, 'Are you for Evensong?'

'*I* am,' said the wife. 'My husband's going to take a pint of beer and meet me afterwards.'

I grinned at her, and we might have kissed again had it not been for that usher.

Chapter Forty-Four

I found 92 Victoria Street within ten minutes of quitting Victoria Station. One brass plaque by the door read 'William Watson, Tailor', another 'The Railway Club, est'd 1899'. The door was firmly locked, but then the talk would not begin for another six and a half hours, it being just then only one o'clock. I might return for it, but really I had only walked up to the door in order to establish the exact location – just in case any railway-minded person should ask me about it.

I turned and retraced my steps, entering the station on the west side, under the awning belonging to the London, Brighton and South Coast end of the Victoria operation. The names of the principal destinations were painted on a long board mounted over the awning, and I read: 'Hastings, St Leonard's, Bexhill, Pevensey, Eastbourne ...'

I bought my ticket, and found the train waiting on the platform with all doors invitingly open. As the guard began slamming them shut I was not so much reading as gazing down at my copy of the *Yorkshire Evening Press*. In Scarcroft Road a York councillor had made a miraculous escape from a burning house. I'd been reading the same words for five minutes, and it seemed impertinent for the paper to be telling me about York while I sat in one of the grandest stations in London, so I folded it up and put it aside. Shortly after, the train jolted into life and we were rolling out from under the glass canopy into a beautiful, sky-blue afternoon. We soon began to make good speed, and I wondered a little – but only a little – about the engine. I had not walked up for a look at it, just as I had not looked at the one that had carried me south from York, and I believe that I only really noticed one station on the way from Victoria: Lewes, where the gulls screamed over the goods yard even though we were still twenty miles from the sea.

I continued in my distracted state as I walked south from Eastbourne station along Terminus Road. Why did I walk south? I had no firm idea, but that way led to the front, which was the main attraction of Eastbourne in sunny weather. After ten minutes' walking I came to the sea, and in my mind's eye the paper fan unfolded.

The frontage was called the Grand Parade, and it was just that: motors, carriages, bath chairs and pedestrians – and every face turned towards the glittering waters of the English Channel. I joined the throng for a while, before descending towards the Prom where a narrower parade was going on for walkers and bath chair patients only. Out on the milky sea there was only one vessel to be seen – a sailing boat – and it brought to mind a sign posted in York station for the benefit of engine men: 'Make No Smoke', which made me think in turn of Captain Rickerby. Since his escape, it had come out that one of the constables meant to be guarding him and Klaason at Greenwich had been a seaman who'd sailed under Klaason in deep waters ten years since, and I'd thought it very big of the Port of London Authority police to admit as much.

I came to a bandstand that projected out from the Prom and hung over the beach. The crowds were particularly dense here even though a dozen notices, fixed all around the bandstand, said that the concerts would not begin until the Saturday. The seaward edge of the beach (which was pebbly, as Howard Fielding had said) was crowded with bathing machines and, as I looked on, one of them rolled forwards, which set the people standing about applauding. A little while after, two men emerged from it, waded a little way out, and began to swim. Some of the crowd clapped again, some cheered, and some laughed in derision for the water must still be freezing.

Won't be for long though, I thought: the day was beautiful, and all the predictions were for a fine summer.

I continued my walk, looking for a lavender coat and a mass of curls under a feathered hat, but most of the ladies wore white that day, and perhaps she did too. Or perhaps she was nowhere near Eastbourne.

I walked easterly until I came to a round fortification sitting on a hummock of grass. It had been built to keep Napoleon off but was now part of a pleasure ground. I bought an ice cream from an Italian with a barrow, and turned around and walked back towards the pier. That seemed promising, being so packed, and as I approached I studied the men and women walking up and down, and the thing in general. The highest of the white wooden buildings on it was crowned with a kind of white, round summer house, and this – as I realised when I approached the pier turnstiles and all the signs announcing the attractions available for my penny – was the famous camera obscura of Eastbourne, being some species of magic lantern that captured scenes from all along the front. I might see her inside there, projected two inches high and flickering in whatever the camera obscura made of the glorious sunlight. But the queues leading up to it were too long.

I walked to the end of the pier and back with no luck.

. . . Or was it just as well?

On the Grand Parade once again, I was practically trampled to the ground as I took out my pocket book where I'd noted the times of the return trains. It was now nearly four o'clock, and there was one at a quarter after: an express too. I would be in plenty of time for A. K. Chambers and his thoughts on the New Atlantics. But I decided to wander inland a bit, and so, with my suit-coat over my shoulder, I walked for nearly an hour amid the comfortable villas, which all had names: The Chase, The Sycamores, The Grove, The Haven. I had half an eye out for a house called Paradise, but the names in Eastbourne were a cut above that.

I returned to the front thoroughly over-heated, although the sun was now going down and making a golden road running out to sea. I was a good way further east than I had been before, towards Beachy Head and the cliffs, where Eastbourne becomes country. The sounds of the Grand Parade came to me faintly, and I saw that the Promenade here was all-but-deserted. A zig-zag path winding through ornamental gardens brought me down onto it, and looking right I saw her. She was gazing out to sea in a blue dress, a straw boater in her left hand. Well, it would never have fitted on top of her curls, and I believed that she only carried it for form's sake. Something told me she was about to look my way, so I darted towards a laurel bush that stood between us, and when I stepped out again she'd gone; and I found that I could hardly catch my breath because she was alive and looking just as before; because I had seen her; and because I now could not.

I then noticed the shelter on the Prom, made to look old and quaint with white plaster, black beams and a thatched roof. She must be in there. The thing was open at the front and I knew that, short of walking directly up to it, the best way of getting a look inside would be to drop down from the Prom to the beach, and walk a little way towards the sea.

This I did. In fact, I walked right to the water's edge, where two lads stood throwing stones at some rocks a little way out. I faced out to sea with the shelter now behind me, not quite directly and at a distance of, say, forty yards. I half turned and saw her on the bench inside it with legs crossed, kicking her top-most boot. She might be sheltering from the continuing sun, or from the slight breeze that was picking up, or just lazing after a long day of doing not much. I decided that she was most likely not working. She was supposed to be lying low after all, and I knew she was in funds. On my visit with the Chief to Paradise I'd inspected the vanity case and all the other boxes in Fielding's tall chest of drawers, and the forty pounds was nowhere to be seen.

I looked again towards the Prom, but this time the other way, for I had to ration my glances at the shelter . . . and there was Adam Rickerby, walking slowly. He looked thinner, though still not *right*, and he seemed to list as he walked. What was wrong with his face? Was his hat on backwards? That was the effect somehow; there also seemed less of his curls under it, and I knew from the way his sister rose to greet him in the shelter that he was poorly. I wondered whether the bullet was still in him; I hoped not, for where would he find a doctor to take it out? I looked forward again, watching the stones thrown by the two lads into the little waves.

What had I done wrong in the Paradise guest house? As far as everybody else was concerned, it seemed very little. But then I was the only one who knew that I'd fallen for Amanda Rickerby.

What had been the result of my doing so as far as the investigation was concerned? One consequence was that I'd given too little time and thought to Tommy Nugent. I ought to have taken him in hand on the Monday: packed him off home – flatly insisted that he leave Scarborough. But I'd been too keen to get back to Miss Rickerby.

Would I have stopped in the house for that second night had it not been for my feelings towards her? And the thought that something might happen between us? I believed I would have done . . . Then again, it was my feeling towards her that had finally made me lock the door *against* her.

Why had she told me to lock the door? I wanted to ask her that, at least. Had she really known of the danger presented by Fielding? In which case, why had she not done more to protect us all? I believed she had been on the point of telling me to lock my door on the first night. She had begun to say it, late on in the kitchen, but she had pulled up. She wanted to make sure of her suspicions, and by flirting with me she was able to approach certainty.

And then again – the question of questions – why had she held my hand in the ship room, having used me for her own purposes for the entire . . . What had it been? Only an evening and a day; and I'd only been in her presence a fraction of that time. Had she taken my hand to apologise for what had happened, or for what was to come? Or had there been some other reason for it?

'Mister,' one of the lads was saying (and he'd probably been saying it for a while), 'we're aiming for that rock.'

He pointed out to sea.

'Want to try?' he said, and he walked up with a handful of stones.

'I'll only need one,' I said, taking the biggest. I shied it and scored a direct hit, no doubt because of not trying at all.

I turned about and saw Amanda and Adam Rickerby in the shelter, both looking forwards. She, I believed, was smiling.

The first boy was eyeing me in amazement, but the second was a bit of a harder nut: 'Bet you can't do it again,' he said, but I knew from his face that I could rest on my laurels, that no second throw was required. I glanced down at my watch.

'Where are you off to now?' enquired the first lad, doubtless wanting to know what amazing feat the hero of the hour might perform next.

'I'm off to catch a train,' I said.

He nodded, and it evidently seemed the right course of action to him, as it did to me for a dozen different reasons.